Shadow's Ghost

Shadow's Ghost

THE LEGEND OF TEX ELEMENT

RAY & ANN DIAMOND

TATE PUBLISHING
AND ENTERPRISES, LLC

Published by Tate Publishing & Enterprises, LLC
127 E. Trade Center Terrace | Mustang, Oklahoma 73064 USA
1.888.361.9473 | www.tatepublishing.com

Tate Publishing is committed to excellence in the publishing industry. The company reflects the philosophy established by the founders, based on Psalm 68:11,
"The Lord gave the word and great was the company of those who published it."

Book design copyright © 2016 by Tate Publishing, LLC. All rights reserved.
Cover design by Norlan Balazo
Interior design by Richell Balansag

Published in the United States of America

ISBN: 978-1-68254-936-0
1. Fiction / Fantasy / Epic
2. Fiction / Fantasy / Contemporary
15.12.18

We dedicate this book to our family, friends, and grandson, Michael Rafael.

ACKNOWLEDGMENTS

A special thanks to our cat Shadow who was the inspiration for this novel. Also a special thanks to Diana for her drawings.

Mystery Links in Shadow's Ghost

Many times through life we wander through the busy schedules we keep and not see what is really in front of us. We hear names and places, but we don't really pay attention. Life leaves us clues to understand what is happening, and yet our frame of reference is not at its peak, and we tend to avoid what is really in front of us.

Maybe we just don't want to hear it or it doesn't fit our pattern of thinking; either way we seem content not to disturb our way of living.

Shadow's Ghost, the novel, has clues in it like the game called Clue. Instead of Colonel Mustard, Mrs. Peacock, or Miss Scarlet, the names of certain characters and the actions they create is like the classic mystery-solving game that was very popular since its creation in 1949.

In this novel, the readers must figure out whodunit. The character's verbal actions they commit and the crime to society they are perpetuating all named after their names (clue) begins in chapter 41.

Chapter 45 has the continuation of new characters and their beginnings and places. One clue is Trinity.

The reader's job is to figure out who acted that part and their motives in today's political realm.

Nothing is sacred in Shadow's Ghost, the legend of Tex Element, except chapter 34.

The poor murder victims in this book are really today's generation.

In chapter 41, there are four names. Who are they?

In chapter 45, there are two names, a religious person and his rented hut and a teacher whose residence the evil one started out from.

Like I said, we wander through life and yet did we see this coming?

Contents

PROLOGUE

The Wise One

After days of preparation, the villagers welcomed their family and friends to celebrate the *Qingming Festival*, a festival that is celebrated once every year in China.

In the center of the village stood a huge—I mean a big, big—tree, and under those branches sat the Wise One. He is considered the oldest in the village and was given the job of retelling the story of "Jie Zitui."

The young and old was so excited to know that they were going to hear the telling of this wonderful tale, and also how it all began with the legend of Blackie, the polydactyl cat.

As daylight began to fade, lamps were being lit throughout the village and around the tree. The Wise One sat quietly; a smile of happiness and calmness can be seen by all. And then he began his story.

"It is said by those who know that the Qingming Festival started from a day the Chinese call *Hanshi*, a day that really means, 'that one should only eat cold foods,' and in that way it became a special day.

Jie Zitui's story begins in the banishment period of Duke Wen of Jin before he received the royal title of duke. He was just one of many followers of Wen during this period. There came a time when all the food was gone, and everyone was starving. Jie cared a lot for the leader Wen that he prepared some meat soup and gave it to him.

"Wow!" Wen said. "This is great. Where did you get the soup?"

Jie then told him he had to cut a piece of meat from his own thigh to make the soup.

The young boys and girls let out a disgusting and nauseating sound—*urk*—when they heard the cutting of a piece of meat from his thigh, but the Wise One just smiled and stroked his long white beard and continued.

Heavy tears flowed down from Wen's eyes. He was so moved by Jie's selfless sacrifice that he said, "Jie, I promise to reward you one day for your kindness."

However, Jie was not the type of person who sought or wanted rewards; that was not the way he felt. He just wanted to help Wen return to his home at Jin and give him a chance to start over again and become part of the royal family.

Once Wen became duke, Jie resigned because he believed that his job was done. To avoid receiving rewards, he decided to stay away.

Duke Wen rewarded the people who helped him in the time of his exile, but for some reason, he forgot to reward Jie, who by then had moved into the forest with his mother. Duke Wen went to the forest but could not find Jie.

Where was he? *Wen thought.* Why did he leave?

The men who worked for the Duke of Wen gave him a stupid suggestion—real stupid!

"Let's torch him out. He will then come out. He has to. Sound good?"

Duke Wen, not thinking clearly, ordered his men to set the forest on fire to force out Jie. However, Jie and his mother died from the fire.

When the duke heard of their deaths, he mourned and locked himself in his bedroom for days. People tried to get him out of his room, but the Duke of Wen lay on his bed crying. Still feeling sorry, Duke Wen ordered the county to have three days without fire to honor Jie's memory.

The legend goes that Jie Zitui died in 636 Bc around the spring or autumn period, but it's not really clear when. The city where Jie died is still called Jiexiu, which means "the place Jie rests forever."

The Wise One stopped to look at the crowd. Some had the sniffles while others were blowing their noses and wiping the tears from their eyes with their sleeves. The Wise One waited till they settled down, and he continued.

They say that Qingming Festival has a tradition going way, way back for more than 2,500 years, and its beginnings

17

are credited to the emperor called Xuanzong. Now, you have to understand that during that time, the wealthy residents of China, so they say, were holding too many—I mean, too much— flashy and expensive ceremonies in honor of those who died. In other words, their ancestors. There were just so many ceremonies each year that the emperor decided to reduce this practice.

He declared that all respects could be formally paid at the ancestors' graves only during the Qingming Festival. So you see, instead of a lot of ceremonies in honor of their ancestors each year, only one was observed. By this action, one can see that the observance of Qingming Festival found a firm place in Chinese culture and has continued to this very day.

As the Wise One finished his story, a slight breeze from the west moved the clouds and the branches of the huge tree.

The smell of evening dew was in the air. The young ones knew it was the right time to hear the tale about the beautiful black cat.

The Wise One sensed their anticipation, and a smile of delight radiated as he began the legend of Blackie, the polydactyl cat.

"The day of this ancient festival called Qingming, a ship landed in Fengdu County, a county located in a municipality of Chongqing, and Blackie the cat was in her sixty-fifth day of gestation. For those who do not know this word *gestation*, it means that the cat was pregnant."

The young boys and girls giggled as the Wise One smiled and stroked his white beard again and continued.

The People's Republic of China has provided a special invitation to all countries to attend this festival; and the HMS Emerald, *a ship commanded by Lieutenant Commander Bernard O'Neill, was honored to be a part of this festival.*

Blackie too was honored but in a different way, more like she was glad that they reached land. She knew she was a special cat that offered friendship to the sailors of this ship. Her presence brought a sense of home, security, and companionship to all the sailors because they were away from home for such long, long periods of time.

Blackie was good in catching mice and rats. Her natural ability to adapt to the ship's surroundings made her suitable for service to the ship, and she was loved by all. But that love had to be put aside; for she, in her condition, needed a place on land to litter her kittens.

Blackie wandered into a city called the Fengdu Ghost City and entered into a cemetery near the Buddhist temple.

A great thunderstorm was taking place on this seventh month in the Chinese calendar, when they say ghosts and spirits come out from the underworld to visit earth.

The Wise One paused as he saw the children's eyes wide open, thinking about the ghost and spirits. He then continued.

But Blackie found a dry and warm nest in a corner where hay was her bed for delivery. In the midst of the thunderstorm, the labor began, and Blackie started to pant short rasping breaths.

Then as lightning crossed the skies, she stretched herself full-length, and a white pus sac appeared from her female surface.

Though one of her babies has arrived, she began to lick away the white sac that the kitten was covered in—biting and chewing then licking away at the covering until the kitten began to wimp and mew.

As the firstborn began life, the mother cat began panting and preparing herself for the arrival of two more kittens, and then the storm took a break.

For the first several weeks, the kittens were unable to do much without being stirred by their mother. They were also unable to control their body temperatures for the first three weeks, so Blackie just kept them warm by using her own body as a blanket. Blackie's milk was important for the kittens' nutrition and proper growth.

Seven days after birth, the kittens opened their eyes. At first, the retina in their eyes was poorly developed, and their vision was poor.

Blackie knew that it would take time for the kittens to be able to see well, and she was pleased.

The kittens played together and built up their strength as they started to improve day by day, play-fighting with one another.

They began to explore the world outside their little nest. They learned to wash themselves and one another, as well as playing hunting and stalking games, showing off their inborn ability as predators. These inborn skills were developed by the kittens' mother, bringing live prey to the nest and showing them special hunting techniques . Their private hunting and stalking skills peaked within five months, and Blackie the cat again was pleased.

Nearing the sixth month, the first two kittens that were born were in danger because they liked to find dark places to hide, and they found one—with deadly results.

The loss of her two kittens brought about such an illness within Blackie that, even later, when a Buddhist priest tried to protect her from her own illness, it was to no avail. The pain was too much.

She was buried in a lonely corner in the cemetery, an unknown grave with no marking, a sad legacy for a devoted mother.

The Buddhist priests brought the third cat to the temple and let him wander around the area and its surroundings.

This beautiful black-fur polydactyl cat had white roots. These cats were known to be black smoke cats. In the sunlight, his fur would show a light-rust color, as if fire was his nature. His leathery nose, black. His paw pads, black. But his heart—pure.

Before his seventh month and during the setting of the sun, he was outside enjoying the greenery left by autumn time as he wandered back into the cemetery near the Buddhist temple. He wanted to continue to tend the grave of the departed one, his mother, whom he loved so much. To do so, he had to pass through many willow branches on the gates and doors of homes, which help ward off the evil spirits. This custom was especially true during the Qingming Festival, which took place during his birth about seven months ago.

A strong Jie Zitui spirit wind led and carried the black cat to a garden that had an opening in the ground, where a spirit fire concealed its entrance.

The scent of food and drink drove the black cat through the spirit fire—and the rest became the legend.

The Wise One knew there was more to this legend and pondered whether he should tell them the secrets of Diyu. Lightning crossed the skies while the sound of a thunderstorm was forthcoming, but the crowd was still eager to hear more. The Wise One stood up and looked at the eyes of the crowd one by one.

Diyu—is the realm of the dead!

An underworld web with various levels, and there are chambers to which souls are taken after death.

Ten courts of hell. Some say there are only four. But no matter how many there are, each is ruled by a judge, a Yama king.

These many kings who judge the dead and preside over the Narakas—we know it as hells or purgatories—also preside over the many cycles of rebirth.

Of all these kings, there is one who is the ruler of Diyu.

His name is Yan, and he alone judges the male black cat who has passed through the midway region of the earth and who is protected by the mother spirit of Jie Zitui. This male black polydactyl cat ate the spirit food of Jie Zitui, which was prepared in the same way it was given to Duke Wen of Jin.

This physical action brought about a changing state of being in this cat.

Within the animal's body, an unseen change took place.

This energy was in a state of constant interaction and unrest with one another.

The earth, water, fire, air, and spirit all revolved around this animal, who is protected by the mother spirit of Jie Zitui.

Then, after a little time in the midway region of the earth, the black cat—named Shadow by the ruler Yan—returned to earth.

Yes, he returned, but not as a cat, but as a new creature in a new body. And only the spirits knows the outcome of its design.

The rain started to fall, but the crowd still wanted to hear more. The Wise One sat down quietly and considered their need to know the outcome. He then stood up and told the crowd the story was still being told but in another land and in another place.

"So go home now, and maybe one day, the folklore will be *yours* to tell."

PART I

The Legend

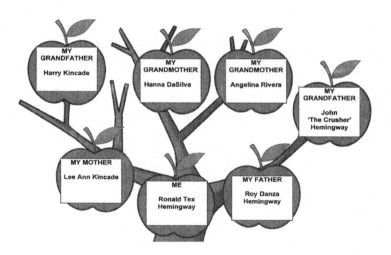

1

A Hamlet in Sullivan County, New York

Narrowsburg is located in the western part of the town of Tusten at the junction of Route 52 and 97. This community calls itself the Eagle capital of New York State.

It is also the home to the Ten Mile River Boy Scout Camp, the Delaware Valley Arts Alliance, the Commodore Murray Cup, and the Delaware Valley Opera.

This community is on the east shore of the Delaware River, near the border of Pennsylvania. It is also between the Catskill Mountains and the Pocono Mountains.

Listed on the National Register of Historic Places are the Arlington Hotel, the Kirk House, and Narrowsburg Methodist Church.

This community was first called Homans Eddy after Benjamin Homan, the first settler in the town.

The bridge that crosses the Delaware River at its most narrow point to Pennsylvania is called the same as the town—Narrowsburg.

There are blue herons, bald eagles, glittering blue waters, green fields, fawns, and towering oaks, and evergreens. All of this is Narrowsburg—a haven to be experienced.

There is also an old farmhouse on County Road 23 near Crystal Lake Road, where Roy Danza and Lee Ann Hemingway was about to experience a little part of this legend. A legend that time brought about in a little hamlet located in Sullivan County in the great state of New York.

2

The Crusher
and the Woodingdean Well

There was one New Yorker who was extremely proud of his family, and his name was Roy Danza. Lee Ann had heard her husband's story about his family so many times that she was able to finish his sentences in her sleep.

To their neighbor Maria, this was something new. Roy started the story, highlighting his dad, who was nicknamed *the Crusher*.

"You know, Maria, that Thame is a town in Oxfordshire, England. It derives its name from the River Thame, which flows past the north side of the town. Now, this town is famous for the legend of James Figg. 'Here I am, Jemmy Figg, from Thame. I will fight any man in England.'"

Roy flexed his upper body with a boxing punching stance in front of the two ladies to emphasize his point to them. He then continued, "That was the cry heard around the Marylebone area of London in the early eighteenth century, where James Figg opened an academy of arms, which included boxing. He stood 6 feet tall and weighed 185 pounds and was ready to accept a challenge to fight from anyone.

They say he lost only one match, and on that occasion, he was said to be sick. Figg was the first recognized champion of England at fighting with bare fists. He was claimed the title Champion of England from 1719 until about 1730. Thame also produced another fighter. And this fighter is the one I'm especially fond of, my dad, John 'The Crusher' Hemingway.

His skills were not only in boxing but in martial arts like wing chun, tae kwon do, judo, and other styles of kung fu and karate. He was also the instructor of defense in the town's police department.

He received a job offer from Puerto Rico to train the academy of undercover police officers who dealt with terrorists and needed this type of defense skills to fight the criminals since these undercover agents were not allowed any weapons in the field to defend themselves. Imagine that. No weapons to defend yourself.

He took the offer, and within a year, my dad lost his heart to a beautiful Puerto Rican girl named Angelina Rivera—my mother. They married, and two years later, they moved to Brooklyn, New York, where I was born. At the age of five, we moved to East Texas near the Piney Woods

30

area. It was there that I met the love of my life and my future wife—Lee Ann Kincade."

Roy bent from his waist and bow to his wife. He then managed to drag her into the conversation so that she could talk about her family life. Lee Ann let out a sigh and then said, "Okay. Woodingdean, which is in England—I was told by my dad—is a place claiming to have the deepest hand-dug well in the world. The depth of this well, they say, is about 1,285 feet. This well was hand-dug between 1858 and 1862.

This place also produced a brilliant engineer, my dad, Harry Kincade. Harry was offered an engineering project job in South America in a country called Guyana. He took the job, and within six months, he lost his heart to a beautiful Guyanese girl, my mom, Hanna DaSilva.

Harry and Hanna married a year and a half later and moved to eastern Tucson, Arizona, where I was born in a development area called Desert Palms Park. Everyone I know referred to Tucson as the Old Pueblo.

My mom's father has Chinese origin and is well versed in Chinese custom and folklores. So as a child, my mother heard all these stories from her dad, and she passed some of these customs and folklores to me in bedtime stories. Those were fun years as a child to grow up in. At the age of seven, we moved to East Texas near the Piney Woods area. There I met the love of my life and my future husband—Roy Danza Hemingway."

They both laughed out loud, feeling a little silly about their stories.

Their neighbor Maria thought the Hemingways were a loving couple, and she knew she was going to miss them. She had to go to Florida to have her left hip replaced, and they all knew this procedure and rehabilitation time would keep them apart for many months. After their lunch, coffees, and hugs, they said good-byes to each other.

The many fun times and laughter they shared together with their neighbor started to fall away into a sad mood when Maria said her final good-byes.

3

Ding-Dong Bell

"Honey, refresh my memory. Why are we sitting out here on these log chairs made by Tommy? I mean, I'm like any other guy who likes sitting under the moonlight with his favorite girl. I like the propane lights hanging from the trees next to our favorite flowing artesian well and our large wooden cross by its side, but come on. What is it with these candles in these altar-type settings?"

"Cuddles, humor me. Remember when we went back home to visit my relatives in Tucson in 1990? There was an All Souls' procession first organized that year by Susan Kay Johnson."

"So what? There were only thirty-five participants involved, I believe. It was crazy."

"Okay, it may have been small, but it kept growing through the years. Anyway, they celebrate it all over the world. They call it the Day of the Dead."

"So?"

"So today is November the second, and it is the Day of the Dead."

"So what is that for us? Come on, honey. Let's go back across the street and open a nice bottle of wine and lie down next to the fireplace and—"

"Roy Danza! Stop being a jerk and just humor me."

"Wow! Did I just got butt-spanked by my wife?"

Roy Danza, at 5'8", 170 pounds, with blue eyes and black hair, got up to put firewood on the little fire between the chairs. The stars and moon were out so brightly that the night darkness around the area had a glow about it. Roy remembered all the traveling they did before arriving in Narrowsburg. When Lee Ann saw that the old farmhouse was for sale, she fell in love with it. What could Roy do but buy it for her? The area had the woodsy feeling like Piney Woods in East Texas, where they first fell in love.

"Honey, what am I supposed to do out here? Should I make a scary face and howl like a wolf at the moon? Howl, howl…"

"Cuddles, grow up! All I want you to do is remember those who died."

"You mean like Janis Joplin, who died of a heroin overdose? Or Jim Reeves, whom we know as Gentleman Jim, who died before his forty-first birthday while flying his private plane into a violent thunderstorm?"

"Why do you mention them?"

"Honey, they are all from East Texas, including Tex Ritter, who died from a heart attack ten days before his sixty-ninth birthday. You remember his song 'There's a New Moon Over My Shoulder.' And, honey, with you by my side, there is always a new moon over my shoulder."

"Oh, cuddles, that is so sweet."

"I'm glad you like it. Not to change the subject, but would this Day of the Dead be more realistic if we would have gone to the Glen Cove Cemetery in Narrowsburg? Ah, maybe not, since Thomas Dunn's family, around the 1800, founded the cemetery and was the only recorded slaveholder in Narrowsburg. I don't think those who are dead would like that."

"Roy, stop being a smart-ass. Try to remember those we knew who passed away."

Roy loved looking at Lee Ann, who was five foot two and ninety-eight pounds, with brown eyes and long black hair. And still she had the power to captivate him.

Roy then started to remember all the stillborn babies Lee Ann had to bury. A pain no woman should bear. Maybe this was her way to say to them that she missed them. Roy couldn't understand how a loving woman, who was diagnosed with multiple sclerosis, went through life with a jerk like him, and yet she still thought he was the love of her life. Tears started to roll down Roy's eyes.

"Cuddles, what's wrong? Why are you crying?"

Roy moved toward Lee Ann and gently kissed her on her forehead. "Honey, you are the best thing that ever happens to a guy like me. I can't help getting emotional about it."

Then, suddenly, the bell over the well started to ring.

Ding-dong, ding dong.

An echo of a baby's voice was crying.

Ding-dong, ding-dong.

"Roy, where is the crying coming from?"

"I don't know. It seems like it's coming from the well."

Roy took one of the propane lights hanging from the tree and raised it above the well. Just below the well in the bucket was a naked child.

"Lee Ann…it looks like there is a baby in our well."

"Let me see. Move over, Roy—let me see!"

In the cool night air, a miracle seemed to present itself.

Not for Roy but for the many stillbirths that Lee Ann went through.

The childless woman now had a chance to become a *mother*.

4

The Enlightened Ones

In East Texas, near the Piney Woods area, Hanna and Harry Kincade turned off the downstairs light to go to sleep. The excitement of spending two weeks with their daughter and son-in-law required a good night sleep before boarding the plane to New York.

The Day of the Dead was coming to a close, and they did not want to get distracted from this day's events.

The night's event, on the other hand, took another turn for Harry and Hanna.

In Hanna's dream, the spirit of Jie Zitui's mother came to her, explaining a vision she needed to see and hear. In the vision, she saw a beautiful black polydactyl cat whose name was *Shadow*. This name was given by the ruler Yan from the underworld. Shadow the cat had the reincarnation spirit of the duke of Wei, known as the General Li Jing from the emperor Taizong of Tang Dynasty.

This black cat is the *only* adopted cat from the White Tiger, who represents the west and autumn season. The White Tiger, who is part of the fifth element, has chosen this special cat because of its dreams of wanting to be human.

The cat, tending of the grave of the departed, showed outwardly signs of humanity. The cat had warrior-and-hero type qualities that only a general warrior spirit could be part of him.

The evil and injustice of Duke Wen and the many wrongs in his life shown to Duke Wei, has given the White Tiger and all the other four elements to bestow to this adopted cat its power.

The spirit mother said, "Shadow the cat will fight evil and injustice from the living and the dead and those who are not of this world. Even those who are the undead will not hide from his wrath."

She told Hanna that the ruler Yan had provided the rebirth and that she, the mother of Jie Zitui, would protect Shadow the cat and its human form. She had provided a birthmark on the back of the right shoulder blade of this child for identification. It was the Chinese number 5 (五). It represented the five elements and their powers.

"You will see this child soon. Tell only those who are involved with this child. No other humans need to know."

And as the dream seemed to fade away, Hanna could hear the spirit's voice saying, "Hanna will keep my wishes...Hanna will keep my wishes...Hanna will keep my wishes..."

Then the dream with the spirit of Jie Zitui's mother came to Harry. She reminded him about the nursery rhyme he learned as a child in school.

> Jacke boy, ho boy newes
> The cat is in the well
> Let us ring now for her knell
> Ding dong ding dong bell.

It was a reference to John Lant's nursery rhyme, who was the organist of Winchester Cathedral in the year of 1580.

Harry, who came from Woodingdean, England—the suburb that claims to have the deepest hand-dug well in the world—is now being told by the spirit mother that he will soon see another wonder: a cat from a different well becoming another form.

"Do not be afraid of this child, Harry. Support your family in protecting the identity of this child. Hanna, your wife, has some details you need to know. Speak to her. Harry will keep my wishes...Harry will keep my wishes... Harry will keep my wishes..."

As the dream was echoing and fading away, the night's sleep took on another form: the form of the *enlightened ones*.

5

The Farmhouse Protection Plan

Roy came back from Peck's Market with diapers, baby food, baby bottles, and milk.

The morning of November 3 was bright, with very little clouds and a touch of light wind in the air. They were up all night.

Lee Ann's face was cheerful and as bright as a newborn's mother. She was still holding the child, whom Roy nicknamed *Tex,* in a soft white blanket.

"Oh, cuddles, I'm so happy. I still can't believe this is real. Pinch me, Roy."

"Honey, it's real, but what do we tell your parents when they arrive this afternoon?"

"We tell them the truth, Roy. I've never lied to my parents, and I'm not going to start now."

"The truth is stranger than fiction. Would they believe us?"

"Yes. They've never lied to me, and they know me. My mother used to tell me stories regarding folklore and customs, the same stories her dad used to tell her when she was a child and growing up. Somehow, she can probably explain this miracle or help me find the answers I need."

Lee Ann paced back and forth in the kitchen, holding the child in her arms, smiling down at it, and then looked up at Roy and said, "One thing I know. No one—and I mean, no one—will ever take this child away from me! I will protect it with my life! Do you understand, Roy, what I mean?"

Her eyes had a demanding stare and were focused upon her husband's eyes; and before he could answer her she said, "Swear to me, Roy, that you will honor my wishes in this matter! And swear to me that you will protect and father this child as if it was your own! Swear to me!"

"I swear, Lee Ann...I swear...I swear..."

It was 3:00 p.m., and Roy was back from Walmart with a playpen, baby blankets, and baby clothes and shoes. While he was preparing the playpen, a taxi parked outside the farmhouse, dropping off Lee Ann's parents. Roy stepped outside to help them with their luggage after he greeted them.

As soon as they entered the farmhouse, Lee Ann ran over to hug and kiss her mother and dad.

Hanna looked at Lee Ann with a knowing smile and said, "Someone is overly happy to see us...or is it? Maybe she is trying to tell us about her new special gift."

Roy's and Lee Ann's bodies froze in that minute. Their eyes opened wide in amazement. They both wondered, *Do they know? How could they?*

The next hour, Hanna and Harry related their dreams to Roy and Lee Ann. They went over to the child and saw the birthmark. Then a plan of action had to be decided now to protect the child's identity.

Harry suggested that Roy and Lee Ann board a flight tonight or tomorrow to their house in East Texas. He said, "Lee Ann must dress like she is nine months pregnant and let everyone at the airport see her. Hanna, the child, and I will take the Amtrak train to Beaumont's train station and take a taxi to our home from there. Then we will call Roy's dad and mom to our house and explain this miracle to them. Then I will call Dr. Kim, who has taken care of Lee Ann since she was a child, to have the honor of providing the local registrar the birth-certificate information. Now, let me see what else..."

Harry looked at his wife and then at Lee Ann and said, "Dr. Kim will arrive from his vacation the tenth of November, and we can say to him that the child was delivered on the eighth of November by a midwife from Guyana, a friend of Hanna who was in the area. We can tell the doctor that we wanted him to have the honor since he took care of Lee Ann when she was a child. And as far as Lee Ann is concerned, she can say she saw a gynecologist at Christus Hospital–St. Elizabeth in Beaumont on the ninth of November, and everything health-wise was okay. Once all of this is done, Roy and Lee Ann will wait a month or two before going back to Narrowsburg. I think this is a good plan. Okay, let's get started. I'll call the airlines to see what's available. Am I missing anything?"

Roy started to think about the situation they were in. They lived in Narrowsburg for less than a year, and they rarely ever went out. When they did, they usually went to Monticello to shop or dine out. No one knew their private life except Maria, and she was in Florida. So this plan could probably work.

Two months turned to three months in East Texas. Grandparents love to spoil their grandchildren. And these two grandparents were no exception. They kept fighting each other for that honor. Roy Danza's dad was the one who named the child Ronald after the president Ronald Reagan. Roy thought, *Who can argue with the Crusher?*

Roy thought that his newly adopted son, Ronald "Tex" Hemingway, would become something special. Maybe it could be a legend that needed time to fulfill its destiny?

A destiny that will contain future stories about a new mother and father with a unique child. And this story will begin in Narrowsburg—a haven yet to be experienced with an extraordinary child, a lovely hamlet in Sullivan County in the great state of New York.

PART II

The Change

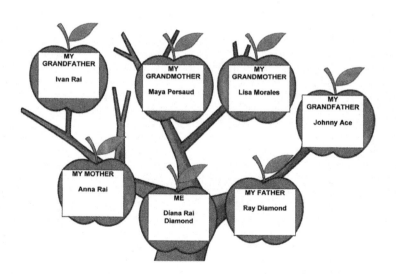

6

A Change Is Coming

Ray Ace thought about the Second Reconnaissance Battalion in the Dominican Republic Civil War, which to him seemed like a pussycat tour mission. All his prior training in close-quarters battle tactics and the other special trainings were not needed in the so-called invasion launched on April 1965.

Ray was trained in special skills, including but not limited to scout sniper school, jump school, military free-fall school, combatant dive school, and ranger school.

He was surprised by orders that his platoon should report to a special fielded operations unit that sent them to align with Project DELTA at Nha Trang, Vietnam, and that their mission was to conduct small-scale reconnaissance and hunter-killer operations.

His platoons captured and interrogated VC/NVA (People's Army of Vietnam), tapped communications, bugged compounds and offices, rescued downed aircrew and prisoners of war, and placed minefields and other booby traps. They also conducted psychological operations and performed counterintelligence operations. Their focus was on the base area and infiltration routes in the border areas.

The funny thing about it was that after he was honorably discharged, there was no mention of the Second Reconnaissance Battalion platoon *ever* in Vietnam. Only the Combined Action Program, with the thirteen-Marine rifle squad, the Navy corpsman, and Vietnamese militia platoon.

One thing about special operations unit, they sure know when to disband once the conflict ends. Ray chucked at the thought.

It had been over two years since he left the Marines, and his hiring skill level during that time was only good in eliminating problems for corporate institutions.

His mentor and teacher was a friend who lived next door to his apartment in a building in Richmond Hill, New York, which had 99 percent airline stewardesses living there. The truth was that his mentor was seeing a lady in the apartment building, not that he lived there.

Ray thought about his eliminating problem skills. If it wasn't for scout sniper school, he would have been out of a job. Even though the money was excellent and two years in the business provided a nice fortune for him, he needed a vacation time from the job, or else the Feds or other problem solvers would come around looking for him. And looking over his shoulder wasn't what he wanted to do in his life.

He needed a place where nobody could find him. A place where a person of 5'10", 180 pounds, with blue-greenish eyes and dark-brown hair was never in, a place no one would ever suspect he had been to.

A new location was great, but he also needed a name change.

How about India? He thought as he packed his bags and started toward his storage facilities to bury his past.

7

❖❖❖❖❖

You Have the Third Eye

Overlooking the water at the capital city Bombay, in the Indian state of Maharashtra, India, Ray realized that he was safe here. His biggest problem was to convince Mr. Rai, Anna's father, that he wanted his blessing and Anna's hand in marriage.

Since the first time he met her, he knew she was the one. She was a lady who loved to read and even had pen pals around the world. She never questioned who he was. When he asked her why she never asked him more about himself, she would always say, "When you want me to know about it, you would then tell me. So why push it, my honorable Ray?" Who could argue with that?

Anna—at 5'5", 105 pounds, with brown eyes, full lips, and long black hair—would tell him that Bombay is the birthplace of Indian cinema. A person called Dadasaheb Phalke laid the foundations with silent movies, followed by

Marathi talkies—and the oldest film broadcast took place here in the early twentieth century.

Her face would light up when she talked about Bombay and its large number of cinema halls that feature Bollywood, Marathi, and Hollywood movies. It was the Hollywood movies that helped Anna with her English and her dream of loving an American. Ray knew this lady had to be his partner for life. But it was hard trying to convince her dad.

It took some time, but Ray was able to have a legal name change from Ace to Diamond. It took a little more time to convince Mr. Rai, with the help of Anna, to finally have an Indian wedding.

Passport and green-card procedures in India took some time. Extra payments of money to the right people were needed so that the paperwork process could go faster.

Thank God for the American dollar, Ray thought.

It took a year before Ray and Anna was able to go to America.

Ray bought a home for Anna in Luxton Lake, Narrowsburg, New York.

One year later, on April 30, Diana Rai Diamond was born, on a month whose gemstone is also the diamond.

Fifteen years went by before Anna received a letter from India that her father was ill. Since it was during the school's summer vacation, they all packed up and went to India to be by Anna's father side and to comfort the family.

During this time, Anna's grandfather Raj was a cemetery caretaker at Santa Cruz Cemetery in Bombay. A bond between Raj and Diana occurred during their stay. She would go to work with him at nights and learn from Raj the legends and superstitions that went along with cemeteries. She would also see the groups of young people who placed their altars at the cemetery and did their black magic ceremonies.

There were other similarly secret happenings, such as devil worshippers trying to take place, but Raj would catch them in the act. He would yell at them and called the police to get rid of them.

Living in India with all its charms prepared Diana's inward senses to increase and brought out the ability to see auras around folks. She developed a kind of "six sense" about people's characters.

Every once in a while, when she would go to sleep, she would have an out-of-body experience, which gave her a perception of what was around her. Like a seer, she could map out the thoughts and feelings surrounding a person. It was a unique gift she now had to deal with, and she was at ease with it. But sharing this information with her parents was hard at first.

She only told her great-grandfather Raj since he was the one who saw the changes developing in her at the very beginning.

Every once in a while, with a slight grin in his face, Raj would pass by her and tell her—in his cute, deep Indian accent—"Daughter, you have the third eye."

8

Tex Achilles's Heel

"Dad, why can't we go to the gun club now? I think I am ready."

"Okay, son. Show me one more time the dry fire practice again. Let me see your feet and leg positioning. Good. Now your upper body must be correctly aligned. Good. Arms, elbows, and shoulders must be locked in the right way. That looks good. Now make sure you have the proper grip of the handgun and that you know the sight alignment techniques. Make sure your breathing isn't hampering your accuracy.

Finally, the position of your finger on the trigger and your trigger pull must both be performed correctly in tune with the rest of your body."

"Dad, can't you see I got it? I have been doing this for two months. And now can we go?"

Roy was thinking that Tex wasn't afraid to learn small lessons the hard way, but he was hoping that Tex would try to learn the big lessons the easy way, from somebody else's mistake.

Now they were on their way to Beaverbrook Rod and Gun Club on Trout Pond Road to put theory to practice. Five minutes later, they arrived. After greeting the people there, a young lady approached them.

"Good morning, Mr. Hemingway."

"Good morning, Ms. Diamond."

"Good morning, Ronald."

"Good morning, Diana."

As Diana passed by, Ron looked at his dad and said, "Dad, why does Diana Diamond always act funny around me?"

"What do you mean?"

"In school, she is always looking at me. In martial arts class, she always wants to be my sparring partner. Then she asks if I need help with my homework, or do you need a study partner before a test is given? What gives?"

"Do you like her?"

"What do you mean?"

"I mean, do you think she is pretty?"

"Yeah, she is pretty, but still weird."

"Maybe she likes you and probably thinks you are weird."

"Why would she think that?"

"I guess being young has its own problems, but don't think too hard about it. Okay, let see some fine shooting, son."

As Roy watched his son shoot, he felt proud to see that the lessons paid off. He always knew his son had a special gift in learning things really quick. In fighting or using any weapon, his son needed to know that he should not make a mistake and assume that adrenaline does not affect us the same way, whether we're being attacked on the street or inside our home.

In a violent encounter, if you have to take time to think, you're at an extreme disadvantage. Thinking means hesitation, and hesitation means freezing. That is why Roy needed to have his son practice and practice until it became second nature to him.

"Dad, did you see my shooting? All the shots went right where I wanted them. Dad, you are the best teacher in the whole wide world!"

"Really? I thought I was boring you with too much repetition."

"Come on, Dad. You taught me all the different techniques in martial arts and in boxing, and as of now, no one has ever beaten me. My archery skills are excellent except for hunting. Why is that?"

"You tell me why."

"Well, every time I try to shoot a deer or any animal, I miss. One time, I tried to shoot a rabbit, and the arrow went up and came down and landed in the rabbit's foot. I can't seem to shoot animals. Why is that?"

"Son, your nature will not permit that to happen, and that will always be your *Achilles's heel.*"

9

Be Patient—It Will Come

The phone rang, and Diana answered her first call on Monday morning. "Good morning, A & D Iron Works…Yes, we do structural steel fabrication and also miscellaneous ironworks including stairs, railings, etc.,…Yes, our plant consists of ten thousand square feet under two five-ton cranes. We also have a yard for painting and a separate area for miscellaneous fabrication of steel… Sure, drop by anytime…You have our address in Honesdale. Thanks for calling."

"Who was that?" Anna asked.

"It seems like another customer interested in doing business with us. Mom, it looks like we are going to have another busy day at the office. I need to do the requisitions. Gotham sites and Monadnock sites are due tomorrow. Have you done the bank reconciliation yet?"

"Diana, I did that on Friday. The ledgers and all the books are up to date."

"Sorry, Mom…my mind is a little off today."

"What's wrong, munchkin?"

"It's Ronald Hemingway. I can't get him out of my mind. I saw him at the gun club Saturday, and he seemed to ignore me. What is wrong with me, Mom?"

"You're trying too hard. You need to learn that you have to back off when things don't seem to go your way. I had to do that with your dad when we first went out. If he is the one, then just be patient—it will come."

Diana, during summer vacation and after school, helped her mom and dad in their business, a business Ray intended to sell soon since the economy seemed to be going south. Diana was also planning to join the police department or the sheriff's department after she graduated from high school. She also intended to get some college credits in night school.

It was Diana's dad who taught Anna and her bookkeeping and office procedures. Ray used to help out his uncle for three years after school when he was twelve. His uncle was a certified accountant who wanted to leave the business to Ray. Born and raised in South Ozone Park, New York, Ray believed that having a business while young would tie him down, and he would never experience the opportunity to have choices in life.

"Mom, Grandfather Raj told you about my gifts, and I can't help but see an aura around Ronald that is subtle, and a luminous radiation of power that is hidden and yet wants to be free. I don't think even Ron knows what is in him. How can that be? A person with powers who doesn't know he has them. How can that be, Mom?"

"Diana, remember when you went to India? You didn't know you had the gift. When the right time came, the gift revealed itself. I guess Ronald has to go through that too. Like I said before, be patient—it will come."

10

Quotes for Change

Looking through the kitchen's large window, Ron saw the small changes in the weather. The summer breeze was moving the leaves on the trees overlooking and shading the farmhouse. One of the tree's branches housed a small bird's nest, which seemed to be empty at the moment. Ron's thoughts seemed to move about in the same fashion as that branch, but his nest of questions was still lingering in his mind.

Why did his parents celebrate his birthday on the second of November rather than the eighth of November? This always puzzled him. Why the change? He turned toward his mother, who was sitting next to the kitchen table, and asked her why. She motioned for Ron with her hands to sit next to her. As he sat down, she smiled at him, and then she cuddled both of his hands in hers.

Lee Ann was very patient when looking into the yellowish-brown eyes of her adorable son. She knew that a partial truth was the only thing she could tell him right now, but her son needed a little more than that.

"Ron, I'm surprised it took you so long in wondering why the change. The reason was that you were really born on November 2. We told the doctor it was the eighth to avoid stigma toward you from people who are ignorant about holidays and different celebration days. You were born on the Day of the Dead. Nothing to be ashamed about. We were just being protective. We never decided to change the date back to your original date. I guess a past president said it best: 'If you want to make enemies, try to change something.' I don't think he meant it for this situation, but he was close enough."

Ron now understood the reason his parents acted the way they did. Society has its own special rules with its own stigmas, and one must try to avoid those complications.

Then he grinned and smiled within. He remembered certain quotes his dad used to say, "Life will not always hand you what you think you deserve."

Ron's dad taught him leadership skills at an early age. Roy believed in its principles like, "Be cautious of labels"— in other words, don't define or judge people or be in a rush to put them in your own special little box so that you can criticize them.

He always told Ron that everyone deserved respect and that *courtesy* and *manners* made a difference in people's lives. He told Ron to take the time to know people and that one should always be humble even under great success and wealth.

Life and nature display a laboratory of opportunity so one can learn and practice leadership lessons. Even in his short experience in life, Ron saw many people pursue glory instead of pursuing excellence. His dad would say, "Whatever your job is, do it well."

Ron anticipated that was what life was all about. He thought about another quote by an unknown author who said, "God, grant me the serenity to accept the people I cannot change, the courage to change the one I can, *and the wisdom to know it's me.*"

11

Love Acts in Strange Ways

It was a Saturday morning in Narrowsburg and the beginning of the first week of school. The cool summer breeze still lingered in the bustling crowds enjoying life in a small town. The tourists were relishing the shops and the restaurants, standing on the promenade observation decks, and observing the beautiful and vibrant Delaware River.

The post office also had its bustling crowd, including Ron, Lee Ann, and Diana Diamond. They were leaving and going to their vehicles, which were parked up a hill next to the post office, when a car backed out from its parking space and almost hit Ron and Lee Ann.

Diana Diamond saw what was going to happen and rushed over and pushed the Hemingways out of danger. This caused the car to strike Diana as she rolled down the hill toward the sidewalk's pavement.

"Diana!" screamed Lee Ann and Ron.

"Oh my God, is she okay?" Lee Ann said while she and Ron watched Diana's unconscious body on the sidewalk's pavement.

They both ran to her while the lady who was driving stepped out of her car and cried out, "I didn't see her! I swear I didn't see her! Is she okay? Please tell me...is she okay?" And the lady limped down and started to cry profusely; and in a soft, whispering voice, she said, "I'm so sorry...I'm so sorry..."

"Mom, call 911 while I'll check on her." Ron stood looking down at Diana's body, afraid to move her in case there were serious fractures involved. All he could do was call out her name. "Diana...Diana...can you hear me? If you can, please try not to move until the medics come. They should be here soon."

Ron bent downward and put his hands over Diana's right hand to try to comfort her. Her body not moving and still no reply from her, he silently wept. He never wept for a single girl in his life. He was just too busy studying and learning the different combat skills that he never really put much thought into girls.

Now a girl whom he thought was weird took them out of harm's way and sacrificed herself for them. That, to him, was the noblest action anyone could do. With his head down, grieving, guilty feelings emerged about his treatment toward her.

She was always kind to him, and in his own arrogance, he could not see a loving person right in front of him. *What is the use of my skills when I can't see what is truly beautiful in front of me?* He thought. This brought another wave of tears upon him.

"Ron, the medics are on their way. She'll be okay. She's tough like you son…"

Ron didn't really hear his mother's voice. All he could think about was Diana's unconscious body lying on the sidewalk pavement—and the tears just kept on coming.

12

Not So Lucky

"Come on, Dad, make a left turn here. This is it, Lucky Lane...over there... do you see her gray Nissan Altima parked in the driveway? We're here! Come on."

"Hold your horses, son. She isn't going to disappear. Don't forget the flowers and candy—and please, don't forget to open the door for your mother."

Ron was so excited to know that Diana was home and that there were no signs of concussion found in her x-rays. All she had was a sprained leg that needed at least two weeks of home resting. Ron knew this because he kept talking every day to Mr. and Mrs. Diamond and always asking for a progress report on Diana's health.

He got all the homework assignments she needed from school and brought along all the get-well cards from the students and teachers.

"Hi, wonder woman. I see you are still lying in bed trying to figure out what other superdeeds you need to accomplish today."

"Come on, Ron, stop playing around. How are you and your parents doing?"

"My mom and dad are in the kitchen talking to your parents and having some coffee. And they are doing just fine, thank you. It's just like you thinking about others rather than yourself. You are truly my wonder woman."

"Ron, I've never seen you act this way before. It's funny and yet very, very cute."

"Oh, by the way, I brought you this week's homework assignment and all the get-well cards from your admirers. The school is thinking of giving you a certificate or maybe a plaque of honor for your bravery beyond the call of duty. Who knows, they may name a school wing after you. If they do, I'll be the chairman of that committee," Ron said with a smile and then a big laugh. "But for today, all that I can bring with love and devotion are these flowers and a box of these devious and delicious chocolates, my lady."

Ron bowed and moved his right hand in a knight's gesture.

Diana raised herself slightly from the bed and said, "Thank you, my knight in shining armor. I accept your flowers and—what you call it—ah yes, the devious and delicious chocolates. Your humble maiden awaits your future commands."

A moment of silence ensued when Ronald heard the word *future*. His eyes started to water.

"Ronald, what's wrong?"

"I can't help it. I can't get the accident out of my mind. Seeing your body lying unconsciously on the sidewalk and thinking I may never see you again. Diana, I need to say this …would you let me not only be your friend but a person who would like to watch over you every day?"

"What are you saying, Ron? Are you trying to say that you want to be my boyfriend? Is that what you are really trying to say?"

Ron, with tears in his eyes, bent on his knees as if he were going to propose to her. "If you will have me as your boyfriend, I will promise that I will honor that responsibility and make you proud of me. Can I be your boyfriend, please? Can I be your true knight in shining armor?"

In all these years, Diana dreamed to hear those words from the only one she deeply knew was the love of her life. Her mother was right. She remembered her mother saying, "If he is the one, then just be patient—it will come."

"Darling, I waited all these years to hear those words. Of course, I will be your girlfriend, and you will be my true knight in shining armor."

Ron rose and went over to Diana to give her a loving hug and a kiss on her forehead. "We must tell our parents the good news!" Ron excitedly said.

Ronald and Diana's parents were also excited about the news. In the back of their minds, they knew this was more than puppy love. They knew that when the time was right, Ronald would ask for her hand in marriage.

"Ronald, did you know that the Diamonds sold their business and are planning to move to the city after this school year?" Lee Ann said.

"I knew about it. They also have two buyers for this house. They are also looking for a small place up here for their weekends and vacations. How about that ranch trailer across from our farmhouse? That's up for sale." Ron turned to Mr. Diamond. "How about it, Mr. Diamond? I'm sure they're not asking too much for it, and having us as a neighbor isn't too bad. We could even look out for the property when you guys are not there. Sound good?"

"Sounds good to me. I'll take a look at it."

That afternoon, the Hemingways and the Diamonds sat across the kitchen table and enjoyed a chicken curry meal prepared by Anna Diamond. Much laughter and conversation about life brought the two families together. A bond had developed because of the love of two teenagers. Two teenagers had found the compass of their love and the significance for their lives.

"Diana, you live in Luxton Lake, and your street is named Lucky Lane. Can't you see the *L* word is there?"

"*Love* may be there, Ron, but lying in bed now, well— not so lucky."

13

Metamorphosis Begins

On October 30, three days before Ronald "Tex" Hemingway's eighteenth birthday, his dreams were full of mischievous thoughts. His mind could not conceive or permit those evil thoughts to be a part of him. Even his sleep was full of restlessness as Devil's night tried to take control. The vision of vandalism and arson was repugnant to him.

A biological process was physically starting to develop in him. The beginning stages of a conspicuous and relatively abrupt change in body structure through cell growth and differentiation took hold. And yet no knowledge of this transformation was revealed to him, as well as any outward physical transformation.

On October 31, two days before his birthday, All Hallows' Evening began. Halloween that evening had dreams dedicated to remembering the dead, including saints, martyrs, and all the faithful departed believers. But to Tex, his dream was a vision of a beautiful black polydactyl cat and the spirit of the Duke of Wei, known as General Li Jing, from the emperor Taizong of the Tang Dynasty in China.

In his vision, he saw five elements. These elements were the White Tiger, Azure Dragon, Vermilion Bird, the Black Tortoise, and the Yellow Dragon of the center. Yet, with all the dedication to remembering the vision in his dream, by daybreak, no knowledge of this vision had been revealed to him. During the night, stage two of his transformation began. Yet there was still no outward physical transformation.

On November 1, one day before his birthday, surprise arrivals occurred. Both of his grandparents came to celebrate his birthday. And as usual, they came to spoil their grandson. Ronald smiled and laughed to see them fight over the honors of spoiling him. After a day of great food prepared by Lee Ann and a bunch of hugs from everyone, Ronald felt excited in knowing that tomorrow was the day he would be eighteen years old.

A *rite of passage* is a ritual event that marks a person's transition from one status to another. Eighteen was the year of more responsibilities and the freedom that went along with this transition. This transitional phase between childhood and full inclusion into society, this rite of passage, was also going to be shared by his loved ones. To Ronald, that meant a lot.

As the evening came to a close and everyone was tucked away, Ronald slept. Tonight was All Saints' Eve, the Feast of all Saints, and the day before All Souls' Day, the Day of the Dead.

Phase three of the transformation had begun, and this dream had turn into a *beatific vision*.

This vision was the ultimate direct self-communication of the spirit world to Tex. The spirit of Jie Zitui's mother came to him and explained the transformation he was going through and the vision he needed to see and hear. He learned that his cat name was Shadow and that he had the power to shape-shift into Shadow, and that he had the power to control natural elements and can manipulate molecules. He also had ghost-type powers so that invisibility could be achieved.

As the night went on, the spirit revealed more powers that Tex could command but warned that all these powers were to fight evil and injustice from the living and the dead and those that were not of this world. Even those who were the undead would not hide from his wrath.

The spirit revealed to him how he came into the world and that his parents who raised him and loved him as their own should be honored. No disrespect would be tolerated from him toward his parents, and that was the spirit world's commandment.

He was told that his parents and grandparents knew of his situation and was told to keep it from him until the right time had arrived.

"Do not reveal your powers to no one except the one you will marry. Do not be in a rush to use your powers. The target and task will be revealed to you. Your entire question inside you will be answered at the right time."

Ron shared this revelation of his vision during the early morning of his birthday with his loved ones: his parents and grandparents.

And it snowed in Narrowsburg that morning.

PART III

The Beginning

14

The Past and the Beginning

Narrowsburg dodged the first punch of a hazardous winter storm one week ago, but forecasters warned of a potentially *catastrophic* second blow in a thick layer of ice and snow, threatening to bring hundreds of thousands of power outages and leave people in their cold, dark homes for days.

The streets and highways in Narrowsburg were largely deserted as people in the town area heeded the advice from officials to hunker down at home.

The Hemingways and the Kincades were all huddled around the warm fireplace, sipping hot chocolates with marshmallows.

It had been a week into the storm, and only laughter and storytelling filled the atmosphere in the old farmhouse. Outside in the backyard stood a series of snowmen the Hemingways and the Kincades had built during the week.

One sculpture was a miniature cat, and the other was a large boy-like figure.

The Crusher chuckled out loud and said, "Let's go outside and spray-paint the cat black."

They all laughed except Ron.

During the week, they were all amazed to see Ron shape-shift into Shadow the cat and the ghost-walk around the house without being seen. He would pick up cups or some handy objects to announce his presence.

Ron's ability to control natural elements and manipulate molecules was an amazing achievement. Walking through the doors and walls was really creepy. It got to the point that Crusher would tell Ron, "Keep out when I'm in the bathroom, or I will fart vitamins in your face. Do you hear?"

Everyone rolled around in laugher from this funny gag.

The family, secretly in the back of their minds, was in awe of the gifts Ron controlled. Their sense of humor kept the phenomenon of these powers, which could destroy as well as heal, to a level of sanity.

Harry looked at Ron earnestly as he spoke, "Ron. What we are doing now by laughing and joking around is to let you know that these powers of yours should not be taken too seriously. What I mean about this is that power can be a corrupting cause in one's life. Humility is the only stabilizer that lets you become teachable, and one truly learns only in this state of mind. When you think you know it all and that you are better than others, this leads to arrogance.

You then start to *justify yourself* in everything, and then the next step will be that you will start to *deceive yourself* until you become *self-absorbed*. Your life will then become bitter. You will not find true happiness, and your purpose in life will have no meaning. This is the danger of corrupting power.

Let's take this information to another level. Your girlfriend, Diana, could be your future wife. To impress her or others would be stupid. What you will need is responsibility. Responsibility is the key. Responsibility to God, to her, and your loved ones should be your first goal. Your neighbors and country should be your second goal—all in that order. If you cannot control yourself, how can you lead people?

Lack of control is also a weakness. Your dad, mom, and grandparents love you. They show this love by being responsible for your well-being. They teach you humility by disciplining you. Respect for authority is important in having a good childhood. We all do what we must so that you can flourish and become the magnificent man that you are today. So come over here and give me a big hug."

While Ron was hugging his grandfather, he whispered in his ear, "Thanks, Grandpa. I always knew you had my back. I love you."

"Love you too, kid."

Then the Crusher laughed and yelled out, "Where are our hugs, hmm?"

So as the hug fest and laughter continued, the snow outside started to dwindle away, and the hunkering down soon became the past.

Then the past opened its door to the new beginning.

15

Wanna Sink a Lake?

Forecasters were partially right regarding the warning of a potentially *catastrophic* second blow of a hazardous winter storm. The thick layer of ice and snow—which threatened to bring hundreds of thousands of power outages and leave people in their cold, dark homes for days—was now over for most areas, but not Luxton Lake.

The streets and highways in Narrowsburg were largely deserted as people in the town area heeded the advice from officials to hunker down at home. But now the roads were plowed and ready to be used.

A white vehicle belonging to Sureway Taxi was outside waiting for Ron's grandparents. According to the news, they decided to leave early that morning since the roadway to Monticello and later to the airport was cleared.

Looking out from the farmhouse window, Ron was sad to see his grandparents leave. Seeing the taxi making a U-turn and heading toward Crystal Lake Road, he wondered, *When will I see them again?* The living-room-window view showed the white snow hovering over the trees and grass, and a sense of a Christmas moment was in the air. This winter wonderland was like having nice presents under a white Christmas tree.

Ron started his way up the stairs to his bedroom to turn on the computer. He sat down in his black swivel computer chair and stared at the screen in front of him. He then started to scroll down the blogs' menus showing people's reactions and stories about Luxton Lake.

> There were 3 or 4 inches of snow on the ground this morning in Luxton Lake, with freezing rain mixing in now.
>
> We are having chilly and windy morning in Luxton Lake. Power's out.
>
> Power out throughout Luxton Lake since 6:30 last night, and the rain and snow have subsided, and wind is less frequent and less severe, but still gusty. According to NYSEG, 969 customers in the area are without power.

Ron laughed and thought, *How could that be? With that amount of customers, it must be all of Narrowsburg and then some.*

Ron could hear his dad coming up the stairs and entering his room. In his hands were two cups of black coffee.

"I thought you might have a taste for some coffee son, since mom made pancakes and eggs this morning a little bit of coffee seems to be the last blend needed to be a perfect breakfast."

"Thanks, Dad. You always seem to read my mind."

"Not always, son. I wouldn't have guessed that you would be checking out blogs this early in the morning."

Ron took a sip of the coffee and stared at the screen and said.

"Dad, the reason I'm checking out the blogs is to check out Luxton Lake. I also remember the conversation we had over Robby Quinn's Irish feast on St. Patrick's Day. We talked about Luxton Lake and its history."

"Yep. I remembered that. A lot of good black families moved to Luxton Lake before the dam was destroyed. Jazz musician and big band leader Noble Sissle, whose orchestra was popular in the early 1930s, led the development of Luxton Lake."

Ron was amazed in seeing his dad dance through the menus on the computer with his fingers as if he were playing a piano concerto.

The screen showed many article regarding Luxton Lake property owners who had big dreams and big plans. There were stories about how people were sad when they lost their lake in 1983. A documentary film was made showing the reactions of the residents of Luxton Lake watching in shock as their lake was drained and their beloved community now left almost waterless.

The Department of Environmental Conservation said, "The one-hundred-year-old laid-up stone dam was unstable and posed a threat to houses below the dam." So what they did—*blew it up.*

Roy stared angrily at the computer screen and then looked at Ron and said, "These conservationists had only four words in their vocabulary, and those words were, *Wanna sink a lake?* Son, that is the problem with most of the government's people. They have too much time on their hands, and they need a reason for their existence in their jobs."

"Dad, remember when Mr. Smith, the jazz drummer who played with Charlie Parker and other music greats, told us at Robby's home that he witnessed the dam being taken down. He said it was a sunny and gorgeous day when they blew up the dam. He first thought he heard the sound of thunder, but it was the explosion and the dam's rocks that were moving about that caused the loud noise. We still have a piece of property on the same block that he lives in…right?"

"Yep, our property is right across Robby's home. You remember that their neighbors wanted Mr. Smith and me to provide them a jam session when they found out I was also a famous musician."

"I know, Dad. Those days are way behind you…or maybe your fingers have gone the way of—*the mummy!*"

At the same time, Ron jumped out of the chair to avoid his dad's lightning-fast hands, those same hands that would have smacked him at the back of his head for the wiseass remark. Ron was laughing and telling his dad it was just a joke and that he was sorry if it offended him in any way.

Roy smiled back and said, "You are fast, son—and also smart. You didn't take any chance to see if I was going to react the way you believe I would have. I like what I saw. Let's get back to the articles."

They then saw that the town's defense for destroying their dam was that it was old and a hazard. To their eyes, it had to go.

The lake's rich history was now a thing of the past. Rotting rowboats and worn-out cabins seeing their last days are the only reminder of what life was in Lucky Lake.

To Roy, this was a sad end to a place that provided enjoyment and livelihood for many decades. Roy looked at Ron and said, "I have to go shopping and pick up a few things for mom. Do you want to come?"

Ron said, "Thanks, not now. I want to check out some more blogs."

As Roy left the farmhouse, Ron turned to the blogs he was looking at before his dad came over. Two caught his eye.

> Three bobcat kittens in the snowy Luxton Lake community grounds.

This was a *meow* to Ron since it brought out the catlike instinct in him. Then he saw a disturbing blog.

> There has been a big large bear sighted in the vicinity of Luxton Lake. Be careful in going out.

Ron thought it was time to play since there were three bobcat kittens enjoying the snow.

Three days later and after a restful night at home, Ron Hemingway sat down in his black swivel computer chair and stared at the screen in front of him. He started to scroll down menus and saw the blogs of people's reactions and stories regarding Luxton Lake.

Two blogs caught his eye. The first was one from the state police, which said,

> State Police and DEC were in Luxton Lake yesterday to investigate a bear torso the Tusten Highway Department found at the end of Lake Ridge Rd. The bear was estimated between 150 and 200 lbs. If anyone has any information about who killed and dumped this bear, please contact State Police at 845-555-1234.

Then Ron saw that someone took a photo of a black cat in the snow and asked,

> Anyone know if this black cat belongs to someone? He is frequently at the Luxton Lake community grounds and visiting houses on Lake Ridge Rd.

Ron leaned back on his black swivel chair. While rocking back and forth, he looked at the ceiling, smiled, and said. "That's funny."

PART IV

Life Goes On

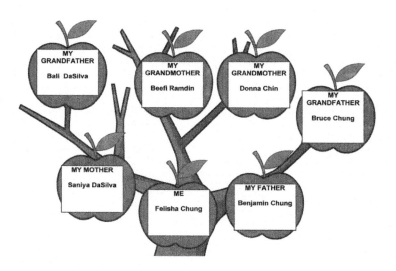

16

The Plumber

The moon, what a large, watermelon-size moon, Glen thought. The moon was coupled with a gentle icy wind and the starlight, a color that painted the Delaware River at night with soft brushes.

The howling voices of the roaring wind through the alleyways on Main Street at midnight were like a sweet, mournful cry that brought a warm chill and comfort to Glen. He stared at the river with amazement, and in his mind, he saw the moonlight bouncing off the water. The cold, quiet thing within him laughed as the moon danced over the waves.

This terrible need inside him cried out. This appetite, this strong desire, was so resilient now that it waited to become satisfied. And yet it was so careful not to reveal the hidden voice from within. Oh, this wonderful, creepy, crackly need made Glen's loins stiffen to hardness. This need had been teasing and prickling at him to find another one. *Yes—find the next one!*

As he stared at the bright moonlight, the clock from within him started to tick away the seconds, and the hand movements of this timepiece went, *Ticktock, ticktock,* along with the beat of his heart, pushing the release of this neediness so that it could be set free.

Oh, I must be careful, Glen thought. *I have worked too hard, too long, to make this work for me. I will not be caught. I need to protect my happy little life. Oh, this is so much fun I can't stop now. I must be careful, yes, I must be careful.*

The basement was dark, dusty, and dreary, even with the forty-watt bulb overlooking the leaking water tank in the corner. Last week, the owner wanted him to check the water pump and the plumbing; but any other fixtures like faucets, they would discuss later. Glen knew he agreed to provide the insulation and the heating tape needed for the house, and the price he quoted for the total work (parts and labor) was $365.00, plus whatever it would cost to put an electrical box below if needed. None was needed.

Glen called the customer early that morning to tell him that he needed a water tank and that he could install a new one for $400.00 in total. The customer said it was okay and that he could pick up the money from Robby the electrician, who was holding some cash from the customer.

Glen knew he was going to fly out to Florida that evening for two weeks and that the appetite controlling him needed to be satisfied there.

So he picked up the money that morning from Robby and went to Monticello to pick up the water tank. With the water tank installed, including the insulation and the heating tapes around the pipes, he went home, showered, and ate a light dinner.

Later, he picked up his luggage, which was already prepared for the trip, and went out to meet the taxi vehicle waiting at the curb of his home. *I must be careful,* Glen thought as the taxi left his home on Erie Street. *I work too hard, too long, to make this work for me. I will not be caught. Oh, this is so much fun I can't stop now. I must be careful—yes, I must be careful.*

It was raining that morning, and the traffic was crazy as Glen drove his rental, leaving the New Yorker Boutique Hotel in Miami, Florida. The traffic down Biscayne Boulevard was crazy when it rained.

Drivers were slowing down on the wet roads, which made other drivers furious. They were aggressive on their horns and screaming out their windows while accelerating out into the lane's shoulder and passing the slowpokes and providing them the fluttering of their middle finger.

So American, Glen thought with a smile on his face.

He knew he needed an excuse to be in Florida. The rain had stopped by the time he reached his destination. The sun shone, and steam rose from the pavement as he drove into Aunt Connie's driveway in Coral Springs. This day trip was the ticket he had to pay for the need and the appetite inside him.

<hr />

That night after a light dinner in the hotel, Glen drove to the Boardwalk in Miami Beach. Parking his rented vehicle in a parking lot near the Boardwalk, he stepped out and started to walk toward the sandy beach area. Gazing out into the Atlantic Ocean brought about the appearance of the thing within, making its usual house call on this tropical night.

Then there was a slight waiting period before the strong need within him wanted to build a legion of hundreds of hiding voices—and they *all* wanted to come out and play.

Please feed me. Please feed me.

The pressure of fighting the need within continued.

I must be careful. I will not be caught.

Walking over to the deli and sushi bar near Indian Beach Park, he bought a ham-and-cheese sandwich and began to eat it as he walked toward the park and watched. While he ate, he waited and watched as the small children played on the manicured grass.

Moms and dads were lounging with conversations while they hawkeyed their kids. Glen waved to everybody. Some of them waved back. Glen knew that he had to be nice. Children liked nice. And then children would love Glen. And of course, he loved the children—oh, very much... *truly.*

He had dedicated a whole life to them. Learning their games and music was all for the kids. Everything he did, it was all for the kids. And today was no exception.

He walked through the park talking and laughing with the kids as if they were long lost friends. He touched their hair, and they laughed. After getting to know the parents of the children, he hugged them and said good-bye. And then he started toward his car while thinking, *Maybe tomorrow will be my lucky day. Who knows about luck? I must be careful. Yes, I must be careful.*

Days turned into nights while nights turned into weeks.

By five in the morning, Glen was all cleaned up. He took an extralong shower, letting the hot water wash away the last of the tightness and relief of the knots in his muscles, cleansing off the small final traces of the clinging fragrance of children. He felt a lot better. He always did—after. Killing made Glen feel good. It was a sugary release, an essential letting go of all the little hydraulic values inside.

The killing was necessary even though it was complicated. It had to be done the right way at the right time. It had always been somewhat draining. Glen was tired, but the tension of the past weeks was gone. The strong need within was gone and quiet, and he could be himself again. Two weeks turned into six weeks. The logistics and planning had to be reenergized. Finding the children's homes and the abduction were problematic. The burial was a work of art, he thought, and the mystery of his accomplishment would amaze any law-enforcement agency. Glen felt good.

He was careful—yes, very careful.

The cost of this need within exceeded the amount he budgeted for. He needed to collect what was owed to him. Or maybe a little more with interest wouldn't be bad. So he started to call his clients.

He called the client who owed him $365.00 and told him he owed a total of $1,200.00 minus the $400.00 already paid. When the client wondered why he was paying more, Glen yelled at him and told him he would mail out the bill to explain the extra charges.

He knew yelling would put the client on a defense mode. He decided to wait five days and showed up at the client's home and presented the bill to him. Glen told the client that he did extra work for him, whom he knew was bogus.

The client told him that he did not authorize that expenditure. Glen then threw a tantrum and started yelling and saying that he deserved $60.00 an hour for labor, which the client never said he didn't deserve.

Glen then stormed out of the house, and in a loud voice—so that the neighbor could hear—he shouted out that the client owed him this money. As he slammed the door to his truck and moved out of the driveway, Glen giggled. *That will work.*

Three days later, Glen received from the client the amount he requested. With a smile, he said to himself, *It never fails to work with these city folks.*

17

The Cool Summer Breeze

High school was over, and graduation brought about a struggle for Ron and Diana as they walked down Main Street holding hands after having lunch at the Heron.

A Saturday afternoon in Narrowsburg was one of the little pleasures they enjoyed since Diana's weekend visit was limited ever since the Diamonds moved to Brooklyn. The ranch trailer across the street from the farmhouse was bought by the Diamonds before they moved to Brooklyn at Elderts Lane. Moving their furniture from Luxton Lake to Brooklyn and keeping some furniture for the ranch trailer was time-consuming and made for less time for Ron to spend with Diana.

Ron only knew that without Diana, life was a treadmill that moved in place and yet no destination to be seen. Ron tried to hide the frustration he felt; but he knew, in time, their lives would be joined.

They smiled and greeted their neighbors on the street who were enjoying with the tourists, the shops and restaurants on Main Street. There was a small bustling crowd around the promenade observation deck, where a jazz band was playing "Sweet Georgia Brown." Narrowsburg Electric sponsored the band, and the crowd was enjoying the entertainment it provided.

Ron and Diana, standing on the promenade observation deck, were overlooking the beautiful and vibrant Delaware River while the music of the band floated in the air.

Ron turned and looked at Diana and said while holding both her hands, "I miss you so much. When you are not here, my mind wanders to the times you are here. I think I'm going crazy. Do I make sense?"

"Yes, deary, it makes sense. I feel that way when I'm in Brooklyn. My dad and mom think I'm a zombie by the way I walk around without you. They laugh at me because that is how my dad and mom were before they were married. My mom thinks it so cute to see me recreate her life in India before they were married."

Ron focused on Diana's face and, with tears in his eyes, went down on his knees and said to her, "Diana, I love you. My life has no meaning without you. I do not have much now, but whatever I have, it is yours. All I can promise you is that I will love and protect you for the rest of my life. I will be your knight in shining armor forever. I am asking for your hand in marriage. Will you marry me?"

Time stood still for them. Time knew that for it to continue, this moment needed to be expressed. The music in the background became a faraway echo. The people in the crowd seemed to disappear with this echo. But the words of Diana's mother played with a strong crescendo along with this music, and it captivated her thoughts: *If he is the one, then just be patient—it will come.*

Her true knight in shining armor was asking for her hand in marriage.

Oh, how she longed to hear those words from the only person she deeply knew was the love of her life.

The cool summer breeze gently slapped her face into wakening. All was quiet, and she saw everyone on the promenade observation deck waiting for her answer. Yes. No. Maybe?

She then lovingly looked down at Ron with happy tears in her eyes and gently said, "*Yes.*"

18

Cousins and Their Tales from the Streets

Felisha Chung, an investigative reporter for the *Stabroek News* and also *The Chronicle News* in Guyana, South America, was enjoying her new life in America with her parents. Richmond Hill in Queens, New York, was like being in Guyana since most of the shops and eating places are catered to the Guyanese and Trinidadian. The only problem this 5'2", 105-pound girl, with brown eyes and long brown hair, was having: getting a job. Her credentials for working in Guyana had no impressive pull when it came for a job at *The Times* or *The Daily News*.

Even though her beauty and personality were impressive, New York City news media wasn't swayed. Her dad, Benjamin, and her mother, Saniya, told her that life in America was great and that she should move here and experience the many opportunities she could achieve "only in America." *What gobbledygook*, she thought.

Being twenty-four years old, she knew there weren't many opportunities in Guyana for her to rise in her profession. Her years in school in the field of journalism and her tutelage under other reporters weren't going anywhere of significant value for her. For the last six months, sending résumés and making phone calls to all the news media in the city that never sleeps had finally taken its toll.

But going back to Guyana was not an option. Like the songs said, "If you can make it here, you can make it anywhere." But Felisha's life going anywhere would have been a start. Then a call from her cousin Lee Ann and a chance to apply for a position on *The River Reporter* in Narrowsburg was like an olive branch from heaven to melt away her life from being a punching bag.

All she needed was a chance, and it looked like one was being opened for her. So she thought, *Lee Ann will pick me up on Saturday, and I should pack clothes for at least two weeks. Okay, Green Acre, here I come!*

The ride to Narrowsburg was exhilarating. Going over the Whitestone Bridge to the Hutchison Parkway and over the Tappan Zee Bridge and on New York State Thruway 87 was the first time Felisha saw life outside the big city. The ride brought about conversation regarding the past and understanding things Felisha and Lee Ann didn't know about each other.

Felisha told Lee Ann that she studied under Chief Master Sang Lee in Guyana and that he was a sixth-degree black belt in the arts of Tae Kwon Do. Lee Ann told Felisha that this must be a small world because her husband was a friend of Sang Lee and knew him very well, and that if she studied under him, she had a good teacher.

Making the trip even more exciting was reminiscing stories from back home. Even though Felisha was born in Georgetown, she would visit and stay at her grandparents' home at 207 North Street, Anna Catherina. She would remember Grandma Beefi, whose room and bed overlooked the road and the cemetery across it.

"Now, Lee Ann, you have been to Guyana and know the road and cemetery I'm talking about."

"I know. It's the road that leads toward the Blackwater bay area, near the wall."

"Yes, that's right. Now, Grandma Beefi said, at night, she would look out of her window and see, on the ground floor of a house, what a woman who lived next to the cemetery was doing. She could see the flickering lights coming from a large cast-iron kettle. Beefi would say that the 'old hige' was mixing potion. Beefi would claim that the old hige would go out toward the cemetery, and a trail of fog would follow her into the cemetery. Everyone in the village would say she was trying to wake up her dead lover."

"Are you kidding me? That's crazy."

"You are right, but that's the tales from the streets. And talking about crazy, Grandpa Bali would tell me the story about a young man who lived in the next village of Leonara

99

who loved a girl in Anna Catherina. As the story goes, this girl would pass by the young man home around 5:00 p.m. every evening and stay to talk to him about everything. Just before it gets dark, she would hop on her bicycle and go home. This routine of her coming by would go on for weeks.

One night, he followed her from a distance to see where she lived. She parked her bike next to a tree in the cemetery and then disappeared behind a large tombstone. Because it was getting too dark to follow, he made a mental note where he last saw her. Next day, he went to the cemetery and saw that the tombstone she disappeared from had her name on it. Shocked and confused, he then inquired around Anna Catherina about the story and death of this young girl. The story was that her parents never let her go out to meet friends or anyone, so she finally committed suicide.

The time of her death was 5:00 p.m. The young man never saw the girl again. Even though he would go to her grave to talk to her, she would not reveal herself again. Months passed by, and the young man was so distraught that they committed him to the hospital for psychiatric treatment. The young man finally committed suicide. The time of death was 5:00 p.m. Now tell me if that isn't creepy."

"Wow, that sure is," Lee Ann replied.

The ride continue to exit 17 west and then to exit 104 near Monticello Raceway and Casino. They were on Route 17B and made a left on Route 55, eight miles from the Casino. Four miles into Route 55, they made a right turn on Route 26 called Crystal Lake Road and then, after 6.3 miles, a right turn on County Road 23. After a 2.5-hour ride and 0.2 miles from the last turn, a charcoal-gray and green-colored farmhouse approached on the right.

Felisha could see, from the short distance, Lee Ann's husband and son coming out to greet them. The beautiful sight of the two-story home and the surrounding trees and lovely landscape with deer and rabbits around it made Felisha feel like she entered a world of possibilities, the possibilities of getting a job and a life that would stop treating her like a punching bag. She remembered *Rocky V*, where Rocky would tell his son, "It's not how hard you get hit and fall down, but how you keep on getting up that counts," or something to that effect. So she thought, *What the hell*; and in her best Spanish accent, she turned to Lee Ann, smiling, and said, "Oh, Lucy—I'm home!"

19

Reporter Meets PI

ABBQ lunch in the backyard and a second glass of wine later made Felisha think that she could get used to country life. Sitting on a cast-iron chair under an umbrella fitted into a cast-iron table made her thoughts seem a lot steadier as the seat she was sitting on. The Hemingways were a happy family who liked to laugh and jest around without being sensitive with the humor.

"Felisha, would you like another steak or chicken?" Roy asked.

"No, thanks. I'm full," Felisha replied.

Felisha looked over at Lee Ann and said, "Lee Ann, you never told me what Roy does for a living."

Lee Ann smiled and looked at her husband and said, "He's a dick."

Felisha choked on her wine and looked, astonished, at Lee Ann and said, "What?"

"You heard me. He is really a dick, or you can call him a shamus. How about calling him a sleuthhound?"

Roy and Lee Ann laughed out loud while Felisha tried to understand the joke.

Ron smiled and looked at Felisha and said, "My mother isn't joking. My dad is a private investigator, and those are the terms they use to describe them. They also use the term *gumshoe, hawkshaw, operative, sleuth,* or *sherlock.* So *dick* is a funny way of expressing it."

As Ron looked at his dad and mom, he smiled and said, "You can say my mother is a personal assistant of a dick."

Lee Ann, Roy, and Ron bent over laughing and trying to keep a straight face while Felisha stood up and said, "I think I could use something stronger than wine because you guys are really out there with jokes."

Ron looked at Felisha and said, "My dad owns an investigation and security agency in Monticello serving the Sullivan County area. My mother has worked with him for many years, and I know she handles all the statements, investigation reports, courtesy surveillance notification, retainer agreement, and much more. Since I was a baby, my mom would take me to work with her in her front baby pouch. At the age of twelve, I was helping out in the family business. By sixteen, I was handling surveillance, which is the most lucrative type of assignment because it is a solid, billable block of time."

Roy smiled as he heard his son describe their business.

Felisha said, "Isn't Ron too young to be in this business?"

Roy said, "My dad got his agency license in East Texas, and at the age of eight, I was helping out. By the age of nine, I was learning how to play the piano. At the age of twelve, I received my first black belt. All this knowledge and more, I pass down to my son, and I pay him good money in the process of implementing this knowledge in the business. Ron makes me proud every day, and I do not force him to choose this life. The choice will always be his. One thing I can say is that he has the skills in doing investigative and security services."

Felisha looked at each one of them and asked, "Is it possible that I could get into this field? What must I do? Does it pay well?"

Roy first looked at Lee Ann, who nodded, and then at Ron, who also nodded. Roy then looked at Felisha and said, "The work of a PI ranges from surveillance, conducting criminal investigations, detecting insurance fraud to other investigative services. The clients are as varied as the work. They include the government, insurance companies, lawyers, private citizens, and any person or organization that needs investigative services.

As far as money is concerned, one could make $300 and $500 an hour for activities like forensic computer evaluation, security consulting, automobile repossession, and a few other specialties. I have made $10,000 in an hour doing bail fugitive recovery work, but now it averages about

$150 an hour in bail enforcement. Many investigators don't have the stomach for that type of work. It's extremely dangerous and a very competitive field, and you only get paid if you complete the case.

To be in this field, you need curiosity, creativity, and perseverance. A strong sense of justice certainly helps. You must have speaking and writing skills. You'll be writing a lot of reports. So the better your grammar, punctuation, and writing style, the better your potential in this field could be. You should read books on investigation. We can guide you in taking an investigative course.

An investigator in New York is required to be licensed and take an examination. The New York Department of State Division of Licensing Services regulates private detectives and administers the private investigator walk-in examination. You can work in our agency and get paid while you learn the business. We can help you with the exam and the other qualifications you need. You want to work part-time with *The River Reporter*? That's okay with us. You can stay here rent-free until you can live on your own. How does that sound?"

Felisha ran over to Roy and shook his hand. She then went over to Lee Ann and gave her a big hug and a kiss. Last but not least, she gave Ron a hug.

Roy looked at Felisha and said, "Does that mean yes, or are you in the emotional hug-fest mood?"

"Both! I mean yes to the job and yes to the hug fest. Thanks, guys. I really mean it. You guys have given me a purpose in life and the family support I need. Can I call my dad and mom to let them know the good news?"

"Sure, go right ahead. You know where the phone is," Roy replied.

"Dad, open up another bottle of wine. This calls for a celebration," Ron suggested.

Lee Ann swayed over to Roy and gave him a big kiss and said with a smile, "You're still a dick."

20

Monticello's Accident

It was raining and foggy that evening on November 23, 2012, and the traffic was light as Ray entered Route 17 west and then to exit 104 near Monticello Raceway and Casino. They were on Route 17B, and the speed limit was fifty-five miles per hour.

Ray looked down at his dashboard and adjusted his speed to forty miles per hour on the cruise control. The 2004 Pontiac Vibe was heading westbound with the sound of Air Supply's "Lost in Love" playing in the air from the iPod attached to the sound system. The song of the tires and the wind and rain was drowning itself out by the relaxing music.

The great moon was invisible with the fog coming and going. Ray thought about the Thanksgiving dinner over at his brother's home yesterday and the conversations about Diana's upcoming wedding. Anna wanted to make this trip so as to bring stuff for the ranch trailer and buy some knickknacks at Walmart in Monticello.

The condition on the road made Ray a little nervous, knowing that deer could shoot out in front of the vehicle and cause a bad accident, but he tried not to dwell upon it. The road ahead changed from one lane to two as they started to go up the steep incline.

As they approached one mile west of Coopers Corners Road, "Even the Nights Are Better" by Air Supply was playing inside the vehicle. Ray glanced quickly at Anna and squeezed her left hand very slightly and smiled.

She in turn blew him a kiss and smiled back. His thoughts were of how lucky he was to be in love and to have a wonderful wife. Ray thanked God in his mind for his blessings, which he knew he didn't deserve.

In the dark night, while the rain was falling and the fog started to intensify, the road started to change from two lanes to one as the steep incline started to take a downward turn toward the right. As soon as Ray turned around the curve, within a second, what seemed like a large trailer was blocking and moving across the one-lane road.

The high beams of the Pontiac reflected its light back through Ray's windshield and blinded him. Ray turned his wheels sharply toward the left, and then the impact occurred. The sound was like a shotgun blast with a crash. Then time stood still. The air bags accomplished their mission with its talcum powder snowing all around the driver's and passenger's front seat.

Nothing became visible but the light and the powdery sprinkle with the high beams reflecting through the windshield.

Brenda from Woodbury, New York, was driving her 2006 Dodge van on Route 17B going westbound. The weather was giving her a tough time in trying to locate the turn she needed to take. Approaching one mile west of Cooper Corner Road, she realized that she missed her turn. The road started to change from two lanes to one. The incline started downhill, and she decided to pull over to the right shoulder after the curve. Seeing no vehicle lights in front or back, she told her son, Peter, who was sitting in the front passenger seat, "I'm going back."

She then started to turn her wheel sharply to the left and accelerated slowly to make a U-turn toward the eastbound road when, suddenly, a bright light came upon her from the downward curve on the westbound lane, and within a second—a crashing sound on her driver's front side.

"It was my fault! My fault! I missed my turn. I'm so sorry," Brenda yelled out.

Ray looked at Anna and said, "Are you all right?"

She nodded and said, "I'm okay, Ray."

"Can you get out on your side?"

"No, the door is jammed."

Ray opened his door and helped Anna through the driver's side door.

Cars were driving by the eastbound lane and told us they called 911 for help. We thank them. Ray walked over to Brenda and said, "Are you guys okay?"

Brenda again started to mumble out loud, "It was my fault! I missed my turn. I'm so sorry."

Within minutes, fire trucks and emergency vehicles were there to light the roads with flares and direct traffic.

Ray felt sorry for the lady, but he knew that he couldn't let emotion dictate his thinking. He then turned to Anna and said, "I'm sorry to say this to you, but watch how her story will change later. Human nature seems sometimes to bring the worst in us."

Deputy Rita Tonga arrived with another deputy, and her attitude and mannerism seemed like she didn't want to be there. She asked Ray what happened, and he told her the facts while providing her his license, registration, and insurance card. She later went to Brenda to get her side of the story. When she came back, Ray asked her politely if he could have the information of the other driver so that he could provide it to his insurance carrier. She said no!

Ray then told the deputy in a polite tone that the insurance carrier and motor-vehicle laws state that they should exchange this information.

She said, "You don't!"

Ray then told her again politely, "How am I going to know whom I had the accident with?"

She then said, "You'll get it in the accident report!"

The deputy did not like anyone to question her. The deputy then wanted the vehicles moved off the roads.

"I told her I was calling a friend to help move the vehicle."

Ray then called Tommy, a friend in the area.

The attitude of the deputy was so unjust that she accused Ray of lying. She said Ray told her he was calling a tow vehicle when he only said he was calling a friend to move the vehicle. Ray was forced to take the towing service on the scene. All of this was witnessed by Anna and others at the scene.

The next day, Ray arrived at Prestige Towing Inc. in Harris, New York. The Ford Ranger driven by Tommy made its way into the front entrance through the muddy road.

Kathy greeted Ray and said, "How can I help you?"

Ray told her that he was the one who owned the Pontiac Vibe in the accident last night.

"The one my driver said the lady was making a U-turn on 17B?" Kathy said.

"Yep, that's the one." Ray smiled. "I'm looking for a rental while this situation gets cleared up," Ray inquired.

Kathy looked over some papers she had over her desk and said, "It shouldn't be any problem. It looks like she is 100 percent at fault, and we will deal with her insurance company. Make sure you send us a copy of the accident report as soon as you get it. Watch out for the accident report. They could get you screwed. We have had these problems before. Anyway, sign this and take the white vehicle out in front."

"Wow, that was quick. Thanks a lot, Kathy."

Ray thanked Tommy for the ride as he entered the white rental and started his way back to the ranch trailer. As he was driving back, he thought that life still had a silver lining to it. He chuckled—if not silver, then white—as he drove the white rental to his ranch trailer.

It took eight days later, after many calls and dropping by the sheriff's office, for him to receive the accident report. Ray told the sheriff who provided the report that the description of the accident was wrong. The report showed that Brenda's vehicle was pulling out of the shoulder onto the roadway, and she failed to yield the right of way to Ray's vehicle. What she did, according to Ray, was made an illegal U-turn across the westbound lane.

The sheriff looked at it again and said, "It was her fault, and any way you look at it, there is no fault to you."

A week later, Brenda's insurance carrier told Ray that he was liable for 15 percent in the accident since the police report alleged speed on his part because box 19 with, the number 19 inserted, meant unsafe speed. Ray told him it must be a mistake.

Ray tried to get a hold of Deputy Tonya, but she had been ignoring his phone calls. On December 19, 2012, at

9:02 p.m., he finally was able to reach her on the phone. Ray reminded her that he was doing forty miles per hour in a fifty-five-miles-per-hour speed limit. He also told her, "How could you state that I was speeding if there were no skid marks on the road? Why didn't you give me a speeding ticket if I was speeding? How do you come to that conclusion?"

She told Ray that it was her prerogative to state what she believed. Ray told her that she left him with no choice but to follow up with legal action against her.

She told Ray to do what he had to do and hung up.

Ray sent certified letters to her boss, Mickey Stevenson, sheriff, and to Undersheriff Eddy Champagne with detailed photos and diagrams, but no one answered back. Ray knew that if they didn't respond to the letters sent to them, they were admitting that they condoned this action and therefore made an *injustice* of the motto of the Sullivan County's sheriff's department.

Those who were supposedly upholding the law turned around and violated the same law by not protecting its citizens from abuse.

When Diana heard of this injustice toward her parents, she told her dad, "I will not join a department of law that corrupts the law."

Ray looked at his daughter with loving eyes and told her, "Because there are a few rotten apples, you can't hold all law-enforcement officers with the same judgment. You can always join and try to make the proper changes within the organization or choose another form of law enforcement that meets with the integrity you expect of them."

Diana, with tears rolling down her eyes, hugged her dad and said, "You're a good man, and I love you, Dad. You have always watched out for me and mom. You try to find the good in a situation that seems hopeless. How do you do this without tearing yourself apart? What is your secret?"

"You guys are my secret weapon. Without you guys, life would have a different scenario."

Ray's mind was wondering whether this was a form of karma. Was this injustice a partial payment for his past life's indiscretions? If it was, then why did his wife had to suffer too? He finally came to the conclusion that this world would always have those who have power and authority and who would abuse it by showing that they are above the law.

PART V

The Story Begins

21

The Wedding and Puerto Rico

Perched high above the Atlantic Ocean on a three-hundred-foot cliff, El Conquistador Resort was a peaceful retreat, Ron thought, as he sipped his morning *café con leche* from his room overlooking the ocean in Las Brisas wing of the resort.

The Island of Enchantment brought back many memories from his previous trips with his parents. Looking down toward La Marina Village, he saw Las Olas wing, where the swimming pool areas once hosted his dad's first musical group in the late '70s called Roy and the Innovations.

While his newly wedded wife was taking her morning shower, Ron reminisced about the places they had already seen and the delicious food they ate at the restaurant Raíces in old San Juan and the touring of El Morro and other sites in the old city.

It was an experience of a lifetime. "Old San Juan is the oldest and the best-preserved historic district in the New

World," Ron read in the advertisement brochure on top of the dresser. He remembered the Museum of the Americas; and across it lay the huge green field in front of El Moro fortress, which in itself, is a dramatic military masterpiece with six levels of terrace, ramps, and rooms overlooking the Atlantic Ocean and San Juan Bay.

To the west, on the far side of San Juan Bay, sits the Bacardi rum distillery, which is the largest rum factory in the world. A new interactive visitor center, Casa Bacardi, depicts the history of the Bacardi family and the processing of rum, but it was the free samples of rum provided that Ron and Diana enjoyed the most.

Ron remembered the history lessons his dad gave him about Puerto Rico. It was originally named *Bourinquen* (island of the brave lord) by the Taino Indians, and that Puerto Rico was discovered by Christopher Columbus in 1493 during his second voyage to the New World.

The best buys to look for in Puerto Rico, he saw, were the traditional island crafts; and Old San Juan had an art center, harboring many galleries that sold paintings and sculptures by Puerto Rican artists. For hundreds of years, open-air markets, known in Spanish as Plaza del Mercado, have been a common sight on virtually every island in the Caribbean, his dad used to say.

Diana was no exception in enjoying these open-air markets. She saw vendors stand behind piles of fruits and vegetables, which had been transported to markets from the surrounding countryside.

In addition to fruits and vegetables stands, they saw that the market also had stands selling local fruit drinks, meats, fish, groceries, and kitchenware—also bunches of medical and culinary herbs, flowers in buckets of water, and dried beans in burlap bags.

A number of the modest, picturesque houses surrounding the marketplace had been converted into small coffee shops and casual restaurants. When one goes toward Old San Juan, there is the Capitol (el Capitolio), which is on Avenue Ponce de Leon. The same avenue was where, many years ago, a disco called the Trip was one of the clubs Ron's dad used to play in with his famous band called the Family Colors. They played seven nights a week for a year and a half.

"That was a sweet gig," his dad used to say. That gig brought about TV appearances, fame, and the call from a French hotel in the Condado area that wanted his band to play for them, which they eventually did.

Then there was the rain forest El Yunque, the Caribbean National Forest, which sprawls across twenty-eight thousand mountain acres and offers some twenty-eight miles of trail. Up the mountains they went. There was a more challenging Big Tree Trail, which led them to La Mina Falls—an experience, Diana said, only to engage in once in a lifetime.

The El Yunque trail took them to some of the highest peaks. All that walking brought about a large appetite, which was satisfied at Richies Café in Rio Grande. This café's view overlooked the tropical forest, the ocean, and the Miramar Resort.

They then continued east on Route 3 instead of Expressway 53. They wanted to take in all of its sights without the speed. Route 3 winds its way down the east coast, past the coastal town of Ceiba and the former Roosevelt Roads Naval Station.

Ron remembered his mother used to work at Roosey (pronoun *rosy*). She was the executive secretary for the admiral of the US Atlantic Command. He didn't remember if it was Naval Force Caribbean (NFC) or Fleet Air Caribbean (FAIR).

His dad and mom first lived in Ceiba and stayed over one of his grandmother's family homes. One of Ron's grandma's brothers was Alejo Rivera Morales, who was one of the founding delegates that signed the Constitution of Puerto Rico and was honored after his death by having his name put on the National Guard Garrison in Ceiba, Puerto Rico.

Ron and Diana took time to go swimming at Luquillo Beach and ate the best steaks in the world at the Hacienda Carabali restaurant.

Puerto Rico, to Ron, was an island that loved to sweep you away to a paradise where palm trees and lounge chairs lined the white-sand beaches, where waiters came around to take your tropical-drink order—which, for Diana, was coconut water.

In Las Croabas, Fajardo, a bioluminescent lagoon is where you can take Captain Jack's little boat at night and run your hands through the fluorescent bay waters and see them glow through your fingers while they pour into the moonlight bay. The eco-sports operators there offered magical nighttime kayaking trips through the mangroves. There are trips to the lagoon every night. The operators told Ron and Diana that they could bring their own bathing suit if they desired to swim in the bay.

Diana really was fascinated with this idea and kept on insisting to come back again before they went back home. They also ate at Playa Puerto Real in Fajardo, where Rosa's Seafood Restaurant is located. Their food was very good, and Ron could see why it was rated one of the best ten restaurants of Puerto Rico.

All these memories would not have occurred if it wasn't for the day Diana said *yes*, yes to his marriage proposal made on his knees on the promenade observation deck overlooking the vibrant Delaware River in Narrowsburg.

Then on Valentine's Day, a Tuesday, Ron's dad's pastor and friend opened the Presbyterian Church in Park Slope, Brooklyn, New York.

In a private wedding with their parents and grandparents as witnesses, they then took the vow.

Ron's dad gave them an all-expense-paid trip for one month as a honeymoon present. Diana's dad gave them the ranch trailer next to the farmhouse, all paid for, as a wedding gift. Their grandparents gave them a lot of money to build their own future in their own way. All this was great, but the best was the wedding night.

Ron remembered that on his wedding night, he told his wife the revelation and the powers he possessed. Diana then told her husband that she also had a gift and that she knew for sometime before they were married about the aura around Ron. She told him that this aura was subtle. It was a luminous radiation of power that he had hidden in him and wanted to be free. The wedding night was a night of revelation and bonding. This bonding, he knew, will last and cement their future relationship to another higher level.

As Diana exited the bathroom with a radiant look and a smile, she said to Ron, "Deary, what's on the agenda for today?"

Ron sat on the bed and looked at his beautiful wife standing barefoot with a towel wrapped around her body. He said, "How about room service all day today and, at night, Captain Jack's little boat?"

Diana ran and screamed with joy and knocked him over with kisses on the bed and said, "Yippie-ki-yay, let's rock and roll! Oh, by the way, should we go swimming tonight in our birthday suits?"

Ron laughed while they rolled in the bed together. He then stared into his wife's eyes and said, "Honey, don't push it!"

22

Spring and the Celebration

Spring fell on a Wednesday, and the young couple's celebration was being held on Saturday, March 23. Three days after their return from their honeymoon, special invitations, with RSVPs, were sent to all those who wanted to attend and to those who couldn't attend.

They say that Emily Post advised anyone receiving an invitation with an RSVP must reply promptly. She also advised everyone to reply within a day or two of receiving the invitation. Narrowsburg was no exception. Just because they lived in a country-type atmosphere didn't mean that protocol was not followed in this upstate community.

Being a community where many artists and writers lived, celebration was what this hamlet was all about. Just a few miles from this celebration was another one that began in 1969. That was where the Woodstock Festival was celebrated, and now Bethel Woods Center for the Arts is located in that area. They are now celebrating their forty-forth anniversary.

Even though the Hemingways and the Diamonds had not requested live music, many musicians and bands offered to play in this celebration, and some even for free. An open invitation was given to them to play only if they were willing to share their artistic music with the other musicians and bands.

Ron's grandparents arrived on spring day to help with the preparation of food, liquor, and decor. Diana's parents arrived the day after spring to join with the Hemingways and the Kincades to help with the necessary preparations for the party. Seating, tables, tents, and lighting needed to be ordered, and a temporary stage needed to be built for the live entertainments.

Ron and Diana were so glad that they didn't have to organize this party. It was their parents' and grandparents' idea to throw this party since their wedding was kept private from the town of Tusten. Their honeymoon was cut short by a week to provide friends and families the joy of celebrating their children's happiness. They were glad that their parents and grandparents were there to bring about this so-called extravaganza.

Ron and Diana stood beside their vehicles parked by the farmhouse and watched the sun fold away its attendance.

Diana looked out across County Road 23 toward the ranch trailer's property and asked Ron five times if everything looked right about the seating, tables, and the tent arrangements. And each time between her questions, Ron, with a slightly different nuance, smiled at her and nodded.

She'd ask Ron three times if he was sure that the stage was in its proper location, but Ron was sure that it was thoughtfulness on her part. She wanted to ask Ron about the outdoor bar area, the trimmings, the helium balloon, the ice machine, and a lot more, but she held back to avoid being obvious. She even forgot herself once and asked in a whisper. Ron told her in a low voice that it would be okay, and she looked at him and touched his arm but did not ask again. At that very moment, the setting sun was breathtaking.

Early to bed and early to rise didn't make the young Hemingway's too healthy and wise.

After breakfast, the smell of coffee and its constant reminder to have more than a cup made the morning rush to close out the last-minute preparations a little unnerving. The Diamonds, Hemingways, and the Kincades were a force to be reckoned with.

With a military standard procedure, they tackled the last-minute preparation with time to spare. Ron and Diana were astonished and thankful to be a part of a family that knew how to handle a crisis.

At 1:00 p.m., the people and the entertainment started arriving, even though the celebration was to start at 2:00

p.m. An area on the farmhouse ground and the backstreet curves was used for parking the vehicles. The other side of the ranch trailer's property was also used for vehicle parking.

A big spread of sandwiches and light finger foods were set at the tables, which were already placed in different areas of the property. These appetizers were for the guests to share before the main courses of dinner was to be served around 5:00 p.m.

Neighbors and family members volunteered to pass out light refreshing drinks to the guests. The band members and the other entertainment members were sitting at a table in the area near the stage, and they all were planning out who would play first and who would follow up. The sound of the drums and guitars tuning up and the checking of the PA's sound system gave a festive atmosphere to the celebration.

After 2:00 p.m., the guests arrived in droves, and the music filled the air to complement the festive mood. The Diamonds, Hemingways, and the Kincades mingled with the crowd of guests and thanked them for their attendance and their gifts for the newlyweds.

A large table that faced the guests was set aside for the newlyweds and their parents and grandparents. But in the meantime, they were all outside greeting their neighbors and town officials.

Greg Amirah, the code-enforcement officer, and Joan Singer, the clerk and building inspector, were a happy sight to see for the Diamonds and the Hemingways since they were so professional and courteous whenever they saw them at the town hall's office.

Roy told Greg jokingly if he would like to play with any of the bands since he knew Greg had a little desire in him to be a professional musician.

Greg, as usual, knew how to take a joke and smiled and said, "I'm only here to celebrate the newlyweds and enjoy the drinks and food. Let the professionals handle the music."

"Amen," said Roy. "Spoken like a true ex-policeman who knows how to detect my bull and yet be courteous with the explanation. Thanks, buddy, for showing up."

They both hugged and laughed in friendship.

Roy Danza heard Maria Mendez, their neighbor, out in the crowd talking to her friends and reminding them of the history of this great town of Tusten and the stories that made this place legendary. If she only knew about Ron and Diana, Roy thought, she would have a new take on the word *legendary*.

Roy also knew that this was an election year, and those who were in office wanted to continue to serve their constituency, and thereby, this celebration was an excuse for them to drum up the votes.

Roy was also glad that the Narrowsburg Fire Department and the Lava Volunteer Fire Department were here too. These unrewarded heroes were never given the recognition they deserved from outside, but the town of Tusten knew their caliber and hoped they could continue to support them when needed.

The town supervisor, clerk, and tax collector were all part of this celebration. Even the superintendent of Highways, Water, and Sewer was there to cheer on the newlyweds.

"Hi, Roy, nice gathering you are having," said Carlos Rodriquez.

"Hi, Judge, I'm glad you made it. I see that your son is also here. How are the preparations going as far as the re-election is concerned?"

"So-so, I guess. I'm not used to this, and the politician in me doesn't exist to make a real go of this. Anyway, whatever the voters decide is fine with me."

Roy looked at the judge kindly and said, "You are a class-act judge, and if the voters don't see that, I guess it's their loss. I wish the best for you."

"Thanks, Roy, I appreciate that."

The judge shook Roy's hand and walked into the crowd and joined his son and family. Roy always had a deep affection for the judge, but he knew, as a friend, he had to step aside to let him handle this role of becoming a politician, which he knew was not in him. It was hard to keep away, but sadly, it had to be done.

"Hey, Roy, how's my little brother doing?" said Robby Quinn, smiling.

Roy turned around and saw his honorary brother, whom Roy lovingly claimed as such by another mother. Robby was in excess of six feet in height and was grinning down on him.

"Robby, I'm so glad you came, and thanks again for your help in setting up the electrical sockets for the band and the appliances around this festival. Where is your shadow, Teresa?" Roy said as he hugged his friend.

"She is over there by the food table, munching," Robby said. And like a retriever who spots his prey, he pointed out with his right index finger and his extended arm above Roy's head and said, "We had to leave home early and didn't have time for lunch. But we fed the dogs before we left, as well as the chickens and the pigeons. They all were grateful for food and the snacks."

"That was really hospitable of you, brother, to take care of your little children before coming here. Really kind and thoughtful of you, and I might even include *neighborly*," Roy said, grinning.

Robby laughed out loud and said, "Now, who got jokes? We should put you on stage for entertainment, or better still, where is the booze? I need a drink." Robby turned around and walked toward the bar area and turned around again to look at Roy with a smile and waved back, rolling his eyes around as if he were drunk. Roy smiled and waved back.

Priscilla and Tommy dropped by along with their precious child, Lucy. Roy thanked Tommy for his help in building the stage and gave him a big hug like a father to a son. Kenneth and Dane Friday—along with Felisha and her parents, Benjamin and Saniya—all came by to drop off their gifts and celebrate with the newlyweds.

Roy walked over to Lee Ann, who was at the table set aside for the newlyweds. He planted a big kiss on her head and said, "This looks like a winning festival. What do you think?"

While Lee Ann was greeting a guest, she turned toward Roy with a smile and said, "Do you really want to know? My multiple sclerosis is acting up, and my right leg is dragging like a zombie, and my eye vision is seeing double, so I guess I'm doing fine. How's your day going?"

Roy looked at Lee Ann's face and saw that she had a twinkle in her eye. He knew his girl had jokes, so he said, "My day is going great. Thank you for asking. Before coming here, I had diarrhea fill my pants, and then I fell in the pond over there." Roy pointed to the pond by the edge of the property.

He then continued, "Then while I was trying to get out of the pond, I stepped on a nail attached to a board that was left by your dad. Yes, by your loving daddy. He made it quite clear that this was revenge because I took you away and married you so young. I then proceeded to go into the house and called 911. They came, they fixed, and I'm still screwed. So thank you very much for asking."

Lee Ann burst out with laughter while Roy tried to hold a straight face. They both looked at each other with laughter and smiled, and Lee Ann said. "Touché."

While the festival continued, Ron and Diana also moved through the crowds. They greeted the guests and thanked them for coming and wishing them well. Diana looked at her husband and said, "Deary, can we go inside and take a breather? I'm a little tired."

"Of course, darling, let's go inside," Ron said.

As they were ready to go inside, a little boy went over to Ron and hugged his leg and said, "Hi, cousin Ron."

Ron looked down and saw his cousin Aditya from Florida. Every time Ron went to Florida to see his family, Aditya was always his favorite. "Hi, cousin. I am glad you came to the celebration. Let me introduce my wife, Diana."

After introducing his wife, Ron gave Aditya a big hug and told him that he will talk to him later.

While Ron and Diana sat inside, they looked at the crowd filling the area and were astonished just by the pure numbers. Who would have guessed that their celebration would be the talk of the town? Even *The River* reporters were there, taking pictures and talking to the guests.

All of a sudden, while Diana was looking out into the crowd, she sensed an aura of evil walking among their guests. Her third eye couldn't control her body language.

"Diana, what's wrong? You seem ill. Are you okay?" Ron said.

Diana looked at her husband with frightened eyes and said, "Ron, we are in big trouble here. There is a person walking around at our celebration that has the embodiment and the possession of an evil spirit within him. He is looking for a new victim for his pleasure."

"Who is he? Can you point him out to me? Show me!" Ron inquired.

"I know he is in the crowd, but there are too many people in the way to pinpoint with accuracy. I need to go out and find him, but for the first time, deary, I'm scared. Ron, me scared? What's wrong with me? I need your help. I can't do it without you," Diana exclaimed out loud.

"I'm here, darling. No one will harm you. I swear to you. No one will dare harm the love of my life. No one will dare!"

Ron held Diana tightly in his arms and kissed her reassuringly while saying to her in a calming but firm voice, "No one will dare harm you, my love, no one."

He knew when he walked away from his car that something was wrong, Glen thought. As he walked toward the festival, something inside him yelled out, *Caution!*

Walking through the crowd, he sensed someone who was dangerous for him was here and that he should leave. Call it a sixth sense or whatever you like. Someone knew he was here. It didn't matter how he knew—he just knew. Maybe it was the smell or the auras of an invader who had left his or her presence in the surrounding midair particles.

Someone knows who I am. Someone must have entered his life while he was sleepwalking.

This was Narrowsburg, not Miami, after all. Even as he did a quick search through the crowd, he knew he would not find anything out of place. And he was right. Nothing was out of place. But someone had been here.

It took him a few minutes to check the tents, the bar area, the tables, and stage area—all the obvious areas first. But all the people seemed to be clueless. Everyone was exactly where they should be.

Glen decided to cross over County Road 23 toward the farmhouse and the private forest areas next, just to be sure, checking where the cars were parked, the street, around the bushes, and trees. They were all fine too, all apparently undisturbed by the aura.

He crossed back over County Road 23 to the festival and found an area where no one was sitting, and he sank into a chair, looked around, suddenly unsure.

He had been absolutely positive that someone had been here, but why? And who did he imagine was so interested in little old shifty eyes and leave their aura there to disturb him? The crowd was talking, the music was playing, and nothing was out of the ordinary. Nothing was really different since he walked in. Nothing changed or was out of place—nothing.

Why would this aura haunt me? I acted normal, even boring. I don't do anything or own anything that might cause comment or raise red flags? I blend in. What have I missed? He questioned himself silently.

Glen leaned back and closed his eyes. Almost certainly, he was conjuring up the whole thing. This was surely just rattled nerves. He thought this must be a symptom of sleep deprivation, and he shouldn't worry too much about the desires and the needs that had a control over him.

And yet the feeling was so strong. He tried to shake it off— just a whim, a tic of the nerves, or maybe a passing heartburn?

He stood up, stretched, took a deep breath, and tried to think of nice thoughts. But none came. He shook his head and went toward the bar area for a drink of Scotch and—*there it was.*

There it was.

He stood behind the crowd and looked, and he didn't know how long, just staring stupidly at her.

Without really knowing what he was doing or why, he pulled his car keys out, fumbled, and dropped it. He reached down for it and quickly slipped away through the crowd; and when he thought he was safe, he then straightened himself out and walked toward his vehicle slowly, as if nothing happened.

His heart was pounding when he finally slid into the driver's seat. He looked back and saw no sign of anyone following him. He started the engine and, with the lights still off, drove as quickly and quietly as he could out into the dark road toward numbness and the new open door.

That numbness was for the journey his strong desire needed to ride, but for the new open door—it cried out.

"Open door!" it cried out.

"Open door," cried the new babies.

"Discover your new twins—*panic* and *terror*."

The outside music echoed with the jumbled heart-to-heart-gossip syndrome, which was a typical performance of any festivity, and yet it seemed to Ron that there was a special electricity in the air, a slight hushed feeling of excitement and tension that one wouldn't find at any ordinary jubilee, a sense that this one was different somehow, that new and wonderful things might happen because they were out here celebrating and discovering the beginning of their new life.

But at this very moment, he knew that Diana needed to confront this situation. He looked at her with fondness. Her beautiful features lit up the evening as they stepped out from the ranch trailer and into the crowd.

The thoughts of her fears and insecurity entered Ron's mind.

There was something missing, some essential piece of the puzzle that he could not explain: her helplessness regarding this aura. She never acted this way before. *What am I missing?*

Diana stopped next to a tent area in front of the ranch trailer to look at the crowd. There it was, only thirty feet away. The aura looked like a dark misty cloud in a perfect surrounding multitude, which had the right setting of good versus depravity, and this—it was striking.

Absolutely perfect revulsion: Jack the Ripper meets Mother Teresa.

"Thank God!" She said and realized she was smiling, and why not? *He was there. Isn't it nice? I wasn't crazy after all*, she thought.

Diana felt a little dizzy, uncertain of whether the back of the chair would hold her weight, as if she might simply pass straight down through the lawn like a mist. Even from the back of the chair, she could tell. He had monitored the area for her aura and had taken his time. He had done it right in spite of what must have seemed like a very close call in seeing her.

She wondered. *Was he teasing me?* He had to have some important reason for being here. *Am I his future trophy?* She thought. *Could he, too, feel the connection between us and just wanted to be playful? He must be teasing me.*

Diana heard Ron's voice in her thoughts saying, *Are you okay?*

The lavish blanket of stunned silence carried on for only a minute. "What?" she said as she moved her head a little closer to Ron's. "I can't hear you."

Ron repeated his question, "Are you okay?"

"Of course, I'm okay. It's just the music and the crowd talking loudly that just stunned me for a moment," Diana said.

Then the buzz of talk from the crowd took a new note as people strained to move forward to pass on good wishes to the newlyweds. The newlyweds had to put on their happy faces and smiled and greeted the crowd, not knowing that this distraction would cause alteration in the sequence of their lives.

The evil one was staring stupidly at her and finally pulled his car keys out, fumbled, and dropped it. He reached down for it and slipped away through the crowd, and when he thought he was safe, he then walked toward his vehicle slowly as if nothing happened.

"Ron, I can't see him anymore. Where did he go? He just disappeared," Diana said.

"I guess you scared the hell out of him. I would be scared if you were after me too," Ron said in a kittenish giggle.

Diana slapped Ron's arm playfully and said, "You're awful."

PART VI

The Need

23

The Twins Begin

He felt fragile, befuddled, and half sick with a combination of panic and terror. He felt this swelling inside him surging upward, a rising that could end only one way: his death.

He backed out of his driveway and yanked his big truck toward Bridge Street. He took a deep breath and looked at his hand on the steering wheel. It was shaking. *But it had been thrilling, hadn't it?* He thought. It had been madly exciting. He almost got caught, and that was a full-of-life feeling, which brought about a new tremor that went along with this crazy high. It had been something entirely new and eye-catching. *Wow—what a thrill!*

And the odd sensation that it was all going somewhere, an important place that was novel and yet not familiar, he would really have to explore this a little better next time. Not that there was going to be a next time, of course. This combination of panic and terror seemed thrilling, but it made him sweat. He would never do anything so foolish and impulsive. Never. But to have done it once made him think, *This is kind of humorous.*

There was no traffic as Glen drove west over the Narrowsburg Bridge into Pennsylvania; and after a quarter mile or so, he turned left toward the water. Across the clean waters of the Delaware River, he could see the back of the Main Street's buildings and the outline of Narrowsburg's waterfront.

He got out and stood between his big red truck and a huge pile of sand. For a moment, he just looked around and stared at the buildings and then down the road toward the water. He looked up. Above the rim of the building, he could just see the glow of the moon. A spring night wind blew across his face, bringing with it all the enchanting odors of country smells: the floral vegetation, the green fields, and towering oaks and evergreens. He inhaled it deeply and turned his thoughts back to the evening's developments.

A small shudder crawled up his spine. *Why am I doing this?*

And the dizziness of it had driven him to the dangerous, unplanned festival, to do something on the spur of the moment. Always before, he had planned carefully. And even knowing this, he badly wanted to do it. He had to do it!

He knew he had to make a fast retreat, and that was all there was to it. His heart pulse still pounded in his ears.

What an irresponsible risk to take. He had never before done anything so brash, never before done anything at all without careful planning. He could have been caught. He could have been seen.

"Stupid, stupid, stupid," he kept muttering to himself. Of course, he was not safe. He had taken a foolish and dreadful risk that went beyond all his cautious ways. He wagered his entire carefully built life, and for what? A future thrill kill—at a party?

"Stupid, stupid, stupid," he kept on muttering to himself. And deep in the shaded corner of his mind, the echo came, *Oh yes, stupid*, and the familiar quiet laughter.

Glen remembered when he lived in East New York on a small street near Pitkin Avenue. A few blocks to one side of his worthless little house, the neighborhood was one of low-income housing, chicken joints, and crumbling churches. Three miles north in the other direction, the millionaires lived.

Rego Park was an overgrown community with regal-type homes that had been built around high walls to keep out people like him. But now Glen was right in between, in a house he shared in Narrowsburg with his brother and the ugliest-looking cat he had ever seen.

Yet the memories still vibrated in Glen. But why was he still remembering his past? Why did this whole series of events seem to be whipping him back through time? He never really had a fond remembrance of his earlier years.

He was wandering down memory lane, self-absorbed in bitter memories of how this all began. Where would the madness end? For a few moments, he thought about life's cruel ironies.

After so many years of people providing good, wholesome care, he was led astray by these so-called caring communities, which drove him in the opposite direction in life.

There is no other feeling anywhere like when you are a twelve-year-old boy and camping out under a starry sky at a Boy Scout camp.

This trip was provided by certain groups and their outdoors initiative to help low-income children to have the opportunity to enjoy the upstate camping world. And even if the sight of all those stars merely fills you with a kind of pleasure, Glen felt, for the first time, the beginning of the killing desire.

He remembered when the fire had died down and the stars were exceedingly bright. The dear old campfire troop leader was taking a small sip of hot chocolate he had brewing on the silvery kettle. He remembered that the troop leader had been quiet for some time until he said, "You children are special. Yes, very special."

He then went back to sipping his hot chocolate and not providing the children any. *What a phony*, Glen thought.

Glen looked away from the brightness of the stars. Around the small and rocky clearing, the last glow of the fire was making its own shadows. Some of them trickled across the children's faces. They looked strange to him, like he had never seen them before. He looked at them in a special way, which brought desires of having sex with them like his homosexual cousin did to him.

He was nine years old when his dad and mom left his cousin to babysit while they went out to church. Every night after that, his cousin would come and crawl into his bed. He would suck Glen's little weasel and later rub his ding dong between Glen's thigh and butt.

This would go on for weeks until, one night, the cousin entered him. The sensation at first was pain and then, later, desire. That same desire stirred up a sensation that night around the campfire as the last glow of the fire trickled across the children's faces.

He could see that the canoe was there, moving gently with the surge of the river's water. That same surge was inside Glen, moving gently through his body.

Oh, let there be a moon, a good plump moon, something bigger to look at. As Glen tried to distract his thoughts, he clutched a fistful of grass.

His face was hot, as if these sexual desires wanted to be visible, but something inside him was watching silently, and this something wanted him to kill and enjoy the act he desired.

High overhead, a slow single-engine plane crawled by. Glen looked away, across the dying fire, off into the future over there somewhere. Even then he knew: needing to kill someone every now and then would pretty much, sooner or later, get in the way of being caught.

This killing desire happened to him when he was still a little kid, and it had shaped him. He had tried to level it out, but it was too strong, too much. It got into him too early, and it was going to stay there.

The growing need was making him kill. And he couldn't stop that. He couldn't change it, but he learned real early to control it.

With that, he gave some shape to his entire life, his whole kit and caboodle, who and what he is.

Being cautious went beyond the actual killing, of course. Being cautious meant building a cautious life too—playing the game that life expects and to imitate people's social existence—all of which he had done, so very carefully. He was just a neat and polite monster. You know, the one everyone talks about, *the nice boy next door*.

24

Fathers Knows Best

Diana, dressed in her tight black running clothes, had been spending way too much time out by the pond. She would sit and stare at the fishes and the tadpoles swimming around while trying to fathom the feelings she felt the night before.

To Ron, it didn't seem like a good place to go to reflect last evening's event. Diana didn't see it that way. Maybe because she knew she had the third eye, and it was challenging her responsibility. Ron knew his wife was a good-looking young woman who wanted to be a police officer. It was not her fault she looked more like a *Playboy* centerfold. Diana's 5'3" height, 110 pounds, and long brown hair and full lips truly made her a centerfold model.

"Diana," Ron said as he strolled over toward the pond. "Nice outfit. It really shows off your feminine figure in a bursting-at-the-seams display."

"Give me a break, deary," she said, feeling embarrassed.

"It would be better if we went inside and talk about this over a cup of coffee," he said helpfully.

Diana showed Ron her teeth. "How about letting me figure this out for myself?" she snarled. "I let this jerk escape." Then she gave a little shudder.

Ron stared at her, amazed. She was tough, a daughter of a Marine dad. Things didn't usually bother her.

She was an excellent martial arts fighter, and no one in school would ever try to threaten her. If they would try to get tough, she wouldn't blink. She would look them straight in the eyes and say, "You don't want to go there."

She had been there, done that, and bought the fight game in their face, and they never bothered her again.

But this one made her shudder.

This was a thought-provoking moment for both Diana and Ron.

"This one is special, is that it?" he asked her.

"This one came to our home...our home, Ron!" She pointed a finger at Ron. "And *that* pisses me off. Sorry, deary, for the temper. He made me feel afraid and helpless, and that's not me."

Ron gave her his happy smile. "Detective Sherlock Diana Holmes needs to solve this case?"

"You got that right," she said. "I want to catch this jerk. I need a small break..." She paused. And then she looked at Ron. "Please help me, Ron. I really need your help."

Seeing his wife looking at him with those adorable hazel eyes and with the sweet *please* dangling in the air, what else could he say but, "Of course, I will, Diana. You know that"?

Catching this evil person doing something awful was the number one priority in her mind.

Ron sat down near Diana on a large rock facing the pond. He remembered his dad teaching him how to obtain the right frame of mind for thinking. "The capacity of our peace of mind is determined by how much we are able to live in the present moment," his dad used to say. "Regardless of what happened yesterday or last week and what may or may not happen tomorrow, the current moment is where you are, at all times.

Monday morning, walking the streets of Narrowsburg brought about a new change of attitude for Ron and Diana. After checking their post office box, they stepped out to see the people strolling down on Main Street.

Narrowsburg and the town of Tusten in which it is located has always historically been a lively place with sturdy ties to the out-of-doors folks. And today was no different.

They both saw that Narrowsburg's Main Street was a confirmation of the American entrepreneurial spirit at work. They could see the many different artisans, antique shops, galleries, and restaurants establishing their new homes in and among the quaint and historical buildings.

And all of this was within a few feet of the scenic and recreational upper Delaware River. What a sight to behold!

The crown jewel of Main Street is the Delaware Valley Arts Alliance, which they knew was responsible for providing the pivotal magnetic force that has drawn artists, musicians, writers, dancers, fashion designers, jewelry makers, and filmmakers to Narrowsburg over the years.

Ron looked at the people walking the streets, and he thought that many of them seemed to live as if life were a dress rehearsal for some later date. He was taught by his dad that no one had a guarantee that they would be here tomorrow. Only today, this very moment, is the only time we have, and the only time we have any control over. When our attention is in the present moment, we push fear from our minds.

His dad would also warn him about bad mood swings that can be extremely deceptive. It can trick you into believing your life is far worse than it really is. He would use the example of the fact that when one is in a good mood, life looks good. You have an outlook that has common sense attached to it and, above all, some wisdom in the mix.

When in a good mood, things don't feel so hard. Problems don't seem like problems, and if they are, they are easier to solve. In other words, relationships seem to flow better, and communication is a little laid-back, and if someone tries to criticize you, you just take it in stride.

But when you're in a bad mood, life looks agonizingly serious and problematic. You have very little perspective. You take things too personally and start to think with your emotions. A bad mood is not the time to analyze your life.

"Remember this," Ron's dad would emphasize, "Not to do so, is emotional suicide."

So the next time Ron would feel bad, his dad would say, "Life is too short for bad moods, and when they do come, they can also go away. If you let it, you're not married to it. If you are, then cut it the fuck loose. Divorce that daughter of a bitch!"

25

The Echo in the Air

They arrived home around 5:00 p.m. and laid down the shopping bags that were filled up with grocery items from Peck's Market. Diana started to put the groceries away while Ron sat down on the kitchen's table chair and didn't speak. He waited for Diana to unload on him. *That's what married couples do*, he thought, but instead he spoke, "Why were you seemingly so anxious to talk to me? On our way home, you started to say something, and then you paused and stopped. Then the mumbling began. What gives?"

"It keeps on bothering me when I can't remember what the jerk looks like. I only saw a dark cloud in place of a person. Then the crowd came to wish us good cheers, then—puff like the magic dragon—he just disappears."

She opened the bag that had the doughnut in it and looked inside.

"What did you expect?" Ron said.

"You know that we had to put on our happy, smiley faces for the crowd. It would have been rude of us to act any other way." She pulled a sprinkle chocolate doughnut out of the doughnut box and bit into it. "I expect," she said, mouth full, "to be in this with you in finding him."

"You don't have the right frame of mind," Ron said, "or the right temperament to follow any clues."

Diana crumpled the empty grocery bag that held the doughnuts and threw it at Ron's head. She missed.

"Get this straight, deary," she said. "You know damn well I deserve to be a part of this. Instead of—" She started to feel her tears falling from her eyes, and she looked at Ron and waved her hands in front of her face to hide the tears from him. "This is bull, Ron!"

Ron nodded. "Although on you, the bull looks good," he said, smiling.

Diana made an awful face: rage and disgust competing for space. "I hate this feeling," she said. "I can't let this go by, or I swear I'll go nuts."

"It's a little soon for me to have the whole thing figured out, hon. I have an idea, but let me make a few phone calls first. Okay?" Ron said as he wandered away toward the bedroom and closed the bedroom door.

It seemed like forever when Ron appeared in the kitchen and sat down on the kitchen chair and looked up toward Diana. He waited until her eyes were focused on him. "I think we may have a person of interest. It may be thin, but it seems like a starting point."

Diana's eyes had a glitter of hope. She said, smiling, "I like thin. Thin is good, and it works for me. Just give me the details!"

She then pulled out another doughnut and brutalized it with the hunger of knowing that a plate of goodies was about to be served.

"So what have you figured out, hmmm?" she said, mumbling with her mouth full.

Ron, knowing her excitement, didn't keep her waiting. He told her about Robby, his Irish brother from another mother, who saw a friend of his arrive at the celebration late. As he tried to approach him to say hi, his friend started to cross County Road 23 toward the farmhouse. He thought his friend left, but then he saw him coming toward the bar and then stopped. Bending down, he picked up something and then started to slip away from the celebration. He thought his friend's action was strange."

"Okay, who was he? What is his name?" Diana shouted out.

"Easy, honey, you need to take a chill pill to calm down. His name is Glen. Okay, are you happy now?" Ron said.

Diana turned her eyes upward with a quizzical frown on her face and said, "Who is this Glen fellow? I don't know him."

"He is a plumber who lives in town. Robby has worked with him on some jobs but does not really know him. He only knows him professionally. I got his address. Want to take a ride and check it out?" Ron asked in a wicked tone.

Diana jumped on Ron, and both fell to the floor, laughing.

"What do you think, deary? I love you, my hero, even if this clue is thin." She then started to kiss Ron all over his face and head like a chicken pecking down on her food.

They were parked across the dark street from the cream-and-dark-red-shingle home on Erie Street. Their lights were off. They had been waiting and watching the house for twenty minutes. The pressure, the growing need, the waiting made time tick by slowly, only to swell more with every tick of the bright night watch on Diana's wrist. But it was a time to be careful. A time spent making sure. A time to be certain that he was the one. Diana looked at Ron sitting on the passenger seat since, in her haste, she wanted to be the one to drive.

She looked at Ron being so relaxed and looking cautiously out of the window.

"Why are you so relaxed, deary? I'm pumped up and so excited to think that we may have the jerk cornered," she said.

"Hon, I've been doing surveillance work for my dad for sometime that this just seems routine to me. Robby told me that this guy lives with his brother and to watch out for an ugly, cranky cat that lives with them. Now, I want for you to stay in the vehicle while I go out and check this house and see who's there. I am going in with my own invisible puff-of-the-magic-dragon routine, and please be a good girl and listen to your daddy."

He then winked at her while he slowly disappeared in front of her.

"Boy, I could never really get used to this, deary, seeing you vanish in front of my eyes. Are you still here, or am I speaking to myself?"

"I'm still here, but I will be going through the vehicle's door. Check my footsteps on the gravel outside your window. I leave those footsteps for you to smile at. Bye now."

Ron slipped through the vehicle door and started making little scraping sounds out in front of Diana's windows. She looked out of the window and down toward the footsteps that were walking toward the suspect's home. She then, while resting her arms on the window's armrest, smiled and said to him in a loud whisper, "Go get him tiger!"

Ron started for the house and decided to go through the back-door entrance. As he entered the home, he could hear the TV on in the living room as he passed through the kitchen into the first bedroom. Nothing seemed unusual except for the luggage in the corner with baggage claim stubs from Miami, Florida, to New York. *Someone likes to travel*, thought Ron.

He then continued to the other room, which had the lights on; and in the middle of the room was a box with dirty coveralls and double rubber gloves that smelled. *Maybe that was for the laundry to take care of,* he thought.

He then went toward the living room, where he could see a young man sitting on a reclining chair next to a cold six-pack of beer. He was looking at reruns of football's greatest games.

All of a sudden, Ron saw the ugliest cat in the world smelling and following him. This cat, to Ron, was a disgrace to feline beauty and should have been a candidate for plastic surgery. The cat looked like he had just finished fighting a skunk, or maybe a porcupine, that must have scratched the hell out of his face. And then to make matters funnier, the cat must have gone a few rounds with Mike Tyson since a piece of his ear was missing.

Other than that, Ron thought, nothing showed out of the ordinary. It looked like *crazy* wasn't in the house. He then decided to go back to the vehicle.

Once he entered the vehicle, he reappeared and said, "Boo!"

"Cut it out, deary. You want to give the love of your life a heart attack?" She said seriously and then smiled. "What did you find?"

"Nothing yet. It seems that his brother is there, and he is still out."

"Will just wait a little more to see if he comes home, and maybe we..." As Diana started to finish her sentence, she sensed the evil aura was coming. "Ron, he is coming. I sense it," she said.

They waited and waited, but no one showed up.

"He knows we're here," she said, detecting him. "He is not coming as long as he feels my aura too. Ron, he must be the one. We must find a way to be sure. No sense in waiting around. Let's go home and rethink the strategy of capturing him. What do you think?" She said, looking in Ron's eyes for answers.

"I think you are acting professional and have become an ace detective, and I like the new you." Ron then leaned over and gave her a sweet long kiss on her cheek and said, smiling, "Let's go home, partner."

The engine started, and the lights were turned on as they drove off silently toward home.

Meanwhile, on a hill where a lonely church glittered next to a large cloudy moon stood a five-foot man with binoculars. He was looking down half a mile away toward a cream-and-dark-red-shingle home on Erie Street. He watched and waited until the dark-colored vehicle passed by.

"Stupid, stupid, stupid," was an echo in the air.

"Stupid, stupid, stupid," he kept on muttering to himself.

26

Watch Out for the Sucker Punch

It had been four days since their last encounter with the cream-and-dark-red-shingle home on Erie Street. Ron took Diana with him to work while they both did background checks and investigation on Glen.

To avoid being discovered, he made sure that Diana was not part of the visual and mobile surveillance with video content. They used different surveillance vehicles to avoid detection, and their tailing methods and tactics seemed to be working. No one in the office knew whose name was listed as the client except Ron's dad. So a bogus folder was established with a bogus client, and the expense was handled within.

Diana had left early on Friday to go see her dad and mom. Ron had just returned to the ranch trailer that evening. He was leaning back in his La-Z-Boy chair and relaxing when the phone rang. He let it ring. He just wanted to breathe for a few minutes. His day needed this break. He could think of nothing that couldn't wait. Besides, he had voice mail on his home phone, so let it earn its keep.

At two rings, he closed his eyes. He breathed in slowly and relaxed his tired body. The third ring, he let his breath out slowly, applying his martial arts training skills in breathing. He knew the voice mail was now taking control and that he had a few more seconds to relax before getting up and pressing *86 on the phone's keypad to check his messages.

He breathed in again slowly while listening to the message that followed. "You have one new message. Please press one to listen to your message."

Okay, he thought while pressing the number 1 on the keypad.

"Hi, it's me."

A female voice, not his mom's or Felisha's, but whose was it? It couldn't be Diana; she was over her dad and mom's home. *Why would she call me at the home phone and not my cell number?* He just couldn't understand why so many people started their messages with, "Hi, It's me."

Of course, it is you. Everybody knows that. But who the hell are you? Why do people do this? He thought about this as his mind started spinning, trying to figure out who was calling, and his context of choices were rather limited. He knew it wasn't his mom. It didn't sound like Felisha, although anything was possible. So that left…

"Diana?"

"Um, I'm sorry, I…" There was a long breath sighing out. "Listen. Ron, I'm sorry I called…I thought you would call me, and then when you didn't, I just…"

And there was another long breath out.

"Anyway, I need to talk. Because I realized…I mean, oh hell. Could you, um, call me? If…you know."

He had no clue. Not at all. He wasn't even sure who it was. Could that really be Diana, he thought.

Another long sigh.

"I'm sorry if…" And a very long pause, and then there was a full breath with a sigh. "Please call me, Ron. Just…" A long pause. Another sigh. Then she hung up.

Am I going crazy, or did I just step into the twilight zone?

The whole thing began to irritate him beyond measure while he paced around the living room.

The simple thing to do was to call Diana. He called Diana's parents' home, and Diana's mom picked up. He heard the voice of Anna, and it was coated with tears. Diana picked up the phone from her mother, and her voice was disturbed with pain and coated with the same tears as Anna's.

"Diana, what's wrong? Did you call me at home?" Ron inquired.

"Yes, I did…" And she burst out and cried over the phone. "I tried to call you on the cell phone, but you must have turned it off because I was getting your voice mail and…" There was another burst of tears, a long pause, and then a full breath with a sigh.

Ron looked in his pocket and pulled out his phone and saw that it was turned off. He must have turned off the phone while he was doing surveillance and forgot to turn it back on. "Okay, honey, I'm here. Tell me what is wrong and how I can make it right. Just tell me!" Ron said as he sat down on the kitchen chair and listened to his wife describe what was going on.

Between the sobbing and crying, he was able to make out what the problem was. Even though her dad had a previous CT scan of his chest, he needed to follow through with an MRI, which he had on Monday.

Then on Tuesday, he had a lung biopsy. The diagnosis was that his lung tissue had invasive squamous cell carcinoma, moderately differentiated. In other words, he had *lung cancer*, and it needed to be surgically removed immediately.

On Thursday, Diana's dad went to a cardiovascular diagnostic center in Brooklyn, New York. He needed clearance to have an upper lobectomy, which was scheduled this Tuesday coming up.

In the meantime, he was experiencing chest pain and needed to have a stress test since he was known previously to have mild coronary disease. The only good news was that he had one of the finest surgeons in this field, Rajesh Kham, MD, FACS.

To make matters worse, Ray was going to have a hip replacement this year, and that had to be put on hold.

What got Diana angry was that her dad and mom didn't want her to know what he was going through. She only learned about it today, and it shook her up.

"Ron, why did they treat me like a stranger? Don't they trust me to tell me what's going on? I love my dad so much and…" There was a pause, a sigh, with crying in the mix, and she continued, "And it's hard to see him this way."

"What does your dad say about all of this?" Ron inquired.

"He thinks this is just another walk in the park. Screw him and his tough-Marine attitude! I just think he's…"

There was a very long pause, and then there was one full breath with a sigh—in deeply and then puffed out abruptly.

"Damn him…damn him…Ron, I love him so much I can't help it. It's killing me inside…"

As Diana put the phone down slowly, Ron could hear her crying heavily and muttering, "He thinks he's so tough, so tough…why do you have to be so tough? Why? Why?"

Ron could hear in the background her mother picking up the phone and saying to Diana, "It will be all right, dear. Don't worry. It will be all right."

Then her mother spoke to Ron, "Is it okay for Diana to spend a few days here until her dad goes for surgery?" she said in an inquiring tone.

"Sure, Mrs. Diamond, it's okay with me. If you need me, I'll be there. Please let me know. Tell Diana I love her and she can call me anytime, day or night."

And with that, she hung up the phone while the echoes of Diana's sobering tears hung in the air.

The whole thing distracted Ron while the scene in his head reeled. He pulled out some cold pizza from the fridge and warmed it up in the microwave. He opened a can of cold light beer and rubbed it on his forehead to cool down the little tiny men that were pounding nails in his thoughts.

After brushing his teeth and a light shower, he rested his head on the soft pillow on his bed and dozed off. He was awakened by an owl in a nearby tree as he walked over to the window to look out.

There it was again, the huge happy face in the sky, the chuckling moon. It felt like life was laughing at him, and the moon was no exception. He closed the curtain and turned away. He circled his home from room to room, touching things, telling himself everything would be all right. *Yes, I guess*, he thought, *this is what married people go through.*

Everything in his life seemed too easy. Being married to the best girl in the world was a plus. Life was good. But one compass reading in life had now exposed itself.

Whatever life tries to tell you, watch out for the sucker punch.

27

Cockroaches Are a Pest

Glen cleared his throat. He felt a little clumsy and light-headed while shopping, but after all, this was a very important moment in a monster's mind.

"Do you want these large set of knives with the rest of the kitchenware since we are having a special on them?" the lady behind the cash register at Walmart inquired.

"No, thank you for asking"—he looked at the lady's name on her tag—"Suzy? You're so sweet. Thank you again for asking," He said in his polite, thoughtful, boy-next-door tone while smiling and thinking, *She's too big to cut up. Where would I put the pieces?*

Pulling out of the parking lot at Honesdale, Pennsylvania, he realized that he was whipped. He thought that he didn't ordinarily require a great deal of sleep, but as soon as he arrived home, he might take a nice, solid twenty-four hours of a peaceful snooze.

The ups and downs of the last two days, the strain of so much new experience, like panic and terror—it had all been draining. As he drove on the main road, passing the shopping centers, he pulled over next to the gas station curve, put his gear in park, and rubbed his throbbing temples.

A terrible, mind-numbing need was chipping away like a draining sinus.

He then tried to sit up straight in the seat while his seat belt was pushing in. It was like a cloudy disorientation that squeezed in between his two frontal lobes. *What is happening to me?* He kept thinking. *And why can't it happen to someone else?*

He felt different, this *panic* and *terror*, his twins. But what did that mean? He wasn't sure what that difference was or what it meant.

He kept thinking that this seemed like a twisted soap opera, and it was far too much. He reached in his left-side coat pocket and pulled out a bottle of aspirin. He took four of them. He didn't care for the taste. He had never like medicine of any kind except in straightforward way.

That's how I roll, he thought.

He finally let out a long sigh and then put his left signal light on; and while they were blinking, he put the gear in drive, looked at the left side-view mirror, and slowly merged into traffic.

The road was empty and lonely as he crossed over the Narrowsburg Bridge into Bridge Street.

As he made a right turn on Erie Street, he suddenly stopped short. "What the fuck is going on?" he said in a low, muffled voice to himself. "This can't be happening again!"

His insides were screaming, *Caution!*

His sixth sense—that was what he called it—smelled out the same aura of the invader who had left his or her presence in the midair particles at the celebration two evenings ago.

They know I'm here.

It took him a few seconds before he turned his car around and went up the hill toward the church, and he turned off the engine.

The lonely church that glittered next to a large cloudy moon had a visitor. This visitor was petrified and alarmed at the thought of being caught. Mr. Smooth was now looking down through his binoculars with such an intent look toward the cream-and-dark-red-shingle home on Erie Street half a mile away.

He watched and waited and kept looking around to see if there was more to this surveillance. He watched and watched and watched. Twenty minutes later, the dark-colored vehicle's engine started, and the lights were turned on, and they drove away.

"Stupid, stupid, stupid," was the echo that flowed in the air.

"Stupid, stupid, stupid," the five-foot man kept on muttering to himself.

When he arrived, he peeked into his home carefully. There was his brother with his headphones on, listening to the sound coming out of the TV and drinking *his* beers. *Lazy fuck*, he thought.

In the corner was the ugly cat turning in circles until it finally decided to lie down. No one heard him coming in. If he was a thief instead of a monster, he thought, he could have cleaned out his own home, and his brother would still be sitting down like an idiot.

"What the fuck," he uttered.

He went into his room and put on a Steppenwolf CD and sat in his chair. The song "Twisted" stirred the emptiness inside him as the lyrics rolled around in the bedroom's air.

"Oh, six a.m.," and then it continued, "but I've...when it comes to being sociable...can't seem to win."

"That me not being sociable," he said, laughing and smiling, as the music continued toward the end of the lyrics.

"Oh...I'm twisted, yeah...All right...can't seem to win."

While the music was playing, Glen got up and twisted his hips and whispered to himself, "I'm twisted. Yes, I'm twisted." And he continued to shake his hips and body with the beat of the music.

And after a few minutes of this, he sat down on his chair, and his usual calm and frosty thoughts returned.

"But I can't seem to win like the music said." His teeth began to grind. "Those fucking cockroaches are a pest! They keep on pestering me. No, I will step on these little cockroaches!"

And then an idea popped into his twisted mind.

He then went behind his desk and pulled out two large machetes, and in his best Al Pacino imitation, he said as he swung the blades, cutting through the air, "Say *hello*—to my little friends."

PART VII

Memories and Dreams

28

Memory Lane

As the plane landed at 4:00 a.m. at Cheddi Jagan International Airport (the national airport of Guyana), Hanna Kincade was still lumbering and light-headed from the news she received from her sister, Saniya, at the celebration of Ron and Diana on Saturday.

Roy and Lee Ann, as well as Angelina and John Hemingway, knew what was going on and kept it from the newlyweds. Afraid that Felisha would open her mouth, they decided not to let her know until after the celebration.

As Hanna walked on the pavement toward the terminal, she held on to Harry's arm for support as she recalled in her thoughts how this airport used to be called Timehri International Airport.

"Funny how things come back to the mind," she said to Harry as they walked.

Harry nodded and said, "Yes, this trip is opening up memories in my mind too. If I'm right, we are on the right bank of the Demerara River in the city of Timehri, about twenty five miles south of Guyana's capital, Georgetown."

And then he continued, "Do you remember on the thirtieth of July 2011? It was in all the news about this same airline, Caribbean Airlines. Their flight number 523 overran the runway in rainy weather and went through that perimeter chain-link fence?"

He turned to the right and pointed to the area where it happened and continued, "The aircraft, a Boeing 737-800, broke in two just behind the first-class area. Thank God there were no casualties."

"Leave it to you to bring out the engineering information and facts about Guyana. The old habit doesn't die, right, dear?" she said while chuckling.

"You know me well. Nothing gets past you. I love you," Harry said with tenderness flowing from his eyes.

And she looked in his caring eyes and said, "Thank you, and I love you right back, Harry."

They go into the terminal to be routed through customs.

Then they entered the vehicle and felt the local climate was a little hot and humid. But a northeast trade wind along the coast welcomed them. And to make their journey a little sunnier, their arrival came at the right time, just before the rainy season, which started around the first of May to mid-August.

To keep the trip from being silent, Harry needed to spew out additional information: "Hanna, there is more than 80 percent of Guyana still covered by forests. That's including the dry evergreen and also the seasonal forests. And then there are the mountain regions and lowland evergreens including the rain forests. All these forests are home to more than a thousand species of trees. Imagine that.

What a country. Yet people can't find work, so they leave the country to find work elsewhere. Very sad." He drifted into silence as the ride continued.

Hanna thought about the news from her sister, and her mind wandered back to the days when she was young.

She remembered a man, an ordinary man of no great importance to the world, but for her—he was her daddy. In her eyes, he was always brave but a little hot-tempered at times. Yet, he was always her father.

He walked with a slight limp, smoked like a chimney, and worked in the cane field from dawn to dusk, but somehow, he always made time for Hanna.

One of those special times was their bicycle for two. Through a child's eye, she would look at him in awe as he would mount the bicycle while her dearest mother lifted her up to sit in front, sidesaddle, with a pillow to cushion her bottom for comfort.

She could still see his legs peddling. With one leg shorter than the other, he managed to maneuver the bicycle, whistling softly at the same time.

Looking back now, she understood what life meant for him. Exhausted, maybe even angry at what was dealt, but somehow, he always managed to smile, even laugh aloud at her curiosity while she pointed at something or someone, trying to distract him.

On one occasion, she remembered him scolding her on the bicycle.

"If you make us fall off this bike, you not riding with me anymore. Furthermore, me not gonna pick you up off the road. You know that, so now keep still."

And with her sharp tongue, replied, "You always pick me up when I fall, Papa. You always do."

And he laughed softly, kissing her lightly on the top of her head, as they rode on their bicycle for two.

Those memories brought tears in Hanna's eyes.

"Are you okay?" Harry said, looking at her tears.

"I'm okay, Harry... really, I am...I am just thinking about lovely memories...that's all."

And with that, she leaned over to him and planted a sweet kiss on his cheek.

Viola's Passages is what they called the Demerara Harbour Bridge. It was a joke of bad taste, she thought, as the bridge expanded its 6,074-foot-long pride. The government, well-meaning, decided to construct a floating bridge to accommodate growing businesses and trade across Guyana. The only problem was that the vehicles on this bridge all bounced up and down like jumping jelly beans, with the musical accompaniment of slow bursting machine gunfire—*bang, bang, and bang*—the sound that made crossing the Demerara River a unique government experience.

Toll was collected only in one direction of travel even though the bridge handles one lane of traffic in each direction. Traffic going west to east pays no toll, so none was given as they went by.

Hanna could see the people riding their bikes, walking and carrying their heavy bags on the pedestrian's walkway on the bridge. She could also make out the raised section of the bridge to let the small vessels pass under.

As she crossed the bridge, she saw an old movie theater that seemed abandoned. Her mind started to drift back to her younger days before she met Harry.

It was a Saturday, 7:00 a.m. The pots and pans were scrubbed and laid out to dry, and the smell of breakfast and lunch wafted into the bedroom of their sleeping parents. Her mother, Beefi, would open her eyes and then nudge her husband, saying, "You smell that?"

Hanna imagined her dad, Mr. Bali, who would then be startled from his sleep and bolt into a sitting position, looking around him, then at his wife, and anxiously ask, "What? What? Fire?"

Exasperated, Beefi had replied, "No, man, them gal must ah been up since four day morning. Can't you smell the food?"

Scratching his head, he glanced at the clock by their bedside and smiled. "You know what day it is, right? So why you so surprise? They bribing us, you know."

In the kitchen, below the stilted house, Hanna and Saniya busied themselves putting the finishing touches to shelves, rearranging and filling empty bottles. When everything was to their satisfaction—and hoped silently to their mother's—they both, at the same time, asked, "You think they are up?"

Looking at each other, they burst out laughing. Hanna, the eldest, said, "I hope they let we go to the movies. We got those new dress and shoes and everything. Besides, we did all the housework for at least the whole day."

"Well, it all depends on Ma," Saniya replied.

Hearing the sound of footsteps coming down the steps into the kitchen, they both ran into the open yard, looking at nothing in particular. Then their father called out, "Hanna? Saniya? Come, come. What you hiding for?"

He could see his daughters giggling nervously, pulling at each other, saying, "You go first?"

"Okay, girls, come on. Your mother is not here yet?"

They approached him slowly. Then Hanna, the elder of the two, said, "Well, you see, Pa, we want to see that new movie with Hema Malini and Dharmendra."

"Oh, you mean *Sholay*. Yes, man, nice movie. You know, I see it in Georgetown three weeks ago."

"What, you see three weeks ago!"

Turning around, they saw Beefi smiling. That was a good sign. "So I see you girls going to the movies. Who else going?"

Hanna answered, "Well, Mom, is me and Saniya and some of the girls down the street."

Nodding head in approval, Beefi replied, "Very good. They is good girls, but still be careful. Don't let no boys come sit next to you. We don't need neighbors talking now. So what time the picture start?"

Both girls replied, "Eleven-thirty."

Then Beefi said, "So get yourselves ready, and look nice now both, you hear?"

As Hanna reflected on those memories of the past, she couldn't help but think that those were the days that made their busy lives exciting—those Saturdays at the movies.

She smiled as she entered the village of Anna Catherina on the West Coast Demerara. Hanna pointed straight ahead, moving her arms up and down and saying in excitement, "Up ahead, look. That is where the village of Leonora is—where we would get our vegetables, Harry. Do you remember that?" She giggled.

"Yes, Hanna, I remember." He smiled.

Then the vehicle made a right turn off the public road and entered Front Street.

"Just a few blocks more," she said as she harked back to memory lane, childhood times, and Stewartville School.

Memories and recollections of old just came flooding the doorways of her mind as the vehicle then made a left on 207 North Street.

29

Raj Wept

Light then darkness. It was floating in and out and fighting the way toward the light. He did not like what was within this darkness—it tasted. The taste, the feel of salt, suffocated him, filled his mouth, his nostrils. There seemed to be no release. He needed help to escape this agony. He fought desperately, hovering within light's reach. Then the voices—yes, voices—he felt himself being dragged, rolled over. He was being pumped free.

Confusion surrounded him, voices screaming his name. Some questioned, and others had stories of what really happened. He lay on the sand with his eyes closed, his head pounding, and swells of nausea with every breath then receded slowly. They were all whispering, each a different story. He grasped at whatever his mind allowed him.

"You can't tell me he was not out there on that broken-down fishing boat of his," a male voice argued.

"I am telling you. I saw Raj sitting on them rocks, minding his own business, and today is his day off. I should know," a woman's voice replied haughtily.

Another said, "All of you crazy, making up you own stories. You people can stretch a ruler into a lamppost. You probably believed you saw something really big and hairy pulling Raj into that ocean—and it had to be Master Curaman."

The crowd hovering above Raj roared with laughter.

Raj groaned. Moving slightly, he tried to remember something—anything that they say happened. He could not.

As dim cries of welcome, softness, and warmth greeted his body, he opened his eyes slowly. The task hurt. Raj felt like someone was plucking his eyelids.

Shapes, figures, they were all twisted, moving before him in waves. He shuddered, looking around frantically, his legs thrashing, both his hands now wrapped around his body, shielding himself. Calming hands pressed him into the mattress, a familiar voice reassuring him, "Raj, you are home. Safe, you hear me? What is it? Do you remember what happened?"

Floorboards creaked from restlessness. Boredom replaced concern on few of the known faces. Some of those faces eased their way out through the wooden door. His mother looked at each one, thanking them as they left the bedroom. Raj looked around the room, blinking rapidly. Everything looked the same. The only thing he could not account for was what really happened.

"Ma?" His voice was still weak. "I can't remember anything. I just feel like I was in the ocean for a long period of time. I know I went to sleep last night. Now it's the middle of the afternoon."

"Sleep, son. Maybe when you wake up, you will remember." She then exited the room.

Slowly he eased his fingers away from the palm of his left hand. Cool air caressed the moist skin. In the other hand, however, there was a pinching sensation.

With less care, he opened his hands. Buried in his flesh was a smooth shimmering shell. Quickly he closed his hands. *My eyes must be playing tricks on me*, he thought. Looking again, he saw it was still there. Gingerly, he touched the shell. His body tingled. It felt like a dose of electricity had just shot through his body.

Easing the shell away from the palm of his hands, Raj saw that the shell had bitten deeply into his flesh, drawing blood as he eased it out. Upon closer inspection, he saw it was not just another shell.

Raj stood up and moved toward the old bureau and stared into the rectangular-shaped mirror. His reflection stared at him like a stranger would. Curiosity, the need for answers, as well as questions, lay behind his dark eyes. He spoke to his reflection, "A few days ago, I saw you, knew who you were—a fisherman, lover of books, and a good son, or at least you try to be. Now all I need is a few answers, and your brain seems dead."

Waving his hands in dismissal, he turned away from his reflection and tossed the shell on top of the bureau. Warily, he stepped out of the old khaki pants and got back into bed, cradling his head with both hands. His mind was shifting from voice to voice, a different story rolling off the lips of the villagers. Men and women he grew up among were each set in their own cruel ways.

Everything that he detested surrounded him. The difference between the villagers and Raj clashed violently. He knew they mocked and laughed at the way he spoke, the way he lived. Privacy was a sin to them. If you couldn't share problems with them, then you were not one of them. Raj knew that the act of helping him had just opened the doors to these villagers.

Before he drifted off into sleep, he decided to close those doors. He enjoyed his privacy, so did his mother.

He was sleeping a tired man's sleep, until it began. In his mind's eye, he saw an angry ocean, waves of fury lashing against rough boulders. Somewhere in his sleep-filled subconscious, he forced himself to move, but his body refused. In frustrated desperation, silent tears trickled from behind closed lids.

When he awoke, there was emptiness inside him, a sense of great loss. Emotions were evoked within him, the kind he had experienced only once. He had tossed the shell carelessly on the bureau, hoping that when he awoke, it was gone, perhaps had disappeared. And then it began to rain, like the day of the funeral several months ago. The house had both its floors crammed with mourners. Friends, neighbors, brothers, and sisters—they all waited for the rain to stop so they could accompany the dead to the final resting place. Extra ice was ordered, and his mother began to wail, saying between sobs, "My son doesn't want to leave this house. Look at the way it's raining. Anybody ever see such a thing. His shell will never leave."

"The shell. Yes, the shell," Raj recalled. It was all coming back.

The rock, and then yesterday, that was special day, the day when he saw the shell, that which represented the feelings he was holding in and not letting go.

How could he? He wanted that shell. It was the only way he knew how to honor and celebrate the boy he loved and couldn't let go.

Yes, yesterday was his brother's birthday and the reopening of memories.

Raj wept.

As the days went by, Raj recalled the stories his brother would tell him about his mermaid friend named Serene. He would laugh and say that was folk tradition. Sometimes he would talk to Bali, his next-door neighbor.

But according to Bali, who was well versed in knowledge, many countries have shared this similar tradition. The common element was that they were the restless spirits of the unclean dead.

"They are usually the ghosts of young women who died a violent or untimely death, or perhaps by murder or suicide, and especially by drowning."

Bali would then go on, "Mermaids are said to inhabit lakes and rivers. They appear as beautiful young women with long green hair and pale skin, suggesting a connection with floating weeds and days spent underwater in faint sunlight. And they also say that the mermaids can be seen after dark, dancing together under the moon and calling out to young men by name, luring them to the water and drowning them."

Raj pondered on his brother, David, drowning death. He couldn't believe that a boy who swam better than him could drown.

Did a mermaid lure David to the water and drown him? The shell his brother was holding in his hand, was it a mermaid's shell? Where is the shell now? Where did I put it?

He remembered easing the shell away from the palm of his hands, and he saw that the shell had bitten deeply into his flesh, drawing blood as he eased it out. And upon closer inspection, he saw it was not just another shell. *Was it a mermaid shell? Okay, where did I put it?*

Raj remembered when he stood up and moved toward the old bureau and stared into the rectangular-shaped mirror and spoke to his reflection. Then he tossed the shell on top of the bureau.

That it! It's upstairs on top of the bureau. That is where I put it!

And as a mouse running from a hungry cat, he stormed upstairs and searched for the missing ornament.

He noticed that the shell had small pearls in its shape. Bali used to tell him that in literature, they said that when a mermaid wept tears, those tears became pearls.

Maybe David's death was no accident.

He was so absorbed in his brother's death that he didn't even think if it was an accident, or was it murder? "I need to know," he said to himself.

Raj then went next door to see his neighbor, Bali, and showed him the shell and told him his story. Bali then lit up a cigarette, inhaled, and let the smoke fill the room while he examined the shell with a Sherlock Holmes curiosity.

Minutes passed by, and Bali then proceeded to his library of books and started to read the section labeled "Under Reported Sighting."

> In 1493, sailing off the coast of Hispaniola, Columbus reported seeing three female forms which rose high out of the sea, but were not as beautiful as they are represented.
>
> The logbook of Blackbeard, an English pirate, records that he instructed his crew on two separate voyages to steer away from charted waters which he called "enchanted" for fear of merfolk or mermaids, which Blackbeard himself and members of his crew reported seeing.
>
> These sighting were often recounted and shared by sailors and pirates who believed that mermaids

brought bad luck and would bewitch them into giving up their gold and dragging them to the bottom of the sea.

All this reading brought more curiosity to both Raj and Bali.

Again, Bali looked at the shell, and his mind was lost in thought. "Tomorrow we will go to the place where David drowned and investigate," he said softly. And then, with so much authority, he inhaled his last drag on his cigarette before putting it out. He raised both of his arms up in the air and said, "The adventure will begin. Tomorrow we will start finding *the truth*!"

30

Dreams Keep on Giving—Dreams

Bali had been up for some time, turning and tossing in his bed, eager for dawn. He had dreamt of a bright-colored feathered friend soaring high, unprepared to land on any of the tall palm trees in the vicinity.

The morning was bright, and a slight chill had blown into the room together with a dragonfly, which in twitchy movements up and down seemed to be looking for and entrance into his mosquito's net.

Strange, he thought.

To look more clearly at the dragonfly, Bali wiped away dew-covered humidity from his eyes, unsure of the dragonfly's progress in entering his net.

Beefi stirred on account of the cold wind coming through the bedroom's window, and Bali covered her with one of her robes. When this proved insufficient, he found the bedcovers on her side and placed it over her robe. He got up and closed the window and returned to bed.

Then he saw in his mind's eyes that the dragonfly was not what it seemed. It was a *winged man* who was trying to enter his net.

He woke up, his mind cluttered with unrelated memories.

Half an hour later, Bali sat alone in the armchair where he had left the book about mermaids. A voice was urging him to get up, go to the bookshelf and find out why he hadn't found the book that had been stirring for so long in his mind.

But *another* voice, equally convincing, was encouraging him to concentrate on the winged man.

A dreamy voice said, *The outsider has not done whatever it came into this life to achieve. It just recently grew up, unheralded, and—who knows—will probably leave unannounced. A mythical child, if you like…*

The voice went on, and it did not sound at all like Saniya, more like Hanna.

A baby whose beginning is that not of a baby who joins the timelessness of fables and, who knows, may be a part of the vagueness of legends. Think about a black cat. Was he not in a well? Was he floating through the underground before reaching water levels? Think about miracle babies and think of myths, the voice concluded.

"But I want to get up!" Bali said to himself, although he hadn't the urge within him to stand up. It was as if a weight heavier than him was holding him down, forbidding him to rise.

189

Then the winged man perched on the tip of his nose.

But Bali was too sleepy to chase the winged man away.

He thought he heard a knock on the outside door, and maybe someone had stumble in. Or was that the noise of Eggaton, the cat, moving in his cot?

Bali saw an eagle descend, watched it enter his room, saw it emerge, holding and clasping in its beak not a winged man but a pearl necklace as it flew out toward heaven.

Everything was so dreamy and motionless. Bali thought he too was not among the living.

Bali woke up.

The quietness had movement, and then sound. Was he imagining Beefi's voice asking if he would like a cup of tea? But what happened to the winged man? And there was an eagle?

For a sleepy instant, everything was real as a dream being dreamt.

Noises came from the kitchen: a kettle being rinsed then filled with tap water, a match being struck, fire burning with a whiff of blue coloring and stomach-churning odor.

There was someone pacing up and down, and it was whistling.

At last the meaning of the noise became clear as Beefi arrived carrying a tray of tea with bread and a jug of cold water from the clay waterpot to wash his face.

Awake was the sign he needed.

Bali saw Beefi hesitate, wondering where to place the tray. Suddenly he lumbered to his feet, showing that he was full of energy. This seemed to Beefi a sign for her to be filled with vitality too.

Bali took in all that came across his eyes, noting the state of disrepair the house was in. Was it appropriate for him to go on an adventure without giving consideration to this as first priority?

Nothing to be remorseful about, he told himself, no sins to repent.

The floor would be varnished, the walls too. All would be well.

He had found a low table for the tray and said, "Where has everyone gone? Where are the children?"

Silence fell.

Bali *awoke* again with a start, and he remained restless for sometime, turning and tossing in his bed in utter discomfort. He had also dreamt of a *cat* of indistinct breed, beautiful and black. There was a rowdy lot of ghostly and evil villains teasing him, the cat hissing, and the wrongdoers having fun tormenting him.

At a fetching distance from the noisy brutes, as though trying to separate herself from them, stood a woman bearing no resemblance to anyone Bali had ever met, a women who, in some mysterious manner, appeared to share an ancestral biological and spiritual closeness to the cat in that she had an untamed stare and sharper teeth than any Bali had seen in the mouth of any human.

At any rate, Bali's attention rested on the woman who, with a suspense appearance, kept looking to her left. Was she waiting for someone coming from that direction?

Bali picked out the shape of a shield she was focusing on. A shield and a sword-wielding mermaid was on this official coat of arms.

"I have seen this coat of arms before," he kept saying to himself. This coat of arms belongs to *Warsaw*. Images of a mermaid have symbolized Warsaw on its arms since the middle of the fourteenth century. All this he knew because of his son-in-law Harry. Harry was of Polish descent and had kinsfolk in Warsaw.

There have been several legends associated with this city, which may have been the origin of the mermaid's association, as it was told to him.

Then a snake appeared, whose arrival created anxiety in everyone, with the exception of the woman.

But there was disturbing movement around. And it exploded in a gust of wind, enclosing everyone and everything in its shadowy activities. The whirlwind was gathering dust, spiraling upward. Whereupon the woman's eyes were touched for an instant, contentment was shown. Also, hesitation seemed to garment her hard stare, tempering it into spicy smiles.

And the snake bit this shadowy woman.

And the skies were overflowing with the colors of seaweed.

Her way of walking was well expressed as a sleepwalker's. The woman then stepped away from the scene and from the rowdy monsters. And the cat followed, stopping only when they came upon a well where a baby's body lay.

At this, Bali woke.

PART VIII

The Adventure

31

The Adventure Begins

Raj was sitting on a large rock, with his back facing the wall that surrounded and protected Anna Catherina's seacoast, and his mind was still pondering, back and forth, along with the morning tides.

In the mornings, he thought, the birdsong sounded quicker and more familiar, and the smell of vegetation was more noticeable.

Meanwhile, the homes, with their zinc roofs, behind him shadowed above the wall while they stretched out their legs and arms on their stilts to let out its morning yawn and awaken the busy kitchens on this day to the orange sunrise that overlooked the Atlantic Ocean.

"Where is he? Didn't he say that he will be here before six o'clock? And it's already six o'clock."

Raj turned his head toward the dirt road that led to the seawall.

"No one is coming. Where is he?"

Looking to his left, he could see Anna Catherina's cemetery, where the grass and tombstones gave off an intense radiance, supplementing the glare of the sun and the applause of the palm trees that swayed with the music of early morning tropical breezes.

"Where is he?"

From a distance around the curve of the wall, Raj could hear someone calling out, "Raj, over here. Raj, please come over here."

Could that be Bali? Raj thought. Raj stood up and walked over toward the person calling. As he neared the turnaround curve of the wall, he could see Bali observing the waves and poking around with a stick, as if he lost something. Raj could see Bali's old khaki pants rolled up to his knees and his sandals dragging and waving around in his left hand.

"Bali, I have been waiting for about ten minutes by the rocks. I didn't know you were here. By the way, good morning, Mr. B," Raj said.

Without raising his head and still staring at the waves, Bali said, "Good morning, Raj. I've been here since 4:00 a.m. I couldn't sleep last night. I had these crazy dreams... yes, crazy dreams, about a dragonfly, a winged man, miracle babies, a black hissing cat, and a mysterious woman who floated as she walked. Now isn't that strange and creepy? Now I found another one!"

As Bali bent down and reached into the water, he picked up a shiny object. "This is the fifth one I found this morning."

Bali put his sandals under his right armpit and pulled out something from his pocket, and in his hands were four more shiny pearls.

"Those are beautiful, Mr. B," Raj exclaimed.

"I know they are. Something told me to look for something. I didn't know what until I saw these pearls. These pearls with the shell that you have will guide us to our answers. Do you have the shell with you?"

"Yes. Here it is, Mr. B." Raj handed over the shell to Bali.

"Now show me where you found the body of your brother."

Raj walked closer to the cemetery, where the five-foot seawall protected the graveyard passage. He then walked one hundred feet toward the seashore and pointed where his brother's body was found.

To Raj, it was true, horribly true. His own senses, oddly sharpened by his past suffering, had confirmed it. No matter how hard he tried, he could never again deny it. The death of his brother. He looked at Bali and said, with tears in his eyes, "My brother"—and he had to say the word—"died, over here." He pointed where the waves met the seashore sands.

Raj thought his brother's mortal body would never again walk this bountiful earth, only his memory. Raj was destined to suffer the slow fading of the emotions. Even though he knew the emotions would fade, the memories would always live with him.

Stricken with the now emotional grief that defied all attempts at description, Raj turned his back and covered his face with both his hands. He stood like that for a long time. Thinking Raj was disoriented, Bali courteously showed him the path back to the seawall near the cemetery.

Raj shook his head and asked Bali to leave him alone, and he lifted himself over the seawall and walked toward the open path of the cemetery. Bali decided to give him a little space to grieve. Raj wandered down through the cemetery path and flanks by imposing mausoleums and tombstones.

He did not know how long he walked, or how many circles around the cemetery he must have covered, or how many minutes passed by, or how many epitaphs with their useless markings of surnames filed past his unseeing eyes. Those had no meaning for him while he grieved. Almost as though in a trance, Raj wandered like another ghost in the zone of the dead, breathing the air coming from the cemetery, which had the rotten and toxic stench of the dead.

He walked back toward the seawall and crawled over it and went back toward the seashore sands, where his brother's body was found.

He then walked into the water while the waves were splashing, and his cream-colored pants stuck wetly to his body. And then, suddenly, a sharp wind mercilessly lifted the folds of his light shirt, cutting him to the flesh.

Exhausted at last from so much aimless wandering, Raj retraced his steps back to where his brother's body was found, leaving behind the place of this emotional journey and returning, without happiness, to the world of the living. But a deep voice drew him wordlessly once again to the scene of his previous weeping.

"Raj, are you okay, son?" Bali called out.

"I'm okay, Mr. B. I am just letting off a little steam of emotional memories that needed expressing in my mind. I'm okay now," Raj answered.

"Let's go exploring if you are up to it. Where is your boat?"

"It's the brown one over there." Raj pointed to the boat tied to a small wooden dock, rocking along with the current.

They both got in the boat, and Raj used the oars and paddle like a true fisherman toward the coastline of Leonora.

The silence of the boat going upstream was barely broken by the slap of the current against the flat-bottomed boat. They were traveling through a region of clearings so regularly spaced they seemed man-made. The river was growing calmer, and the water's resistance to their progress was hardly noticeable.

Then they entered a grassland area, with small groves of palm trees and extensive marshes created by the floodwater from the previous rainfall. They both looked up and saw a flock of seagulls cross the sky in regular formations, which reminded Bali of a war movie of squadrons and reconnaissance planes.

The seagulls circled the boat and then flew toward the riverbank while their milky white bodies landed on shore with flawless grace. Then with a slow movement of their tiny feet, they cautiously advanced one quick step at a time, bending their heads down and probing for food. Other seagulls would go by the water and dive down. When a fish was caught, it started to struggle for a moment in the long bill. The seagull then would shake its head, and the victim disappeared as if by magic.

The weather was gradually changing. The current became stronger, and the riverbed was narrowing. They were leaving behind the sugarcane jungle, and the humidity was blunting the senses and distorting their perception of every sound, smell, or shape. As they moved up the river about two miles, a tropical breeze arrived, and their trip became cooler and lighter. *He never travels this far up*, Raj thought, *This is new territory.*

The look of the current was changing radically. The bottom, he thought, must be rough and rocky. The sandbanks had disappeared.

The river was narrower, and the first foothills were beginning to rise along the banks, exposing a reddish soil that sometimes resembled dried blood and then faded to a pinkish color.

A dry, burning heat started to envelop them, transporting a pure light that beat on them like a drum and bestowing an absolute, inevitable display of its presence.

Everything became silent, and it seemed to be waiting for some revelation that would be devastating.

The clouds opened, discharging the rivers of the heavens. The dull scream from their very soul was silent, yet their throats were on fire. They wanted to see the mermaid, and one did appear, whose figure had floated like a white dove through the waters—a woman whose body was under the rush of a mountain waterfall. And her brief cries of surprise and joy were upon her lips as she saw the journeymen.

The movement of her limbs in the rapid foam that carried her beauty struggled to escape the waterfall's current. This scene was so exotic to them. The movement of her body and the way she swayed was the textbook of erotic happiness, which surely came only once in a lifetime.

Something had struck the controls of their mind, in the most secret part of their soul, and they couldn't do anything to prevent it. They didn't even know what was in them.

She smiled as she looked at them. Her breasts, thighs, and partially hidden fishlike body were exposed to them with a candor not typical of any woman in real life. Her long black hair was as wild as the mane of a mythological beast.

She then burst into a childish, almost innocent, laughter.

With her gestures, the downward breeze brought the scent of her skin, and her sudden, intense glances soon filled Raj with overwhelming tenderness. Her acceptance of him made him feel that she could rescue him instantly from his confusions and obsessions, his discouragement and failure, or his simple daily routine.

She dipped her fingers in a bottle of oil and rubbed her hair, and at the same time, she sang a song whose sadness left them helpless, and they experienced the awful deception of the inevitable outcome.

All eroticism suddenly had vanished from their eyes.

They tried to scream, as desperate drowning men do, but couldn't open their mouths.

With their last ounce of strength, they were able to paddle the boat toward the shore. They wondered in their desperation if this adventure would lead them down a one-way path.

A path of oblivion, the kind that would last forever.

32

Wai-Wai People

In the air was the sound of hand drums, banging, banging, and banging in line with their heartbeats. Raj looked at Bali and said, "Do you hear that?"

And Bali, joining Raj's wide open-eye fear routine, shook his head up and down, as if he was playing along with the drums.

They turned and saw that they were in a village-type setting, next to a cave, with a large fire burning near its center.

They saw faces among this noisy, exotic crowd, dazzling with stuff of many bright colors, beads, and feather, which brought about a powerful aroma of adventure to Bali's nostrils. The people were of medium height, their skin lighter than that of Guyanese Indians, Bali thought; and in their general appearance and language, they resembled the Wai-wai tribe.

In Bali's youth, his dad took him to see them. He knew they were great hunters and celebrated for their dogs, which were also trained hunters. There was something wrong with this picture, Bali thought. The Wai-wais are mainly found in the surrounding area of the interior region. He knew that the Wai-wais are the smallest tribe in Guyana with a population in total of probably around two hundred. But what was troubling him was that there is only one Wai-wai community in Guyana, and it is located in the most southern region of the country known as Konashen.

So what are they doing so far north? He wondered.

Then he saw *yaskomo*, the medicine man also known as shaman. He knew it was him because he had three servants to wait on him alone, each olive-skinned.

The *yaskomo*, with his brows bound with a larger-than-life bone, wore a thick woolen blanket in all the colors of the rainbow and had it thrown over his head like a cloak. All three of his servants wore crosses around their necks. Bali remembered the studies and the books about these people.

There was a Western influence that has severely changed their traditional culture and religion. He knew that many of them have converted to Christianity. The missionaries were well-liked among much of the tribe, but when the missions had to leave Guyana because their residence permits were not renewed, 700 Wai-wai people followed them to Brazil. Some 150 Wai-wai people left in Guyana fell under the influence of the Christian Brethren Bible Outreach at that time.

He remembered why the permits weren't renewed; it was because of the authoritarian government of Forbes

Burnham. Under his administration, there were heavy persecution, violent imprisonment, and forceful extradition of Christian missionaries; and for that reason, many of the tribes chose to migrate to Brazil.

But then again, Bali thought, *What are they doing so far north?*

The Wai-wai in Guyana lives in the far south of the country, near the headwaters of the Essequibo River.

He couldn't help but see the village people cooking and doing their daily chores. They are great nomadic hunters, but he knew they are also farmers. However, the light, thin soil they have to work with and an annual rainfall of four meters can make it very challenging to produce enough food.

Their traditional method of farming was the destructive method of slash and burn.

His eyes went back to the medicine man. He was sitting down, and one of his servants was fanning him with a huge leaf, which drove away the tiny flies that rose from the mangrove trees next to him.

The fishermen by the caves near the shores were catching fish by dazzling them with torches, and after grilling those delicious fish on the open fires, they brought them to the shaman.

He could smell the aroma.

Then he heard a clamor among the natives, and he thought that they were celebrating their arrival, and he turned to look.

The custom of the tribe, he knew, was for them to pick up their tambourine and start to dance and sway on their waists with an enthusiastic, exotic movement.

The drummer, while playing, was inhaling some sort of tobacco smoke from a pipe made out of a bone. Bali turned his head toward the waterfall and watched the fishermen taking a short break, sitting on the sand area and watching the magical sea roll its shinning pebbles into the caves along the shore.

Then he saw a woman sitting on a rock, leaning against a palm tree, and she was weaving. He saw others twisting cotton into yarn. He took a closer look at what the woman was weaving, and it was a hammock. He could see that the hammock was being weaved on square hammock frames.

On the other side of the camp, there were men and women using their artistic skills by making pottery, woven combs, bone flutes, and other crafts he couldn't make out.

Bali was told by his father that women play a crucial role in the culture of the Wai-wai. In terms of Wai-wai concept, the men's success in terms of wealth and power are dependent on female labor and reproduction. The size and stability of a village also depend on cultural values and how relationships are tied. For the Wai-wai, the relationship between a father and daughter lends a sense of control to the father over his daughter and son-in-law.

That is not too far off the beaten path of regular Guyanese families, Bali thought.

Mansiya is their name for marriage. For women, marriage cannot take place until after they have reached their first period at around the age of thirteen, and most women are married by the age of seventeen.

Something was funny about this village. A village size is the indication of the level of political strength and riches, but this village size was about thirty.

Then suddenly, the medicine man got up and went over to the mermaid and spoke to her.

But then it rained, and everyone ran to take shelter under the caves. They all looked up at the cloudy skies. Some of the tribe members were praying for sun, but their answer was more showers of rain falling on the trees and the colored-stone sculptures on the ground.

Then the *yaskomo* looked up into the sky, shook his hand back and forth, and with a yell toward the sky, the rain stopped falling.

Bali and Raj stood amazed at what they saw. The sun came out, and the clouds took their exit.

Raj looked at Bali and asked, "Who is that man?"

Bali replied and spoke like a professor and said, "He is called the *yaskomo* of the Wai-wai and is also known as a medicine man or shaman. He can heal and perform 'soul flight.' Soul flight can serve several functions, like flying to the sky to consult cosmological beings, like the moon or the brother of the moon, and to get a name for a newborn baby.

It can also fly to the cave of peccaries' mountains to ask the father of peccaries for abundance of game. Then it could fly deep down in a river to achieve the help of other beings like the mermaid we are looking at now. But the greatest of all is that they are able to reach sky, earth, water—in short, every element. Yes, the yaskomo of the Wai-wai is a powerful servant of its people."

Then the mermaid spoke out loud and said, "The Wai-wai people are a noble tribe of people. Not only are they great warriors but keepers of the land. They know that the rain forest produces the air that they breathe and keeps the soil in their place and provides food—like nuts, fruit, and fresh fish—and all sources for natural medicines. And now a great disaster has come to your way of life.

There is an evil presence that has come to this land, which will bring destruction and chaos. And for that reason, I'm here. The yaskomo has summoned me from the deep oceans. The presence of these two men is part of the solution. Let them pass. And when it is time for them to leave, let them go."

And as the mermaid was speaking, some men turned around and looked at Raj and Bali funny. The men didn't look like they were part of this tribe. They had on white trousers, and the others were roundheaded with blubber lips and thick hair that looked as though it had been cut under a pudding bowl.

Raj and Bali looked at each other, and with a big lump caught in their throat, they gulped.

"Maybe, Mr. B, those guys over there...," Raj said, wide-eyed, pointing out those who were wearing the white trousers.

"Looks like they didn't get the memo."

33

Buds for Life?

The mermaid whose fully aquatic body was under the rush of a mountain waterfall continued to smile as she looked at them, her long black hair swinging wildly back and forth with the sprays of the waterfall hitting the waters.

She then moved slowly, possessing major aquatic adaptations. Her arms were used for steering; and her fishlike body paddled her movements toward them, as a propulsion, while she let her long hair shelter her breasts and her fishlike body.

She was not exposing them to the enticement of her body, only now with her telepathic mind.

While she looked at them, still smiling, she transmitted certain information she wanted them to know without using any known sensory channels or physical interaction. Their feeling, perception, passion, affliction, and experience still remained, but could this be real? Raj and Bali thought.

This was the first time they had experienced this phenomenon. Bali knew that telepathy was a common theme in modern fiction and science fiction. The books he had read in the past had many extraterrestrials, superheroes, and supervillains having this telepathic ability.

Good afternoon, Bali DaSilva and Raj Ram. Do not be frightened or think I am using some sort of mind control. The reason I am talking to you in this manner is to avoid those who are around that want to do harm to you. By those, I mean not letting them hear what we are talking about. If you understand, just smile at each other and move your heads up and down.

At this moment, Bali and Raj looked at each other, smiled, and bopped their heads up and down like two idiots on drugs having the munchies.

Good. Make like you are looking at the scenery. Go toward the water, take off your sandals, and put your feet in the water. But do all of this slowly so that you will not attract attention while I speak to you both.

Bali and Raj did as they were told. Bali sat at the edge, his legs dangling over the water that splashed him with a coolness he would have enjoyed more on other occasions. He pondered what would be told to him.

Bali sensed the invasion of something trying to read his thoughts without even touching him. How could that be?

Bali, you had dreams last night that were disturbing. Let me interpret them for you. The dragonfly is a reference to Satan. The winged man is a soldier of his and was once an archangel who possesses immense power. The wings on an angel mean a rank of authority. The more wings, the higher the authority. Almost all angels do not have wings, unlike as humans believe they do. This winged man possesses the body of one of our merman, who had Raj's brother killed and drowned. And the pearl necklace was the clue to let you know that it was a merman. The eagle that flew toward heaven was the brave warrior, Raj's brother, David.

As Raj heard this, tears started to flow from his eyes. Tears of happiness upon knowing David's death was not in vain. *David*, he thought, *yes, my brother, David, was a hero.*

My name is Princess Serene, and I was a good friend of David. He knew about what will be coming and was going to warn both of you of the impending danger. Somehow he was trapped, killed, and drowned.

The spiritual woman in your dreams protects the black cat. This black cat's name is Shadow, and he is from Diyu, the realm of the dead, and is the adopted son of your granddaughter. Your daughter's husband Harry has the ancestral line of the Warsaw family in his blood, whose shield shows the mermaid wielding the sword of justice.

This sword of justice must be used against the evil spirits that escape from the realm of the dead. They must be stopped, for they are dangerous and will create chaos. That is why you were chosen to relate this information to your daughter so that her grandson will come and do battle with the evil ones.

214

Go over to the cave areas and eat some food. The yaskomo will make sure you will have plenty to eat and drink. He will put a spell around you for protection so you will not be harmed. In your dream tonight, Bali, a voice will provide more information. Raj will not be privy to the other information for now, lest he will wind up like his brother. I could not bear the responsibility of another death. So be patient with me, Raj. I am only thinking what is best for you.

When she finished, she went back toward the waterfall and dived under it and disappeared.

Raj and Bali got up and walked barefoot toward the cave and sat down. The yaskomo raised his right hand up and pointed to the ladies who were cooking by the fire to provide food and drinks to them.

Two ladies in grass skirts, with dark hair and brownish skin, brought them two cups of hot cocoas and some fried plantains in clay plates. They thanked them and gulped the cocoa in one swallow. They were thirsty. As they ate the slices of plantains, they felt the gradual return of strength in their bodies. They later were fed fruits, nuts, and fresh fish. Their bellies were full.

The landscape of the jungle was beginning to change. At first, the signs were erratic and not always very clear. Even if the temperature stayed the same, Bali thought that this high temperature was as unmoving as a stubborn child refusing to budge. But sometimes the extension of the daylight brought with it a cool tropical breeze. And then it came.

An exotic gust, which seemed to come from another climate, played with Bali's moods and mannerisms. Looking around, Bali saw that this wind change was affecting everyone's state of mind. The crowd in the village sensed a relief from tension, which brought about a desire to talk, to have a gleam in their eyes, as if they knew that something long awaited was about to happen.

In the last light of the afternoon, a prime-blue line appeared on the horizon and became easily confused with the pending storm clouds amassing at a distance. To Bali, it was impossible to determine the outcome.

In the meantime, two young ladies, with a smile, brought them two bottles of El Dorado Rum.

"I guess they want us to have an early sleep juice potion," Raj said with a smile.

"You can have both of them," Bali said with a smile back. "Look Bali. The ugly men won't be coming back."

Raj saw the men who were looking at them funny walking away into the jungle.

The evening light was dimming, and Raj was on his second bottle of rum.

Bali looked at Raj and smiled and, in jest, told him that he should have another drink.

216

"Good, I will have another drink. Oh, I drink till I start sweating, till I feel as if my tongue's on fire... Se-Serene! What a woman! Or maybe I should say, what a... mer... madwoman! I need a drink to cheer me up. I also need one to get me talking. Unless I have a good drink, I can't talk. Don't know why? I feel so...so tired...never mind. Tomorrow you'll be gone, Mr. B...you will probably leave me on my own, ahhum. What do I care?"

Looking on the ground, Raj saw the sheepskin blanket provided to them in case the evening air had a slight chill. Raj continued his ranting, "Yeah, see, that's a good skin the ladies gave us. It probably was taken from a small sheep with a big head. Ha-ha-ha...oh, by the way... do you want that? Take it. You're not drinking...are you going to leave me the rest of the rum? Stretch out on the ground, Bali. Wrap yourself in with the skin and get some sleep, why don't you? I'll put some more wood on the fire and look after things, keep the fire going. You try and get some sleep. Why don't you get some sleep?"

As Raj tried to get up, he staggered around the fire, and then deciding sitting down would be a better option, he said, "Well, I'll just have another drink, if you don't mind. Now I'm beginning to feel good! You should eat and drink what you've got while you still feel like it...there's nothing nicer than a full belly. This rum's terrific, just what I needed. Bah! This is lousy firewood, makes your eyes run, all this smoke...hum? You were saying?"

Raj eyes looked at Bali, waiting for a response. Seeing none, he continued his rant, "No I don't hate it. This adventure's good. There's a nice pool to swim in over there." He raised his arm and pointed shakily toward the water area.

"No place is all good or all bad. You have to make the best of it. Yes, sir, I like people, I do. You'd better get some sleep. Me too...oh, it's getting late."

Raj then turned his head up toward the stars. "Mr. B... look at the shiny North Star way up in the sky. Look at all the little stars...no sleep for me. It's nearly time to get out there. Did you know that I rise early every morning, long before daybreak? You try and get to sleep, Mr. B...why don't you lie down?"

Bali got up and looked at Raj and smiled and said, "Looks as if you're only staying awake to keep asking me questions, Raj. If I answer you, you will then ask me something else. Is that it?"

"What is this you're saying? And what happens next, what...I finish up drinking all your rum. Hum, hum, don't worry, I won't get drunk. I only get drunk when I drink lots and lots of blood...yeah, blood... like a vampire... yeah, me, Raj, a vampire...don't worry, Bali, you can sleep in peace. I'll take care of things. I know how to keep an eye on everything. I'm like a dolphin...I can sleep with one eye open...ha-ha-ha...I can see you're sleepy. Okay...oh, I can draw two circles on the ground if you want me to. Let's make-believe those are your eyes. Then if I step on them, you'll go to sleep at once… ha-ha-ha…oh, Bali, but you are brave as well and can stand up to any man. You could even hunt a demon…steady on…tallyho…and all that…"

Then as Raj's drunken head hit the green surface of the ground, he said his last words before sleeping, "Mr. B…you're my best friend…in the whole…whole wide world and…"

PART IX

A Voice, a Legend, and a Family

34

A Voice in the Jungle

Since the beginning of time, man has searched for explanations to life's mysteries regarding the *truth*. Politicians, clergies, and those who teach the fundamentals of education have been trying to program mankind to their special points of views in regard to what truth is.

As children, we are taught what is right and what is wrong, and it always seems that what is right is harder to achieve than what is wrong. Why does that become a major problem? Could it be because society agrees that the right thing to do is more acceptable for moral stability, and yet we still draw near to what is not acceptable?

Why do we like playing with the dark sides in our lives? When will the forty winks take a hold of my mind so that I can at least enjoy one night of sleep, Bali thought.

Bali, instead of getting his forty winks, got his mind scrambling with questions that always bothered him, the questions he thought about and for which he never really found an answer that made any real sense. And yet these questions still lingered in his mind.

But then, suddenly, a man's voice entered his mind, providing information about *the real enemy* and his determination.

Bali, in the beginning of time—before the creation of this world as we now know it and before mankind was created— there was the creation of angelic beings that had the gift of eternal life. The leading cherub angel of this creation had four wings, which was at that time the highest rank of authority among the angelic creation. I'm sorry to say that most angels do not have wings.

This leading angel was perfect in beauty and in wisdom, and he also had the exalted position of being an honor guard to God's throne. His name was originally Lucifer, son of the morning. I will be providing scriptures in your mind for your knowledge.

Then the voice brought out scripture.

> Son of man, take-up a lamentation over the king of Tyre and say to him, "thus says the Lord God, 'You had the seal of perfection, full of wisdom and perfect in beauty.
>
> You were in Eden, the garden of God; every precious stone was your covering: The ruby, the topaz, and the diamond; the beryl, the onyx, and the jasper; the lapis lazuli, the turquoise, and the emerald; and the gold, the workmanship of your

settings and sockets, Was in you. On the day that you were created they were prepared.

You were the anointed cherub, who covers, and I placed you there. You were on the holy mountain of God; you walked in the midst of the stones of fire, you were blameless in your ways from the day you were created, until unrighteousness was found in you.'"

Then the voice continued: *The king of Tyre is also a reference to this angel Lucifer, and even though he was created by the Word of God, it was God the Father who placed him in that exalted position.*

Just like the first created woman on earth, who let the serpent deceive her into thinking that she could be smarter than God by using her volition *to defy God's commandment "not to eat" by eating the forbidden fruit off "The Tree of Knowledge of Good and Evil."*

She then found out that God was smarter than her when she ate the forbidden fruit that contained the sin nature and the consciousness *of understanding what* human good *and* evil *was.*

Going back to Lucifer in the beginning, when he was first created perfect, a flaw developed in him by his own free volition. *He was so in love with himself that his arrogance brought about the lust of power to rule over everything God has created.*

He wanted to be the authority. *In other words, he wanted to be God. Just like the woman who wanted to rule over man*

225

in the garden, *Lucifer was the first with that thought, and he wanted mankind later to follow in his footsteps.*

Again, the voice brought out scripture:

> But, you said in your heart, "I will ascend to heaven; I will raise my throne above the stars of God, and I will sit on the mount of assembly in the recesses of the north. I will ascend above the heights of the clouds; I will make myself like the Most High."

Then the voice continued: *Because of this rebellion by Lucifer, he was able to persuade one-third of the angelic creation to follow him in this revolution. The angelic ones who followed Lucifer are called fallen angels, demons, or angels of darkness. Then there are the elect angels, the ones who follow God.*

In heaven, a trial was convened to judge Lucifer and the fallen angels. Lucifer was the defense attorney for himself and the fallen angels, and that is when his name and title changed to Satan.

This new title was given to him because Satan *means "adversary and accuser." He is the adversary of God and the accuser of those who are the children of God. Satan and all of his fallen angels* lost *that trial and were condemned to spend eternity in the lake of fire.*

Bali interrupted the voice and said in his thoughts. *Since Satan and his angels have already been condemned and sentenced, why has this sentence not been executed since he still exists in the world today?*

The voice continued: *Satan lodged an appeal at the conclusion of his trial: How could a loving God cast His creatures into the eternal lake of fire? Mankind was created to solve this appeal and the angelic conflict. Just like the angels had volition to choose for or against God, mankind also was given* free will *to make the same choice.*

That is why God permitted the woman to use her own volition, as well as the man, Adam, to use his own volition, which he did by choosing the woman's fallen state over God's perfect destiny in the garden.

The woman was deceived, but Adam knew *what he was doing by taking the forbidden fruit. And thereby, through Adam, the sin nature is passed through all the generations at birth. So* every *baby that is born will have a sin nature, and you can thank Adam for that. These are the answers you wanted to know about why we choose the wrong over the right. It's in our nature—the old sin nature. This battle between the angels of darkness and the angels of light will continue and not conclude until the end of human history.*

Then the voice brought out scripture:

> Therefore, just as though one man (Adam) sin entered into the world, and death through sin, and so death spread to all men, because all sin.

The voice continued: *God never abandoned or deserted the human race because He has provided a redemptive solution. He sent the* Word of God, the Second Person of the Trinity. *We*

227

know him as the Lord Jesus Christ, *the one who is the same Messiah to the Jews, who became perfect humanity and who died on the cross as a* substitute *for the sins of* every person.

Sin will never be used against mankind in the last judgment, *only his works. The works that they believe is better than the righteousness of God. And by believing in Christ, His righteousness is then imputed to us for salvation. Anyone can be saved by* faith *in Christ alone. Beware of those who try to impose additional steps for salvation. Those who do this do not realize that they are working for the ruler of this world.*

Guess who is the ruler of this world? It is Satan since the fall of Adam. Adam was the original ruler, but he lost it when he chose the forbidden fruit and rejected God's plan for his life. Mankind has the same choice, to accept the love of God and believe in the Son of God for salvation.

Then the voice brought out scripture:

> For you see The God so loved the world, so much, that He gave His uniquely born Son, that whosoever believes in Him will not perish but will have eternal life.

The voice continued: *No one should add anything else for salvation, or it will be considered by God as works and make salvations grace worthless.* Grace *means "God does* all *the work." There are clergies who say faith in Christ alone is too easy. They are falling in with the ruler of this world, and his deception is to make you an unbeliever and therefore not a child of God.*

228

The voice brought out scripture again:

> For by grace you have been saved through faith; and
> that *not of yourselves*, it is the gift of God; not as a
> result of works, that no one should boast.

The voice continued: *Since the creation of mankind, Satan
has tried to stop the human birth of Jesus Christ by creating
obstacles in mankind's history. One of these obstacles was in
the time of Noah. A group of fallen angels who are demons*
deliberately *procreated with the daughters of men. This was a
sexual invasion, described in Genesis 6, that many scholars seem
not to understand, or they simply avoid it.*

*The account in the scriptures talks about 'the sons of God,'
which in the original language is* Bene ha' Elohim, *and they
only mean a segment of fallen angels that have produced half-
human, half-angelic creatures called the Nephilim.*

*Remember, all angels are the sons of God because they have
eternal life. Not all humans are children of God, only those who
believe in Christ. They are the ones who receive eternal life by
believing in Him and are therefore* born again. *Being born
again means that God the Holy Spirit will provide you a spirit,
a new birth, a spiritual birth—therefore you are* born again.

*This attempt by Satan to contaminate the purity of the human
race and thereby stop the virgin birth of Jesus Christ, who had
to be true and pure in his human state; otherwise, he couldn't
go to the cross to die as a substitute for the world. Satan almost
succeeded in corrupting the human genetics in the human race.*

Only eight *people were left in the human race that were pure humans: Noah, his wife, his three children, and their wives. That was the reason for the worldwide judgment of the Noachian flood—the total destruction of the mixed-breed offspring. The angelic demons involved were incarcerated in darkness and chained with eternal bonds to prevent further attempts to destroy the line of Christ.*

God also removed the ability of all the angelic demons to appear as human beings to stop them from procreating. Since that time, the demons still at large must remain invisible, but they can manifest themselves only through demonic possession— that is, by entering the body of an unbelieving man or woman.

And as the last words from the mysterious voice disappeared, as suddenly as it came, Bali pondered all the information given to him. Thinking how helpless the human race must be, he hoped that this information would be set free into the world so that others may have the *choice* to believe.

Bali listened to the voice, and he *believed.* So as his body floated into the land of visions and fantasy, he smiled, because now he knew who the real enemy is.

35

Oops

The tropical breeze with the morning dew, along with the smell of vegetation and the chirping sounds of the birds, was a wake-up call for the self-appointed adventurers.

Raj woke up with little men playing cricket in his head. His first words were, "Time out!"

Bali turned and rose on his left elbow, with his left hand cupping his chin. He looked at Raj and said, "What up, son? You look like you went a few rounds with Floyd Mayweather. I know you didn't win against the money team because you still have saliva running down the right side of your mouth."

Raj wiped his mouth with the left sleeve of his shirt and said softly to Bali, "Stop raising your voice to me. What are you trying to do? Are you trying to raise the dead from this"—Raj turned his head and looked around to make

sure no one was listening—"from this godforsaken place...
hmm?"

Bali, with a slight smile on his face, said, "Raj, I'm not
speaking loud to you. It's the rum you had last night that
has amplified your hearing to a point that you probably have
construction workers drilling a new Guyanese pavement in
your head."

"No, it's a cricket team," Raj said as he got up. With his
head resting on his knees, he mumbled, "Oh, it hurts...why
you guys don't stop playing? Ohm..."

The morning air took on another smell and sound: fried
fish and the clapping of hands, dancing back and forth,
preparing the roti bread on the makeshift clay ovens. The
sizzling sound of fried fish was now making Raj's stomach
growl, like two dogs in heat wanting to take a piece of each
other. And then another surprise. Who would have thought
the Wai-wai had these beans? The smell of Caribbean
coffee beans roasting on the fire had both men standing up
and looking at the ladies cooking.

Raj said, "Do you think they see us, Mr. B? Should
we wave our hands to let them know we're ready to eat?
What do you think, Mr. B? Should we stroll over there
nonchalantly and ask for some breakfast? What do you
think? Huh?"

Bali turned to look at Raj's tongue licking his lips. His
breathing was stimulating his chest with up-and-down

motions, and his eyes were wide open, focused like a hound directing the hunter to the prey.

"Relax, Raj. Can't you see the yaskomo letting the ladies know to bring us breakfast? Give it a break. Just sit down like we are two perfect gentlemen waiting for our morning tea," Bali said as he sat down and leaned against a coconut tree.

"Fuck the tea, Mr. B. I need coffee, and plenty of it, to drown my cricket team."

Raj sat down next to Bali and took a look up the tree to make sure no coconuts would fall down and introduce another team in his head for a face-off.

"Watch the language, Raj. This isn't a sailor's convention. Please tone it down."

"Sorry, Mr. B. It's those fucking aliens in my head that is pissing me off! Oops, sorry, I fucked up again—oh shit... *oops*."

36

Princess Serene's Diary (circa 2013)

My name is Princess Serene, and I was born on March 3, 1967, in the Aquatic Caribbean kingdom. In Triton years, I'm just a newborn baby. As a child, I have been a student of history and legends and, in the 1990s, of the World Wide Web, including television and its programs. Oh, by the way, I have photogenic abilities. In other words, I can speed-read.

I do not use a cell phone, Twitter, or have a Facebook account. All kingdoms in the oceans have been blessed with telepathy. This is the transmission of information from one person to another without using any known sensory channels or physical interaction. Simple terms: mind to mind.

Having this telepathic ability makes communication with family, friends, uncles, and aunts better than what the AOW (above the ocean world) uses.

My dad's name is King Alexander. And please do not think that my dad is named after a popular Greek legend that turned Alexander the Great's sister Thessalonike into a mermaid, and after her death, had her living in the Aegean Sea. They say she would ask the sailors on any ship she encountered only one question: "Is King Alexander alive?" To which, the correct answer was: "He lives and reigns and conquers the world." They say this answer would please her, and she would accordingly calm the waters and bid the ship farewell.

And if there were any other answer, it would enrage her; and she would stir up a terrible storm, dooming the ship and every sailor on board. Again—not my dad.

All my life, I have been trained and taught to live above and below the ocean and to draw oxygen from the water and be able to use all the power of the sea to make me wonderfully strong and swift. My training and teaching include hundreds of scientific secrets and the art of defense and offensive tactics. My work includes solving the ocean's secrets and recording all the underwater sea creatures and their marvelous wisdoms. Enough about me for now.

My diary must start with the story of my great-grandfather, a famous Greek undersea god —his name, Triton, the messenger of the sea and the son of Poseidon and Amphitrite, god and goddess of the sea independently.

Like his father, Poseidon, Triton carried a trident, a three-pronged spear. In Hindu mythology, it is the weapon of choice of Shiva, but they changed the name and called it *trishula*—that, by the way, is *Sanskrit* for "triple spear."

There were many stories I heard as a child, and one told of my grandpa staying with his parents in a golden palace in the depths of the sea. Another story was that he lived in the waters off Aegae. These and other stories were told to me by my older brothers and sisters when each took turns reading to me at bedtime.

By now, you are probably wondering, Where is your mother? My mother, Queen Marisol, died when I was only a baby; but I do have great pictures of her, as well as wonderful stories about her from my brothers and sisters. My dad loved my mother so much that he never married again.

To get back to my grandfather's stories, everyone wanted to say that my grandfather lives here, and others say he lives there. To make matters more confusing, there are two stories of the Argonauts that place my grandfather's home on the coast of Libya.

One story said that when the Argo was driven ashore in the Gulf of Syrtis Minor, the crew carried the vessel to the Tritonian Lake, where Triton, they say, was the local deity boss, who was rationalized by a guy named Diodorus Siculus as the "then ruler over Libya." Triton welcomed them with a guest-gift, which was a hunk of earth, and then guided them through the lake's muddy passages back to the Mediterranean.

And the other story claimed that when the Argonauts were lost in the desert, my grandfather guided them to find the passage from the river back to the sea. Talk about keeping up with ancestral roots in my family. You can say the historians who wrote this must have been smoking the funny stuff and drinking the crazy stuff. Anyway, let me talk about Uncle Pallas, the uncle I never met.

They say grandpa was the father of my Uncle Pallas and foster parent to the goddess Athena, but what happened was that Uncle Pallas was killed by Athena during a fight between the two goddesses. Talk about family feud. I guess we could have used a Dr. Phil in those days.

We are often compared to other merman- or mermaid-like beings, such as merrows, selkies, and sirens. And we are also thought of as the aquatic versions of satyrs, and there is some truth to this.

And there is a description of us as that of the centaur-Tritons, who were also known as Ichthyocentaurs, depicted with two horse's feet in place of arms. These are not Grandpa's lineages or genetic factor. I don't mind the fish body—that's cool—but horse feet and arms? Come on, I don't think so.

To make matters worse, there is another crazy description of us with our heads growing hair like that of marsh frogs, not only in color but also in the impossibility of separating one hair from another. Sisters, if that were true, I would have killed all the marsh frogs in the sea by myself. Come on, give me a break!

Then they say that the rest of our body is rough with fine scales, just as the shark, and that under our ears, we have gills and a man's nose. But they say our mouth is broader, and the teeth are those of a beast. Okay, it's true that we can transform into these looks, but only to put fear into those who want to do us harm. We do not look this way in general.

It's true that some of our eyes seem to be blue, even though mine is brown, but do we have hands, fingers, and nails like the shells of the murex? Girl, please, I don't want to go anywhere looking like that. Our hands are smooth, as well as our breasts and belly.

The bottom half of our bodies has a tail like a dolphin's instead of feet, but we look good. And that's just how we roll, or should I say, move smoothly.

I live in a palace in the lowest point of the ocean, where no other diver had ever penetrated. My father is the king of the underwater city called the Aquatic Caribbean, a community established off the coastline of Guyana with a population about five hundred.

My uncle is the King Oscar of the Aquatic Warsaw, an underwater ancient city in the Vistula River, roughly 160 miles from the Baltic Sea, a kingdom city where the original mermaid's association was established.

The king's wife, named Melusina, is depicted in the coat of arms of Warsaw. She is the chairlady, the head warrior, of the association, and of course, my favorite aunt, who likes to baby me and tell me stories about her warrior days.

There are twelve kingdoms around the world, and we are about seven thousand strong.

It is true that our class and images are connected with being called mermaid-like creatures and that we are both male and female species, but we do form a guardianship, and we do protect the magical nautical oceans.

Yes, we are a race of sea-gods and goddesses, born from the line of Triton. And I, Princess Serene, a mermaid, am the last of my father's line.

37

Legends and Love

It was early morning. The sun was still sleeping upstairs, and the aquatic lights of the community were still pulsing, waiting for the alarm clock of day to wake up the dawn's lights. And then, when it did, the shinning streams of lights pushed through the many layers of ocean and fell noiselessly to the oceans depths.

Princess Serene had plenty of time this morning, but healthy sleep was not part of her agenda. Scary things were always a challenge for her, but this big task was an honor, given by her dad to accomplish. Baby daughter was out and playing in the big leagues. She smiled and said to herself, "Wow! Okay, I can do this!"

She needed a little time to think and be alone. She needed to get her bearings. It was quiet in the early mornings; only the sentinels and other guards were up. She knew the community library would be empty, so she decided to read some books before meeting the journeymen later that morning.

In the library, there were signs of love on the walls. She often wondered what love is. She saw it displayed in movies and read it in books, but she never felt it. She heard her father describe what he and her mother had and how wonderful she was as a queen, a mother, and a wife.

She would see pictures of them, and oh, how happy they looked together.

Even Uncle Oscar and Aunt Melusina looked happy together. Nothing what her dad described about love seemed to fit the mold in this community. Maybe she was too young to really know what love is. Could it be that her dad first met her mom in the kingdom of Warsaw, and in that kingdom, love has a better chance to survive?

In the library, she found a book about Pendour Cove and the Mermaid of Zennor. Princess Serene remembered her history lesson regarding the United Kingdom. As she recalled, Pendour Cove is a beach in Cornwall, and it's about one mile northwest of the village of Zennor and immediately to the west of Zennor Head.

As she was reading about this local legend, it was being described by another mermaid. What was strange was that she used the title *Mermaid of Zennor*. Serene knew all the communities and kingdoms in the oceanic world, but none was named *Zennor*.

So she kept reading the book, and it said that if you sit above Pendour Cove at sunset on a fine summer evening, you might hear the singing of Matthew Trewella of Zennor, who fell in love with a mermaid and followed her out to sea.

That was strange, Serene thought, a human going into the sea. This sounded interesting, so she read on. According to the legend, Matthew Trewella was a good-looking young man with a good voice. Each evening, he would sing, in a solo, the closing hymn at the church in Zennor. A mermaid living in the neighboring Pendour Cove was enchanted by his singing.

This mermaid, dressed in a long dress to hide her long tail, walked a little awkwardly to the church. Initially, she just marveled at Matthew's singing before slipping away to return to the sea. She came every day and eventually became bolder, staying longer.

It was on one of these visits that her gaze met Matthew's, and they fell in love.

Hold on a minute. How is that possible? Serene thought as she continued reading.

The mermaid knew, however, that she would have to go back to the sea, or else she would die. As she prepared to leave, Matthew said, "Please do not leave. Who are you? Where are you from?"

The mermaid replied that she was a creature from the sea and that she had to return there. *Matthew* was so lovestruck that he swore he would follow her wherever she went. Matthew carried her to the cove and followed her beneath the waves, never to be seen again.

It was said that if one sat above Pendour Cove at sunset on a fine summer evening, one may hear Matthew singing faintly on the summer breeze.

This is interesting, Serene thought. So she found other books about this mermaid, and these stories had a little different twist.

> Long ago, a beautiful and richly-dressed woman occasionally attended services at St. Senara's Church in Zennor, and sometimes at Morvah. The parishioners were enchanted by her beauty and her voice, for her singing was sweeter than all the rest.
>
> She appeared infrequently for scores of years, but never seemed to age, and nobody knew whence she came, although they watched her from the summit of Tregarthen Hill.
>
> After many years, the mysterious woman became interested in a young man named Mathew Trewella, "the best singer in the parish." One day he followed her home, and disappeared; neither was ever seen again in Zennor Church.
>
> The villagers wondered what had become of the two, until one Sunday a ship cast anchor about a mile from Pendour Cove.
>
> Soon after, a mermaid appeared, and asked that the anchor be raised, as one of its flukes was resting on her door, and she was unable to reach her children.
>
> The sailors obliged, and quickly set sail, believing the mermaid to be an ill omen. But when the villagers heard of this, they concluded that the mermaid was the same lady who had long visited their church, and that she had enticed Mathew Trewella to come and live with her.

Serene thought, *This is why I've never heard about a community in Zennor or Pendour Cove. If this is true, then they made their own community by themselves. That's possible.* Anyway, she'd have to talk to Aunt Melusina. She knows all the gossip of the seas.

As Serene kept searching about this love story, she found a chair had been built to describe this story. It was said that the parishioners at St. Senara's commemorated the story by having one end of a bench carved in the shape of a mermaid.

And then she read another shorter account of the legend, and it was related to a person named Bottrell on one of his visit to Cornwall. It was said that the mermaid had come to church every Sunday to hear the choir sing, and her own voice was so sweet that she enticed Mathew Trewella, son of the churchwarden, to come away with her. Neither was seen again on dry land.

Wow, Serene thought, *they say that this famed mermaid chair is the same bench on which the mermaid had sat and sung opposite Trewella in the singing loft. And that this mermaid chair at St. Senara's Church can be seen to this day, together with the accompanying legend.*

Serene kept reading different accounts of the story about this mermaid, and she saw that it was retold in later collections of Cornish folklore, generally following the original accounts collected by Bottrell. She read *The Fabled*

Coast about the mermaid chair, and it was described as a fifteenth-century carving.

I wonder if they are still alive, she pondered.

Some believe and say that the bench itself inspired the legend rather than the other way around.

Interesting. I got to give Aunt Melusina a call. She'll know what to do. She looked up at the different clock zones on the library's wall. *It's too early to call her. Anyway, I need to meet up with Mr. DaSilva and Mr. Ram and provide them the information and tools the Shadow cat would need.*

It was morning, and there were still questions that needed to be answered. Princess Serene moved upward toward the early dawn's light.

The sun was up, and the lights of the Aquatic Caribbean Kingdom were off while the mermaid and mermen were going vigorously to their jobs. Another day as the dawn lights gleamed its way, parting the beautiful layers of this colorful ocean.

The sentinels and the guards, who were the guardians of the kingdom, could see the luminous beams fall silently to the ocean floors, which gave this new day its foundation.

38

Homelife and a Portrait

Beefi never admitted to herself, but leaving Georgetown and marrying Bali was the best thing ever in her life. Somehow, in Anna Catherina, the morning mist seemed to burn off as soon as the sun rose, fresh and clear each morning. Despite not having a profession, despite the fact that she had to spend most of her life indoors, at home—cleaning, cooking, or watching out for the children as they grew up—Beefi was really an outdoors creature. This was where she read best, thought best, and worked best, given the chance.

As she ate breakfast this morning, Mrs. Basmaty, her next-door neighbor, brought her some fresh bread and jam from the corner market. They shared tea and early morning gossip.

Beefi loved sitting on her upstairs porch in the soft warmth of the evening while looking down at the people below. She also loved to simply walk down Front Street, past the soft, crumbling stones that lined as fences around the stilted buildings and the rose bush and the hibiscus plants that grew along the walls so luxuriantly in the tropical heat. That was what made her happy. She knew she was content.

When it became too hot or oppressive, she and Bali packed a few things and left, taking a hirer car off the public road and going to her sister's house outside of Georgetown, where she would stay a few days or maybe a week. She would read, talk to old friends she had known all her life, even occasionally help pick *bora*, or gooseberry, as she had done as a child. Bali would sit inside, enjoying the air-conditioner.

Late that afternoon, Bali arrived home, strangely rested. Beefi had been in disarray: the phone didn't work, and the neighbor was missing her son and wondering why he didn't come home last night. No note, no message to anyone, just plain gone.

She started in with Bali, and as soon as she told him there was no phone, he went upstairs to his bedroom and then came down, without a word. With a sweet kiss on his wife's head, he headed out. Bali only stayed for a few minutes before he grabbed his phone book, wheeled out his bicycle—by now the fastest means of transportation available—and pedaled slowly to his friend's home to call his daughter.

His ride to his friend's house brought back memories of when he started living alone before marrying Beefi. His mom died earlier in his teenage years from cancer, and his dad took to drinking because he couldn't live a day without her. The drinking took a toll on his father. One day, he just walked into the ocean and never came back.

The home in Anna Catherina had scarcely changed in the past fifty years. In the beginning, he had not bothered to put electricity or any of the other conveniences of modern life. Its whole purpose, after all, was to be a place to escape to. Now it served its purpose better than any well-equipped house. He had water in the well outside, a good supply of candles for the night, and an endless store of wood, which he chopped himself. There were two comfortable chairs, a stout oak table, and all the books he might need.

Bali had lived as he always did, rising at dawn and going to bed at dusk to conserve his dwindling stock of candles, and he managed to behave as if nothing had happened. And he wanted to hold on to that feeling for as long as possible.

Then he met Beefi. She was beautiful, not well educated, not refined in any way, but had a coarse sensuality that Bali had rarely experienced. They were drawn to each other because warmth and affection became so priceless in those earlier days. Both of them were starved of it, and both managed briefly to forget everything else in each other's company. Then they married, and the world called him back to reality, and their dreams of escape vanished.

Responsibility came with a baby on the way. Electricity, indoor plumbing, and all the modern comforts, including furniture, were attached to the home, and the outside world now became a part of their inside existence.

All these past memories started to drift away as his bicycle pedaled its way up his friend's long arched driveway.

———◆⬧◆———

After his belly was full, Raj had a desire to draw. He was no ordinary fisherman. He was also a man of dreams, and he knew he had a talent. He was able to capture on paper, cardboard, plastic, leather, canvas, and even on boards, the images of life as he saw it. He knew he could also draw on temporary areas like blackboard or whiteboard or, indeed, almost anything. This was his gift, and he was not ashamed of it.

Having this gift has always been a popular and a fundamental means of public expression throughout human history, and this gift was one of the simplest and most efficient means of communicating visual ideas since the beginning of time. And here he was, in an adventure, and no visual memories were present to capture this moment. He started to go through the lists, with regard to sketches, in his mind.

His artistic nature knew that smooth paper is good for rendering fine detail, but a more "toothy" paper would hold the drawing material better. Thus, a coarser material is useful for producing deeper contrast. He was able to get some smooth papers and some charcoal pencils from the villagers. He started to look around and saw gorgeous women doing their daily chores, and the community life itself was an inspiration that needed capturing, so he started to draw.

When he finished one portrait, he noticed that Bali was in a deep discussion with the mermaid. Looking at her, he couldn't help but think how unique and beautiful she was. So he started to sketch her. He moved closer to the waters and in different angles to get the best light on her features.

The princess, noticing his movements back and forth, came over to him curiously, wondering what he was doing. Raj, in his life, always considered himself somewhat of a playboy. He would use his artistic gift to trap some unexpected girl to fall for him. Sometimes it would work, and at other times, he would get a big slap for his efforts. The pain didn't matter. It helped him pass the time and made life a little bearable.

"I've been worken' bak and fort' tryen' to seize a little sketch here and a little image there. It's unforgivable in me, I know, but a divine command not be ignored so easily," Raj said in his funny accent while he stirred his body back and forth to go along with the bad accent and his account for why he was drawing her.

A little round of applause greeted these words from the mermaid, limited only by the fact that Raj's accent was so terrible that some of his phrasing was lost, but it didn't matter. He was playing with her and enjoying the attention of a beautiful princess.

It was insincere. He would have said the same to any pretty girl he was caught sketching. Someone whose face was worth outlining needed such compliments, even though he would forget them the moment the next pretty girl presented herself for drawing.

But Serene frowned and tried to disguise her pleasure. "I would have thought, sir, that if my face was so much in your mind, then you might have been able to remember what I looked like without following me around like a needy cat. Or perhaps your mind is so weak it cannot hold an impression for very long?"

Raj grinned at her and said, "I have a friend who tells me that the apprehension of true beauty is hard. We may try to capture the moment and bring the emotional feeling out from it, but we are too tainted as humans to keep it alive within us for long. This is my greatest heartbreak, for however much I observe and however much I sketch, all I can take with me when I leave your company is the weakest imitation, a below-average performance of your beauty, just as man himself is below the beauty of the heavenly angels."

It seemed like an easy reply for Raj, for Bali was shaking his head back and forth and looking down at the water.

Boy, oh boy, what a big foot Raj put in his mouth, Bali thought. Bali had once talked to him about his drawings and used that same example to try to explain what it meant to be an artist and what other great painters thought it meant. From then on, Bali thought, Raj needed to handle this on his own, but he knew he was trying to do the best he could.

Raj concealed the sudden drop in the brilliance of his smoothness by deciding it was high time that he must show that he was overcome with remorse and shame by his disrespect. By doing this, it would allow him to give her a shorter reply if she needed new answers. So Raj said the following, with his head bent down, expressing humility, "I'm sorry, my princess, if I disrespected you in any way. I'm truly sorry."

"May I see this sketch you have done of me?"

Raj was ready for that as well. He had worked up a fine sketch of her face and how the radiant splendor of her oval features blazed itself off the page. And on the bottom, he had carefully written her name.

Serene inhaled as she saw it.

"Keep it, my princess, if you wish. For now I have seen the original close-up, and I realize now the injustice my meager hands tried to replicate."

Can anyone really resist the sweet talk of image-taking?

Can, in particular, a young girl in Triton years, who didn't look a day over twenty in human years—conscious of her demands and disenchanted with love, especially in the Aquatic Caribbean kingdom—remain cold when given a portrait that, despite Raj's false modesty, was extraordinarily good, considering the jungles of Guyana and the simple nature of portrait making here? Was this not a flattering portrait of her, which seemed to remain true to the original?

Serene kept the picture and had it waterproofed. She brought it home and put it in her diary. Every time she opened her diary, she would gaze at it.

Was it in any way astonishing that when she looked at it and remembered—all at the same time imagining—that this was how she existed in the young journeyman's heart, she wondered that, at last, could she have now fallen in love?

39

Hanna and Bali

Hanna and Harry stepped out of the vehicle that was parked at 207 North Street. As the driver took out the luggage from the trunk, Hanna admired the hibiscus plants lined up on her right side next to the white fence. To Hanna, they seemed to stand at attention, waiting for her to salute them smartly so that they could return their salute and a robust welcome back to the oldest daughter.

The large rose bush in front of her on the left side was swaying back with the tropical breeze, as if they were greeting her and saying, *It has been a long time, but you are back now, and everything will be all right.*

Beefi came rushing down the stairs, with a white apron around her waist and loving tears in her eyes, saying, "My big daughter is home now. Papa, she is back. Papa, she came home."

The big hug they shared seemed to last for an eternity. Then Hanna said, "Where is Dad? Is he okay, Mom? Oh, Mom, sorry. You remember my husband, Harry?"

"Hi, Mrs. DaSilva, you are looking well," Harry said, giving Beefi a gentle hug out of respect.

Beefi pointed upstairs as she looked at the driver. "Please bring the luggage upstairs, on the porch. Thank you." As she turned toward her daughter and her daughter's husband, she said, "Papa is lying down on his bed resting. He will feel much better when he gets the chance to see you—I mean both of you. Come upstairs, and I'll have some cool refreshments and something for you all to eat. Oh, Papa will be happy to see you all. He has been keeping me up, waiting, asking me if Hanna has arrived yet, calling the airport... Papa, she is here now."

As Hanna and her mother walked up the stairs, Harry paid the driver and added a nice tip. To which, the driver replied, "Thank you, sir, thank you. My name is Bruce. If you will ever need a driver, please call me, day or night. Here is my card."

With that, the driver entered his car. While starting the engine, he waved good-bye. His vehicle backed up into Front Street and drove straight up toward the public road.

As Hanna and Harry walked toward the end bedroom facing the rear of the house, they pushed open the bedroom door quietly and stepped in. While their eyes slowly adjusted to the slightly dark room, they saw Bali lying on the large bed, with the mosquito net rolled up. His eyes were shut, and he was breathing softly.

With a low whisper, Hanna walked toward the bed and said, "Daddy, I'm here. Harry is with me too. Daddy, are you okay?"

Bali opened his eyes slowly. With a wide grin, he said, "My munchkin came home. Just to let you know, I still kept our little secret from Mama."

He opened his arms wide, and Hanna rushed to fill up the void with a loving hug. With tears in her eyes, she said, "You never forgot, Daddy. After all these years, you never forgot."

"How could I, munchkin? You were the adventurous and brazen one. How could I tell, especially with that little sad, questioning look?" Bali's warm, loving eyes cuddled hers.

"What's wrong, Dad? What was the emergency you told Saniya? You said you only wanted me and Harry to come? Why?"

Bali raised himself slowly from the bed and told Harry to shut the door. He waived to Harry to come toward the bed. He whispered to both of them the events that occurred in the past days.

He needed Hanna to speak to her daughter and her husband to advise them the importance for their son to come to Guyana. Bali told them that he never told his wife what was going on, and he did not want anyone else to know. This had to be kept between them, here in Guyana.

He let them know that his next-door neighbor Raj only had a general idea but did not know all the facts.

He also told Hanna that he knew about Shadow the cat and that it was revealed to him by the mermaid, as well as in his dreams.

That morning, the quiet conversation was kept closely guarded in a lightly dark room.

With the whispers of an old running fan cranking out small silent breezes, Hanna promised her dad that she would call Lee Ann and Roy after lunch.

In Bali's bedroom, the sound of Beefi setting up the dining room table could be heard, with the crackling sounds of plates and utensils. And her voice rang out, like a chow bell on a wagon train cattle-herd roundups, "Come and get it. Come and get it before it gets cold."

As Bali sat around the table with his daughter and her husband, his mind wandered to her childhood days, the days that brought heaviness and tenderness. He couldn't keep his eyes off his daughter. He would smile and stare at her like a dopey kid falling in love with his first puppy.

Hanna saw her dad's stare, and she blushed, saying, "Cut it out, Dad. It's making me blush. Come on, stop it."

And he would stop for a while. But her presence there brought him joy, and he would still sneak a stare or two when she wasn't looking.

Every once in a while, when they were eating, Harry would ask a question to Hanna, and her mannerism and the way she stroked her chin brought back the floodgates of past memories.

It was his utmost preference that Hanna resembled him, and she had almost nothing of her mother in her, maybe a little in looks, but nothing in temperament. When she grew up to be both beautiful and talented, his pride and appreciation were so great he could barely contain himself.

His reward for her accomplishment was to offer her all he could provide. He gave her books, movies with her sister, and a sense and independence of nonstop inquiry. He denied her false ceremonial rituals and instead offered her freedom to choose her faith.

Anything she wanted was hers. And only once did he lose his temper with her, and that was when they were riding on his bicycle when she was about the age of eight, and she almost fell because of her fidgeting. They had their only serious fight, which Hanna won. But she only did it once. Hanna had so many of her father's mannerisms, even the way she stroked and cupped the side of her chin when trying to think of something to say.

In bringing her up, Bali knew that Hanna should learn to be more polite and sophisticated than he was, refined in a way he could never be. His own passions to speak out created in him a sort of disfavor that he hoped Hanna would share but learn to control better.

He knew exactly what sort of girl he wanted. He could see her growing up in his mind, and the outcome of his aspiration came about one day when she was still a child, and it happened on the public road.

Beefi was in a hurry. She wanted to prepare the food at home, and it was getting late. She could not understand and was completely perplexed by Hanna's outburst, and she smacked her across her face to make her hurry up.

Hanna screamed even more and kept on screaming until her face was red with a mixture of violence and hopelessness. She was dragged back, still screaming, to the house and sent to her room until she learned to behave.

Hanna never knew how much this frightened her father, how many nights he stayed awake, unable to sleep for fear that the disorder that Beefi, his wife, had would also be a part of his beloved daughter's personality.

This terrified him and became the anxiety that too often kept him awake, wondering whether his wife would continue to exhibit the overwhelming control that allowed Hanna little room to breathe. Her performance that day, however, was mere crabbiness and rebellion, not a sign of emerging recklessness.

Hanna did not behave. Indeed, it might be argued that she would never really behave again.

But this incident could have opened the floodgates in Hanna's developing personality. She could have had a reason not to make well-mannered conversations or not to change her clothes and show poor posture, like not to sit with her knees touching. She could have used this reason to disobey, but she didn't.

What she did do was slip out of the house the next day when she should have been reading quietly in her room. Gracefully she went out through the back way, then down the stairs, past the outdoor freezer, then through an opening in the fence, and into the street.

It was the first time Hanna had ever been outside by herself. She was frightened by her adventurous dare, but only for the first dozen steps or so, and then she was exhilarated thereafter.

She walked brazenly to the public road, and then fear opened her eyes wide, and she was immobilized.

What she saw was her father coming home and walking straight toward her. She thought her life was over.

Are they going to chain me up with a ball and chain like in the movies? No more books to read? Is Dad going to stop loving me? I'm cooked, Hanna thought. *My life is gone as I know it.*

"Hi, sweetheart. Did you come to greet me? I missed you too." Bali picked her up and hugged her so tightly she couldn't breathe.

"Daddy, I can't breathe," Hanna said, gasping for air.

"Sorry, my little munchkin. It's just that Daddy loves you so much," Bali said as he put her down and took her little left hand with his right hand and started walking down Front Street.

Hanna looked at her daddy with a little sad, questioning look.

Bali smiled down at her as they walked home. He squeezed her tiny finger softly and said, "It's okay. We'll keep this little secret to ourselves."

PART X

Egypt, Ghost, and Possession

40

Egypt and the Teacher of Darkness

"West of the moon, east of the sun, where does creation begin?"

In the kingdom of darkness, a teacher spoke to his students.

"What are the elements that all Egyptians believe that are common? Why are there many conflicting existences? One belief held is that the world had arisen out of lifeless waters of chaos called Nu. And out from that water first emerged a pyramid-shaped mound called Benben.

The teacher, dressed in a long dark robe, moved toward a shape in the air that resembled a blackboard screen setting. He started to draw an image of a sun. He then continued:

"They say the sun is closely associated with creation, and it is said to have first been raised from the mound as the general sun god Ra or as the god Khepri, who represented the newly risen sun. Then there are many versions of the sun's beginning. I will only list two for now." He moved toward the blackboard and drew a hill and then a flower on the hill. "It is said to have emerged directly from the mound or from a lotus flower that grew from the mound in the form of a heron, falcon, scarab beetle, or a little human child."

With a swoop of his hand, he waved off the images on the blackboard. He then proceeded to draw an egg with an equal sign to a hill and a wave of water symbols. He then continued, "You probably remember the common element of Egyptian cosmogonies. For those who have forgotten what the word *cosmogonies* means, it's the plural form of the word *cosmogony*, which is a noun, and it means 'a theory or story of the origin and development of the universe, the solar system, or the earth-moon system.' This we studied in our last class. It was the familiar figure of the cosmic egg, a substitute for explaining the 'primeval' waters or the 'primeval' mound.

One variant of the cosmic-egg version teaches that the sun god, as a 'primeval' power, emerged from this 'primeval' mound, which—if you think about it—looks like the shape of an Egyptian's pyramid. And they say that this stood in the chaos of the 'primeval' sea. What I'm trying to say is that this is one of the ways that the Egyptians tried to explain the creation theory.

The teacher then sat down on a throne-like chair and pointed to his servants to bring in four drawings. He had two placed on the left side of his seat and the other two on the right side of his seat. He then continued, "To my right, you see two drawings of a young woman, and to my left, you see the same. All these drawings are the same woman. The only difference is that two are sitting and two are standing. This woman is the goddess called Maat.

Maat was also personified as a goddess regulating the stars, seasons, and the actions of both mortals and the deities, who set the order of the universe from chaos at the moment of creation. Her ideological counterpart was Isfet. Maat is the goddess of harmony, justice, and truth—represented, as you see here, as a young woman, sitting or standing, holding a Was Scepter, the symbol of power, in one hand and an ankh, the symbol of eternal life, in the other. On the first two drawings, she is depicted with wings on each arm, and on the second drawings, as a woman with an ostrich feather on her head.

"Maat was both the goddess and the personification of truth and justice. And the drawings with the ostrich feather represents truth. The Was Scepter she is holding represents power and dominion, and it appears often in relics, art, and hieroglyphics associated with the ancient Egyptian religion, as you will have a chance to see after class. As you can see in the drawings, it appears as a stylized animal head at the top of a long, straight staff with a forked end. This scepter is also associated with the gods we discussed before, like Set or Anubis. The pharaohs of Egypt used this as the symbol of their power and dominion over their kingdom."

The teacher stood up and motioned for his servants to move the drawings and replace them with new drawings and paintings of tombs and coffins. He then continued, "As you can see with these drawings and painting, the Was Scepter was very important in funerary context. It was responsible for the well-being of the deceased and was thus sometimes included in the tomb equipment—as you can see here—or in the decoration of the tomb or coffin." The teacher then pointed toward the paintings and drawings.

"The scepter is also considered an amulet. The Egyptians perceived the sky as being supported on four pillars, which could have the shape of Was Scepters. In these paintings over here, they are depicted as being carried by gods, pharaohs, and priests. Not only do they occur in paintings and drawings like these but also in carvings of gods, as you will see over by the shelves. The reason why these lessons are now given to all new students is that your position in the future are tied in the knowledge I am about to impart.

One of Maat's role in creation was to continuously prevent the universe from returning to chaos, and her primary role, not only in Egyptian stories, is to deal with the weighing of souls that takes place here in the underworld. The Egyptians call this place Duat. We know it as Diyu. Her feather is the measure that determines whether the souls— which we consider to reside in the heart of the departed— would reach the paradise of afterlife successfully. One must go through this process.

Here in the underworld, the heart of the dead has to be weighed against her single feather in the Hall of Two Truths. A heart that is unworthy is devoured by the goddess Ammit, and its owner is condemned to remain here. We are the condemned, and as you all know, we are ruled and judged by the Yama kings.

Three spirits from purgatories escaped yesterday through the various levels, mazes, and chambers down here and are roaming the earth as I speak. We have been chosen and given limited powers to capture these fugitives. Temporary soldier's bodies to function in the upper world will be provided for you. All this information about the different god and goddesses of the Egyptians will help you understand these three spirits so that you can capture them.

We also believe that they are trying to find the Was Scepter or any amulet that can override the judges' power and therefore rule the underworld and cause chaos on the earth. A great reward will be granted to anyone who succeeds in capturing one or more of these spirits. One of these rewards will be that you will be given a good and pure heart and be sent on to Aaru. The guardian Osiris will let you pass through the gates."

The teacher then dismissed his class so that they could familiarize themselves with the objects in the corner of the room. Watching the students familiarize with the objects, the teacher smiled and said, "In the Hall of Two Truths echo *pandemonium*. And for those who don't understand the meaning of that word—please, look it up for yourself. Okay?"

41

The Rise and Fall of Amabo

The bright sun rose in the east and glided over the green mountaintops and fell upon the rippling waters of the Essequibo River. Then it lighted up the forests and evergreen plains around. The northeast wind played gently against Amabo's cheeks and in his long hair as he stood gazing on his fallen foe.

In his hand was the *Book of the Dead*, along with the papyrus picture that showed the weighing of the heart in a tomb scene. Amabo grinned as he looked at the papyrus showing Anubis overseeing the weighing and the lioness goddess, Ammit, awaiting the results so that she could consume those who failed.

"Who's balancing the scales now?" Amabo murmured to himself as he glanced over at the fallen foe. "And they can go to hell with the single Shu feather." He looked, with a snaky glitter lurking in his eyes, at Isolep, his trusted female mouthpiece.

Only the sounds of rippling water and the roar of the waterfalls kept their voices. The busy insects and singing birds froze in a moment of time, and these silences came to his ears, and he knew that they knew that the secret Temple for Ages was violated. Their guardian was dead, and nature had fallen asleep from her responsibility.

And as the strong, possessed body leaned upon his sword, he thought of the deed he had done—behold!

The grinning Isolep, with her beaming eyes and short head of hair, having crossed the gulf of the dead with him to the now bright Essequibo River, stood by his side.

Then the Guyana's rain forest vultures came wheeling downward to look upon the dead guardian, and with them came a raven, black as midnight. And when Amabo saw this raven, he knew him to be Dier's bird, Dier's thought, and Dier's memory.

Then Dier flapped his wings and said, "The deed is done. Why linger here, Amabo?" Then Dier flew past Isolep's ear and whispered, "Beware of Amabo, the master! His heart is poisoned. His curses have increased."

And the bird flew away to carry the news to Dier's possessed body in the campaign halls of the People's National Congress in Georgetown.

When Isolep drew near to look upon the dead guardian, Amabo kindly detained her, but she seemed not to hear. A sparkle was present in her eyes, and her luscious, full lips grinned. She seemed as one walking in a dream.

"It is mine now," she murmured. "It is all mine now, the *Book of the Dead,* the stored wisdom of ages. The weakness of the world is mine and yours. I will keep, I will save, I will mound up—and none shall have shares or portion of this treasure that is ours alone."

Amabo, in another life, held first the prestigious positions in ancient Egyptian society as a *scribe.* His view of the scribe was important in the transmission of religious, political, and commercial information to the rulers and the people.

Remuhs was the patron of scribes and is known as the one "who reveals Maat and reckons Maat, who loves Maat and gives Maat to the doer of Maat." In the *Instruction of Amenemope* text, Remuhs urged the scribe to follow the precepts of Maat in their private life, as well as their work. Maat was the norm and the basic values that formed the backdrop for the application of justice, which had to be carried out in the spirit of truth and fairness, and *Amabo* believed in fairness.

Even though ancient Egyptian laws were essential, including an adherence to tradition as opposed to change, Amabo in his heart believed in change, especially the need for social justice. He knew the need for the importance of rhetorical skills, and this he developed.

Amabo believed in the text where the Creator declared, "I made every man like his fellow." Amabo called out to the rich to help the less fortunate and share the wealth rather than exploit them, and his words were echoed in tomb

272

declarations: "I have given bread to the hungry and clothed the naked," and "I was a husband to the widow and father to the orphan." But in his lust, he wanted more.

He rose in fame and became the vizier and had the responsibility for keeping justice. And then he became the priest of Maat and later a judge, who wore the images of Maat on his robes. He was pleased with his success, so he began to learn and play different musical instruments and became quite good in playing the harp.

Now, Amabo was called by his peers the sweetest musician in the entire world. It was said by some that his household was with the songbirds and that he had learned his skill from them. But this was only part of the half truth, for wherever there was vivacity or beauty or things noble and pure, there was Amabo. And his astonishing power in music and in song was but the outward sign of a blameless soul.

And he was as grander of speech as he was skilled in song.

His words were so persuasive that, they say, he had been known to change the sea, to move great, lifeless mountains, and—what is harder—the hearts of pharaohs and kings. He understood the voice of the people, the whispering of the revolutionists, the murmurs of change, and the roar of the politicians.

Then he was revealed for what he was, a traitor to his nation's laws and its people. He almost destroyed the

Egyptian nation. His two close friends, Dier and Isolep, were also sent to death by the pharaoh and then to the underworld by Maat. *How ironic*, Amabo thought.

He now had the *Book of the Dead*, but he now needed codified ethic of Maat, the spells from the *Papyrus of Ani*, known to the ancient Egyptians as the *Book of Going Forth by Day*. He needed the lines of these texts, which are collectively called the "Forty-Two Declarations of Purity." He needed to fool the gods in believing he and his followers were pure, and these spells would achieve that purpose.

While he looked toward the sea, a brown ship with sails all set came speeding over the waters toward him. It came nearer and nearer, and the sailor rested upon their oars as it glided into the quiet landing port.

Out came Dier, rushing toward him, heaving his possessed skinny body to move with the flow of the evil spirit within him. "Amabo, Isolep, we got trouble coming."

Amabo watched the stars as they came out one by one and the moon as it rose, round and pastel, and moved like an empress across the sky. The night took its time to wear away, and the stars grew soft, and the moon dropped to repose in the wasteland of waters.

And at daydawn, Amabo looked toward the west; and midway between sky and sea, he thought he saw a figure of a man wielding a flaming sword, gliding above the land mists. And then the object seemed to float upon the edge of the sea, moving nearer and nearer.

Amabo looked at Isolep and Dier, who were also looking at the object. With a sense of fear moving up and down his newly possessed body, he said, "Oh shit—he's here!"

42

Saturday Breakfast at Mom's

"**M**om, you still make the best pancakes in the world," Ron said as he gulped down the last two pieces from his plate and started on the scrambled eggs and coffee.

"I'm glad you liked it, and thank you for the compliment." As Lee Ann finished washing the pots, pans, and dishes, she turned around and asked, "How are the Diamonds today? Any news about Diana? And is she okay?"

"I talked to her this morning, and she seems to be taking everything in stride, not like last night. All in all, they are doing fine, and Diana told *me* not to worry about her and her dad. How the tables have been turned, from night to day. She'll be okay, I guess. Mom, I know you didn't invite me for a Saturday breakfast only. I can tell by your voice this morning on the phone…and I know Dad isn't hanging out in the bedroom for nothing. What gives?"

As the cheerful sun from the east revealed itself through the living room windows, Ron was given a mystifying story from his dad and mom, which gave him pause to reflect and fathom the gravity of the situation coming from Guyana.

He knew that Grandma Hanna and Grandpa Harry would never make up a story like that to get him to go to Guyana, and they would never lie to his dad and mom. How could he go and leave Diana in her time of need? What would the Diamonds think about his character? He needed to talk to his wife again, and to the Diamonds also.

He called his wife from his dad and mom's home so that they could relay any additional information about the situation.

"Hi, deary. Before you say anything, pack light. Guyana is hot," Diana said while giggling on the phone.

"How did you know?" Ron said in astonishment. "Was it the third eye?"

"No, silly, it was the third cup of coffee. I mean, we received a call this morning after my third cup of coffee from Hanna and Harry, and they told us the severity of the state of affairs. And this is a game changer for this world, and you know that. You also know that you were born for this kind of circumstances, and if you don't go, deary, you would really piss me off. Just kidding. Be safe, and I love you."

After talking with the Diamonds, Ron passed the phone to his dad and his mom. The in-laws and his parents were on the phone for at least twenty minutes, going over detail and strategy about the trip. One thing was certain: secrecy about his going there was foreseeable.

Ron had practiced the different powers he had with his dad alone. Except for the ghost-type powers of invisibility that everyone had seen and the power to shape-shift into a black cat, only his dad saw and helped him practice the other powers, like how to control natural elements and manipulate molecules.

Ron was wondering if Guyana had the old phone system. He knew that since the 1960s, development of electronic switching systems telephony gradually evolved toward digital telephony, which improved the capacity and quality of the network.

But because the development of digital data communications methods, like the protocols used for the Internet, it became possible to digitize voice and transmit it as real-time data across computer networks. This gave rise to the field of Internet Protocol (IP) telephony, also known as voice over Internet Protocol (VoIP), a term he knew and understood.

Had Guyana replaced the traditional telephone network infrastructure? Would he be using the great-grandfather system with the analog telephone adapter, which interfaced a conventional analog telephone to the IP networking equipment? Or would he use an IP phone system? He thought about question after question and more questions.

When he was young, he would watch on TV the series called *Star Trek*. In this series, they needed to have a transport for matter energy. Ron knew he was the transport as well as the matter energy, so none of this would be a problem. He tried it already with his dad over the regular phone lines and the cell phone lines, and there was no problem.

He thought that the only thing he could really say like a real *Star Trek* fan was, "Beam me through, Bali!"

43

Poof, I'm Here!

With the early morning arriving and the next-door neighbor finishing her morning tea at the DaSilva's kitchen table, Bali reminded Beefi to bring lots of fruit for her grandson, who would be arriving later that morning.

Beefi would mumble in her Guyanese Creolese language, "Dah mouth dat man tek fuh court women ah de same mouth he ah tek an put she ah door."

He heard her and smiled. He knew what she meant. *When a man is courting a woman, he is very concerned, kind, and considerate. But when the novelty of the relationship is over, he finds faults and is unkind.*

Then he said back to her, grinning, "Seven years nah too much fuh wash speck off ah bird neck." This meant: *Some people will never change their ways and attitude.*

Beefi and her neighbor Mrs. Basmaty slunk off silently through the early morning sunrise, and Beefi gave up trying to see who was going to have the last word.

As both women were walking down Front Street, Beefi looked back at the house and then to her neighbor. While biting her tongue, she said, "Curse when yuh ah guh, nah when yuh ah come out." It meant, *You must not curse the place that you have come from because sometimes, in the future, you may have to return there.*

Even though the Guyanese proverb didn't really fit this situation, she needed something to say, the last word maybe, as they walked to Leonora's Market. A warm early morning breeze and the sun on her backside spanked her for her vile comments.

Mrs. DaSilva certainly thought herself one of the most straightforward women in Guyana, and the sight of her cheerful family gathering around a telephone was an edifying experience to her. They were so smiling, so loving, so conversant, and so up-front!

What is wrong with this picture? she thought.

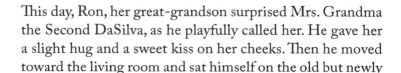

This day, Ron, her great-grandson surprised Mrs. Grandma the Second DaSilva, as he playfully called her. He gave her a slight hug and a sweet kiss on her cheeks. Then he moved toward the living room and sat himself on the old but newly refurbished rocking chair, which had scarcely been touched since Hanna and her sister playfully broke it.

Putting the groceries on the kitchen table, she turned toward Ron and asked him, "How was your trip? Was there any problem coming here?"

Ron smiled and answered, "It was a breeze, and you could say"—he leaned his head slightly to the right toward his grandparents and Bali, and while his eyes were wide open, he raised both of his eyelids and grinned—"Poof! Yes, you could say, poof, I'm here!"

While Bali and Ron's grandparents were laughing, Beefi ignored them and decided to take the fruits downstairs, washing them first, and then prepared them in a large fruit bowl. She pondered what her great-grandson was trying to say, and then she murmured to herself while walking downstairs, "Yuh can't suck cane and blow whistle." It meant, *Do not try to carry out two tasks at the same time.* Pondering her great-grandson's reply was a task within itself.

Maybe it was an American thing, she thought, while washing the fruits and the other vegetables in the large gray-colored sink.

Beefi smiled as she looked out the back-kitchen's window. She could see the neighbor's children, even through the plants and palm trees in her garden. Their laugher and playing out in the street brought back memories of when she was a young girl.

Her thought of childhood memories came to a sudden halt, hearing the murmuring of voices upstairs and the moving around, as if they were wondering whether she was listening.

I guess the servant should know her place, she thought while scrubbing the fruit so hard that the inside was bleeding through. Then she realized why she was so grumpy. No sleep, no life. *One day, life will say no more, and who am I to complain?*

She prepared the fruits in a large flowery-patterned bowl and started her way up the back stairs and said to herself, smiling, "Nah mind how pumpkin vine run, he must dry up one day." It meant, *Every life comes to an end sooner or later.*

44

What's in a Name?

"How did the *Book of the Dead* and the *Book of Going Forth by Day* ever arrive in Guyana? We are talking about ancient Egyptian books at least over three thousand years ago. Why are they so dangerous?" Ron asked as he looked at Princess Serene with a doubtful look.

Knowing that Ron needed answers, Princess Serene told him to sit over by the cave next to the waterfall. She looked at him carefully and knew, though he was young, that he had the warrior's mentality. She said, "Ron, let me take the last question first. The ancient Egyptian books and artifacts were first kept by scribes and Pharaoh's official guards. As to these items and why they are dangerous, you must understand what they include and how the text was written. They were written in both black and red ink, regardless of whether it was in hieroglyphic or hieratic script.

"Most of the text was in black, but the red ink was used for the titles of spells, including the opening and closing sections of spells and the instructions on how to perform the spells correctly in rituals. And they also included the names of dangerous creatures, such as the demons that help with these spells. The first *Book of the Dead* was developed in Thebes toward the beginning of the Second Intermediate Period around 1700 Bc.

The most powerful earliest occurrence of the spells included in the *Book of the Dead* came from the coffin of Queen Mentuhotep, of the thirteenth dynasty, where these spells were included amongst older texts known from the Pyramid Texts and Coffin Texts."

The princess saw that Ron was listening intensely, and his eyes were locked into hers. She then continued, "Now, how they got here is stranger than fiction, but it is true. This starts from a battle and then a victory. One of the most famous victories in 1177 AD was during the Battle of Montgisard, where some five hundred medieval Order of Knights Templar helped several thousand infantrymen during the Crusades to defeat Saladin's army of more than twenty-six thousand soldiers. During that battle, one of the knights found, in Saladin's camp, the *Book of the Dead*, Egyptian artifacts, and the *Book of Going Forth by Day*. He then took it to Rome, where it was kept by the Vatican for 510 years.

A dispute arose between the Dutch and the English in 1667, where the Dutch decided to keep the blossoming plantation colony of Suriname, which they conquered from the English, resulting in the Treaty of Breda. The English were left with New Amsterdam, a small trading post in North America, which you know as New York City, and the Dutch had Guyana.

Now, going back to the Vatican, a problem arose with the new pope at that time. He believed that these items were dangerous and needed to be buried or hidden in a faraway place so that no one could find it. Europe, Asia, or the Middle East were not an option or a place for these items. He needed a country not yet really explored, and South America looked promising.

To do that, he needed somebody strong and courageous enough for the challenge. A Templar knight was truly a fearless knight, for his soul, they believe, was protected by the armor of faith just as his body was protected by the armor of steel. He was therefore doubly armed and didn't fear either demons or men.

And in 1139, they received major benefit when the pope at that time exempted them from the order of obedience to local laws. This ruling meant that the Templars could pass freely through all borders and were not required to pay any taxes, and were also exempt from all authority except that of the pope. But that order doesn't exist anymore.

"What was strange and yet useful was that there wasn't any direct connection between the ancient Order of the

Knights Templar and the order known in 1667 as the Knights Templar, even though they had the same official motto, which said, 'In this [the sign of the cross], you will conquer.'

The church at this time had a falling out with the Masonic knights organizations, and no one would suspect any interactions. The pope, knowing this, had a secret meeting with the organization, and they agreed to handle the task in secret, with financial support from the Vatican.

A group of twelve men disguised in plain clothes went to the Netherlands, posing as businessmen, and chartered passage to Guyana with the Dutch West India Company's vessel. Guyana's territories, at that time, were administered by the Dutch West India Company. During that colonial period, the Netherlands was heavily involved in the slave trade.

The Dutch planters relied heavily on African slaves to cultivate the coffee, cocoa, sugarcane, and cotton plantations along the rivers. No one would suspect that they were Masonic knights and on a mission of concealment. But the primary mission of the order was as defense force protectors of the ancient Egyptian books and artifacts.

At that time, there were nine native tribes residing in Guyana: the Wai-wai, Machushi, Patamona, Arawak, Carib, Wapishana, Arecuna, Akawaio, and Warrau. But the strongest tribes that dominated Guyana were the Arawak and Carib tribes.

The knights became part of the different tribes and married within the tribes. They eventually built a temple deep in the jungle and trained their male offspring on the art of military defense to protect the books and artifacts buried in a secret location within the temple. There was always a guard at all times, protecting the entrance to the temple. But a second area was developed as a burial place, where the *Book of Going Forth by Day* is hidden, and that area is protected by the rest of the knights' family."

"I see what you mean—like, don't put all your eggs in one basket," Ron said, grinning. "Sorry for the interruption. Please continue."

"You're exactly right. That was their playbook," she acknowledges and then continued in a more serious tone, "There are over 186 spells and the summoning up of demons that make these books and the artifacts a curse against the good and pure of hearts in this world.

A section of the Egyptian *Book of the Dead*, written on papyrus, shows the weighing of the heart that the Diyu underworld uses in secret. This well-kept secret shows how to use the feather of Maat and how it is applied toward the measure in balance, which only the Yama kings of the realm of the dead know.

The ruler-judge Yan of Diyu, who brought you into this world as Shadow, requested you for this mission. You will be provided with a flaming sword after the coronation by my dad. There are only two swords in the world with this extraordinary capability, and you have been chosen for this honor."

Ron lowered his head toward the ground and lingered there, only for a moment. He then raised his head and looked at the princess and said, "Tell all those who are involved that I am humbled and honored to be chosen for this task."

The princess nodded slowly and said, "I can see that the Judge Yan has chosen well. You will be given a new name at the coronation, and that name will be the name you will be known for in this world. Is there a name or nickname you like?" she asked, smiling.

Ron thought hard for a moment and said, "I fancy the name *Tex*. Is that okay?"

She smiled and said, "Tex is fine. But because you hold all the five elements, how about *Tex Element*?"

Ron, with a smile, jumped to his feet, moved his head side to side, and shaking his arms, said, "I like it...*Tex Element*. Oh, by the way, do I need to wear a costume?"

45

Hungry Ghost Festival

Three months later, after completing their meditation in the forest, twenty-five exhausted disciples returned home to the shiny golden temple on the east side of the hill, overlooking a Mahayana town in India.

Their saffron-colored robes were still damp from the rainy season, and their sweat and body odor remained as if it were another layer of skin. They chanted their repeating mantra in harmony, low and deep, with a lingering hum, reverberating, with their hands midway in front of their bodies wedged together in a prayer-like form.

They climbed the many stony stairs, which seemed endless, to celebrate Buddha's joyful day and to report their progress to Buddha. This was the eighth lunar month, a month of joy. This was the fifteenth day of the eight month, the day of rejoice for the monks.

Instructions were given on how to obtain liberation for their dearly departed loved ones, who had been reborn into a lower realm. The kitchen was laced with cooking smells as they prepared the food offerings to the *sangha* on this exceptional time. This was a blessed day for the monks, for they had attained enlightenment during this high period, and Buddha was very pleased.

With little personal possessions—comprised of their three robes, an alms bowl, a cloth belt, a needle and thread, a razor for shaving their heads, and a water filter—the monks, with their stained, sewn-together earth robes, rejoiced.

There were those whose loved ones were reborn and found in the heavenly realms, the realm of the gods, and those monks were pleased. However, there were those who were reborn in a lower realm known as Avici Hell or the realm of hungry ghosts. These spirits took on the form of a hungry ghost. They were called that because they could not eat due to their thin and fragile throat, in which no food could pass through, so they were always hungry because they had bloated bellies.

Those who had done evil and unjust treatment to others while they were alive and didn't care for the needy suffered, and it was for this reason they were reborn in the realm of hungry ghosts.

A Buddhist monk named Haimerej Thgirw, originally a brahmin youth, was ordained and became one of the Buddha's chief disciples at this temple. Haimerej was also known for having clairvoyant powers, an uncommon trait among monks. He didn't go to the forest to meditate with the other monks; but instead, he stayed behind, preparing the rituals for this festive time.

On the first day of this month, Haimerej opened the gates of this temple, symbolizing the gates of hell. On the twelfth day, he lit the lamps on the main altar. On the thirteenth day, he held a procession of lanterns. On the fourteenth day, he organized a parade in town, which was held for the releasing of the water lanterns.

Incense and food were offered to the spirits to avoid those visiting homes, and spirit paper money was also burnt as an offering. During the month, people in town avoided surgery or buying cars, swimming, and going out after dark.

It was also important that addresses were not revealed to the ghosts. But this last function, the monk didn't do. He wanted at least one spirit he could control.

While this festival brought about family reunions in which people from the big cities returned to their small hometowns to visit and clean their ancestors' graves, while Haimerej rented in town a Trinity hut for the spirit to dwell in.

A large feast was held in town for the ghosts on the fourteenth day of the seventh month, where the people in town brought samples of food and placed them on an offering table to please the ghosts and ward off bad luck.

By the long curve of the river that passed next to the imposing mausoleums and tombstones' cemetery on the east bank of town, Haimerej could see family members offering prayers to their deceased relatives, providing food and drink and burning hell bank notes and other forms of joss paper.

Joss-paper items were believed to have value in the afterlife and were considered to be very similar, in some aspects, to the material world. And he saw townspeople burn paper houses, cars, servants, and televisions to please the ghosts.

And there were families who also paid tribute to other unknown wandering ghosts so that these homeless souls did not intrude on their lives and bring misfortune. But Haimerej wanted the intrusion.

On the west side of town, a stage was built. A live performance was held, and everyone was invited to attend. The first rows of seats were always empty, for this was where the ghosts sat. The Chinese opera started after sundown, and the music was at high volumes. This loud sound attracted and pleased the ghosts, but the Buddhist monk had his own ritual and attraction.

While walking down the street, he saw that some of the shops were closed because they wanted to leave the streets open for the ghosts. In the middle of each street, he saw altars of incense and stands with fresh fruit and sacrifices displayed on it.

That evening, he could smell in his nostrils incense burning in front of the households' doors so that these families would have more prosperity while they continued burning more incense.

In the Trinity hut, the monk spoke to a spirit, who was enjoying the feast set before him.

"Who am I speaking to? And what title do you hold?" Haimerej asked.

"Title…," said the laughing spirit. "If you need a title, I am a teacher to the new students in the underworld. My name is llib Sreya, and I was once a leader of a freedom movement. I don't like authority figures, unless I am one of them. So what do you want? And make it quick, I'm hungry."

"Great teacher of the underworld, I need a spirit to help me get control of my religion so that I can be the one that the people can rely on."

And as he said this to the spirit, the Buddhist monk got on his knees and bowed down toward the floor with his arms stretched out, facing toward the feast table in the room. And he continued, "I implore you, great one."

The spirit looked at the monk, impressed with his speech and his respect for him. The spirit said, "I like you. You know how to treat a spirit. Okay, let's make a deal."

As the night burned on, the monk and the spirit made a blood deal. The spirit offered three spirits instead of one. But one of the three, he told the monk, was the leader, and the other two were his servants.

"He is a good talker, that leader," said the spirit, laughing. "He would always come to my residence in the underworld, and we would have great conversations. I told him, when the time is right, I will help him bust out. But watch out for him. He is a sly one."

And the spirits laughed out loud with an explosive roar.

Fourteen days after the festival, to make sure that all the spirits, including the hungry ghosts, found their way back to hell, the townspeople floated water lanterns, some on the riverbank, and some set them outside their houses.

Many lotus-flower-shaped lanterns on paper boats lit up the river while directing the ghosts back to the underworld. And when the lights went out, it meant that the ghosts had found their way back.

As the night wore off and the stars grew pale and the moon dropped to repose in the wilderness of the river, three lotus-flower-shaped lanterns stayed lit, and three spirits *didn't* go back.

46

Possession Has a Price

She rose before dawn every morning to have home fried potatoes, sunny-side eggs, and freshly fried plantains ready for their breakfast. Later, they would sit on two old mahogany rocking chairs on the balcony in their two-story home in Georgetown each evening to wait for the Guyanese sun to set.

It had given her such a sense of fulfillment doing the shopping herself every day, making all his favorite foods, or feeding him the first bite of dhal puri or chicken curry with her own hands. And to her relief, he had not brought up the old discussions of other religions and which one was the best. Even following some of the religious rites, they persuaded themselves to be an example to others, and they moved themselves to keep a fast or two.

But then the religious rites were over, and Daewoo was still fasting daily. Sometimes he would keep them two days at a time, not eating from sunrise the first day to sunset the second. When she questioned him about it, he claimed it helped his digestion, or he needed to lose weight, or he was doing it in sympathy with all the people starving in Africa and all those other children starving all over the world. Unclear about how to respond to these claims and limited somewhat by the seeming absence of side effects health-wise, Daewoo's wife tried not to dwell on it.

But it got worse, to the point that he started wearing the same clothes day after day, ignoring the fresh cream-colored khakis and shirt she laid out on his bed every morning. She would sneak out with his dirty clothes at night while he slept and hid them in the bathroom's hamper. This didn't always work since, sometimes, he would retrieve them the next day and reprimand her for putting them there.

Then he would stop bathing for a while and only resumed when his body odor was so ripe that even the members at the campaign halls were prompted to ask her what was happening to the congressman.

Then there was the radio incident. All of a sudden, the radio started bothering him, making him irritable whenever she played it in his presence. He would try to be sneaky by turning it off when she was not looking, and if she complained, he would storm out of the room in a sulky mood. One day, she came back from shopping to find it had vanished altogether. One day, a radio; the next day, a silent home.

And then there was the night when Daewoo had thrown off the bed covers and blankets and turned on the bedroom's light. He started rearranging the furniture. She watched, frightened, as he dumped all the chairs in the guest's bedroom. He then proceeded to move the desk against the corner wall and dragged the heavy wooden trunk clear across the floor to the other corner of the room. Then he put his skinny shoulder against the frame of the bed and, with her still hovering on it, started pushing the queen-size wooden-frame bed toward the wall in short groaning thrusts like some overly enthused ox.

"Daewoo, what are you doing?" she cried out, not knowing whether to get up and assist him or sit there and allow her body to be jolted sideways with each thrust.

"It's too soft," he mumbled through his exertion. "This is bad for my back."

He then pulled a sheet out of the closet and spread it out on the space he cleared on the floor. Then he grabbed his pillow off the bed and walked toward the corner next to the bedroom door and switched off the light.

"Daewoo, please come back to bed," she called to him in the dark, still sitting up in bed. "Why are you doing this to me?"

But he did not answer her, so she waited until she could hear his breathing grow soft and then into a brief snore before she could lie down and try to sleep herself. Sometime during this crazy night, Daewoo threw his pillow back on their bed.

She awoke that morning to find him stretched out on the bare floor, the sheet draped over the upper half of his body and over his head.

She had been unable to solve the mystery of his newly found behavior. She had tried to reason with him, even imploring him with great, big flowing tears, both silent and disturbing. Yet not even the threat to leave him had any form of advantage for her because he was set in his own ways.

He would go back to the same responses, maintaining that he was doing everything for his health and blaming her for wanting too much sex every time she asked him to start sleeping on the bed again. She was tired, so tired, of being the one who was at fault. Daewoo not eating, his fasting, and the muteness of their lives were breaking their marriage away. How much longer could this go on? How much further, and how much more was she supposed to endure?

The tears, thick and salty, started flowing down her cheeks as she sat down on the kitchen's table chair, both arms on the table, her head hung over her arms. She knew this wasn't her fault. She couldn't believe that this was happening to her. Perhaps she should let it out, tell her side of the story, and unburden it to someone.

She had kept everything bottled up for too long, and it must be time to let it out. Maybe she could make a trip to her

299

parents' house tomorrow morning and reveal everything to her parents. Let herself be ashamed no longer, she thought.

Dier was tired of the nagging from the wife of this skinny and bony body that he now possessed. This body couldn't operate with too much food, so a little fasting now and then would make it work smoothly, he thought. He needed someone who was in tuned with the legislature of this country in case they needed to pass some controlling laws or to avoid the passing of some laws that would restrict them from accomplishing their mission.

Only this person had the easiest body he found to possess since this person really didn't care about anyone, a true politician in the making. Speaking words of encouragement and showing the people their smoke and mirrors are what politicians do, yet the biggest lie is making the masses continue believing those lies.

Having the media on your side is a plus for any politician.

Doing the opposite and having their special agenda— "well, what's in it for me?"—that's what the politicians really cared about. Let the masses believe that they're only in it for community service and that they care for the children and the senior citizens. *What a joke*, he thought. *They buy this garbage all of the time.*

He knew that the politicians like to blame the other parties for their failure and incompetency. And if the other party doesn't agree with their spending and looting of the government's treasure chest, they tell the masses that the other party are the ones who don't care for equal rights and they are causing the war against women, children, the elderly, the environment—whatever works.

There are always stupid people who will join the politician's crusade and vouch for their character.

The masses don't see that the politicians like to go on expensive vacations and get the best seats in the house on shows and dinners, and they let the taxpayers foot the bill, all in the name of openness and fairness. But the backroom deals in secrecy are the way we go.

"Love it, I really love it, how the masses are so stupid they believe what we tell them," Dier mumbled under his breath.

And he thought, *If the media likes us and our fairness agenda, then party time is always available for those who can control the masses. When the media is getting close to our lies, then all we have to do is create a crisis.*

Yes, a good crisis should never be wasted. But this body he now possessed and the wife that went along with it was a high price he had to pay for being the servant of Amabo. The only good part about it was that the name *Daewoo* sounded a little like *Dier*—oh well, it was wishful thinking.

Walking toward his office, Dier looked up and saw the prominent cast-iron clock tower over the Stabroek Market that dominated the Georgetown sky line.

"Looking good, clock, but I see that I am already late for my meeting," he murmured as he started to pick up the movement with his skinny feet with a little jogging on his way toward his office. Today he was to get briefed on the situation around Guyana by his secret agency, which kept tabs on almost everyone, even the tribes of Guyana.

At the meeting, he was briefed on the universities, education, Caribbean community secretariat, the hotels, the sugar corporations, airport visitors, and the towns and jungles of Guyana. Nothing was coming up interesting for him after the first half-an-hour briefing. Then suddenly there was the jungle report regarding the Wai-wai tribe, whom their spies said had a visitor yesterday. The rumor said that he was some fierce warrior who came from the underworld, and something about a cat named Shadow.

They all laughed and thought it was silly, but their instruction was to provide everything, even the silly and stupid ones.

Dier smiled and thanked them for the briefing and told them to follow up on the Wai-wai rumors, even the silly ones. He laughed with them as he escorted them out of his office. Dier told his secretary that he would entertain no phone calls or appointments and to charter, if she could, a small vessel today and let him know when it was available.

As the secretary closed the door, Dier walked over to his revolving chair, slumped down on it, and turned it to face the window looking out toward Georgetown's seaport.

"It is true," he murmured to himself. "The rumors are not rumors at all."

He remembered many years ago, during his imprisonment in the underworld, that they all heard about the story of Shadow the cat.

It was the supreme ruler of Diyu, who gave the power of the five elements to the human body of this cat. The Yama kings boasted that this person would be one of the greatest heroes in history and that the power this person possessed would be equal to none.

The other spirits chasing them was a joke, but this person wasn't a laughing matter. He had to tell the others.

"Where is the vessel?" he kept repeating out loud to the secretary. "Where is the *fucking* vessel?"

PART XI

Celebration and a Winding Road

47

Coronation Ceremony in a Lost World

As the Guyana coastline disappears from the sandy beaches, the swamp's marshes begin to highlight the interior mud-swept sea that is carried north by the Amazon River ocean currents. There were two travelers working their way smoothly below the shallow brown waters to a river entrance that avoided the heavy afternoon showers and thunderstorms that this region is noted for. Passing though the barricades of white sandy hills in the interior, they reached their final destination.

Princess Serene signaled Ron with her right hand to surface above the Semang River. The underwater view was fascinating to Ron since this was the first time he traveled a long distance under a river.

The princess smiled and looked at Ron while shaking her head back and forth. She was amazed to see a human who could keep up with her.

As they approached the King Edward VIII Falls, Ron was dumbfounded at the narrow 840-foot-tall plunging waterfall located where the Semang River plunges off the edge of the Pakaraima cliff in northwestern Guyana.

"What a stunning sight," said Ron.

"Ron, the existence of this waterfall is not widely known, but we believe that it is one of the tallest waterfalls in Guyana," the princess said as they turned the bend of the Semang River approaching the ceremonial site. She then continued, "The exact location of this waterfall has been very difficult to pinpoint for the outside world for the last several decades due to a common confusion of a waterfall with a similar name—King Edward VI Falls—which is a series of rapids occurring along the Courantyne River on the eastern border of this country. That is why we chose this place for the ceremony, among other reasons."

Ron saw the princess's father sitting on a large throne on the base of the cliff, near the roaring waterfall. There were also many other kings of the underwater worlds with their wives, dignitaries, leaders of the different tribes of Guyana, and other VIPs.

The ceremonial area was lit up with banners, flags, and tents fit for kings, and there was also a musical group with trumpets and all. A feast of food contoured around the tents, and the fires and the makeshift ovens all warmed up the official welcoming.

"Wow…is this all for me?" said Ron with his eyes wide open in astonishment.

Nodding with a big silly grin on her face, Serene said, "Welcome to the lost world, my future prince."

Ron was led to a royal tent by two young ladies dressed in simple-styled gowns in white satin, with a mermaid design that formed an embroidered border on the hem and bodice.

The light-gold royal tent had four golden lanterns inside on each corner, a round dark hardwood table at the center, and four royal sitting chairs bordering around it.

Princess Serene came into the tent with her hair up and wearing a slim-fitting sheath gown embroidered in gold and trimmed with black-and-white ermine tails at the hemline. It hugged her beautifully around her slender body as she walked toward him.

Ron was perplexed since this was the first time he saw any mermaid walking. "How is this possible? I never knew mermaids can walk." Ron pointed his right finger toward the area of her feet.

Princess Serene smiled, and with a bright gleam from her eyes, she said, "This is a secret that only a few know. You are special, and for that reason, the secret is being exposed to you. Every aquatic person here has that ability, and today is the day that it is being revealed." As she continued to speak, one of the two young ladies who led him into the tent earlier laid out on the round table a black uniform with cape and boots.

Both of the ladies left the tent, and the princess continued speaking, "Ron this uniform has been given to you by the ruler-judge Yan, and it will automatically fit to the form of your body as a second skin. The material is waterproof, fireproof, and can stand even a nuclear blast—not that I'm telling you to look for a bomb to try it out," she said, chuckling.

While walking toward the table, she pointed to Ron to sit across the table from her while lifting up the black uniform and pointing with her fingers toward the chest area.

Ron could see a gold-colored flaming sword's image emerging from the center of the uniform. Then she said, "This represents the sword that you will be given today, and as you can see at the back of the cape, the symbol of the five elements—the same one as your birthmark on your back, specifically on the right shoulder blade."

"How did you know that? Only a few people in this world know that," Ron said, looking at the princess with curiosity.

She smiled and said jokingly, "Watch out, Ron. You know what they say about curiosity…it can kill a cat."

"Come on, Princess, stop joking and tell me how." This time, he looked at her piercingly.

The princess stopped joking and looked at him seriously and said. "Sorry, Ron, I know that you also like to be private in your personal life, so let me tell you how I know. The ruler-judge Yan has told only my father and myself. This secret about your powers and the abilities you possess has been also entrusted to us. We are your second family, if you will have us. And if you permit me the honor to call you my brother, I—"

Ron cut her off, and with a smile and a nod, he said, "Sure, sis. I like it better than calling you princess every time we meet. Yeah, *sister* has a nice ring to it, and since you would be the first sister in my life, yes, Princess—oh, I mean, sister—I like it."

Ron got up and walked around the table and gave his newly found sister a brotherly hug.

The princess continued to explain the protocol of the ceremonial procedures he was about to embark: what he was to do when he received the sword and why he must assume a secret identity that protected his friends and family from becoming targets of his enemies.

She then stepped out of the tent so he could put on the new outfit. When Ron called the princess back in, she was amazed at how impressive he looked at 5'9", 185 pounds, with black hair. She said, "Brother, you look like a real superhero."

Ron then replied jokingly to her, "Sis, you can't print that word *superhero* for me since I heard only Marvel Comics and DC Comics share ownership for that phrase. I once looked that up and found that they have a United States trademark for the words *superhero* and *superheroes*. So you can probably say I'm just your *superbrother*—okay?"

They both laughed out loud, and the princess was almost doubling over with laughter pains as she grunted out, "The hell with them…you're in Guyana…and I, Princess Serene, bestow you the title of *superhero*."

This time, Ron doubled over with laughter pains as they both giggled and joked about being superheroes. The time flew by, and then a guard came to the tent and called out the princess's name.

She left the tent for only a minute then returned. She looked at Ron and said, "The ceremony will start in ten minutes. Now, you remember what you are supposed to do? Something is missing here…is it the uniform? How can you have a secret identity when everyone can see your face? Not good, not good."

While the princess was puzzling with her own question, Ron turned around and looked at a small mirror hanging on the tent and started to transform and morph his face with part of Shadow the cat's eyes and ears, like a mask covering the upper side face, leaving the mouth and jaw exposed.

Looking at his own transformation, he said to himself that this was both believable as a disguise and recognizable with facial expressions. He then turned around and looked at the princess and said, "Sister, is this okay?"

The princess put her hands over her mouth, her eyes wide open, as she started to jump up and down like a child on her bed and said, "Oh yes—yes, that is great! Brother, you look awesome!"

She then stopped jumping and looked at him seriously and said, "If I were your wife, I would be jelly. Oh yes, real jelly. You look so cute, brother."

The princess went over to Ron and gave him a big hug and said, "How about having a mysterious figure nickname, such as the Dark Ghost Who Walks, or the Cat Who Cannot Die, or ... maybe Guardian of the Dark Caribbean?"

Ron stepped back and looked at his new sister with his yellowish-brown cat eyes and smiled. "Princess, *Tex Element* is fine with me, or Shadow's Ghost is also nice. Those two names are mysterious enough, so come on, sis. We have a party to attend!"

Twelve king's honor guards—six on the right and six on the left—escorted Ron up the flower-laid path toward the throne. To the right of the throne was Prince Steven from the Aquatic Warsaw Kingdom, who was representing King Oscar. To his right side was the official coat of arms of Warsaw; and on its shield, it displayed a sword-wielding mermaid holding a golden shield in her left hand on a red field, with a large golden crown above on a white field.

On the left side of the throne stood Princess Serene, and by her side were two swords in its own scabbard.

The scabbard, also known as the sheath, is a protective cover provided for the sword blade, and it was made out of gold. The first scabbard on her left had a small shield bearing the coat of arms of Warsaw, and on her right was a shield bearing the coat of arms of Caribbean.

Arriving at the steps of the throne, six honor guards went to the right of the steps, and six went to the left, and they turned at attention to face the onlookers. Ron walked up the steps and stopped after the last fifth step. He bowed and kneeled with his right foot on the floor.

King Alexander of the Aquatic Caribbean Kingdom stood up from the throne and extended his left hand toward his daughter. She placed the scabbard that bore the coat of arms of their kingdom in his hand. He then took two steps toward Ron, stopped, and removed the king's sword out from the scabbard and placed the blade on Ron's right shoulder, and he said, "The Aquatic Caribbean Kingdom and the representatives of the eleven other kingdoms have acknowledged a new warrior in its presence. I, King Alexander, of the Aquatic Caribbean Kingdom, and those here present as witnesses will have the honor to see my new adopted son named Tex Element, whom I now bestow the title of Grand Prince in the Order of the Flaming Sword."

Then the king tapped Ron's right and left shoulder with the blade once and said, "Rise, Prince Element, and take your place next to me."

Ron stood up, bowed, and thanked the king. Then he walked in a slow movement toward Prince Steven and stood next to him. Prince Steven turned and congratulated Ron by shaking his hand.

Everyone in the audience clapped their hands in salutation, and the trumpets and the musicians started to play the national anthem of the Aquatic Caribbean Kingdom. While everyone was singing the national anthem, Prince Steven walked over toward Princess Serene and picked up the scabbard that contained the flaming sword and presented it to the king.

When the anthem was over, the king called out Prince Element to kneel before him again. The king then unsheathed the sword and handed it to the kneeling prince. At the same time, he said, "Prince Element, do you swear that this sword is to be used to act justly, defend the helpless, fight evil, protect widows and orphans, and avenge what is unjust?"

Ron said in a loud voice, "I swear."

Then the king continued, "Prince Element, do you also swear to fight evil and injustice from the living and the dead and those that are not of this world, even those who are the undead you will not let hide from just penances?"

Ron again said in a loud voice, "I swear."

While still kneeling, Ron handed the sword back to the king, who slid it into the scabbard and passed it on to Prince Steven. Then Prince Steven bent down and fastened the scabbard to Ron's belt.

Ron then stood up and, facing the onlookers, withdrew the sword, and made three infinity circular motions with it in the air. And while still holding the sword in front of him, he started to float up slowly, his body spinning until he was at least twelve feet in the air. He then elevated the sword high in the air and shouted out loud the words, "For justice!" And the flames shot out of the sword toward the heavens, and everyone was amazed.

He then floated back down, and when he touched the ground, he wiped the blade against his left arm before replacing it in the scabbard. He then faced the king, bowed, and turned around and began walking down the steps. As he landed on the last steps, the king's honor guard took their formation and escorted the new prince back toward his tent. On his way back, he shook the crowd's hands and thanked them all for coming.

Afterward, the people clapped their hands and shouted three times, "The Prince Tex Element!" Trumpets blew, music played, and singers at the ceremony offered hymns of praise.

As he entered the tent, he transformed his face back to normal. He then realized that there was another table in the right-hand corner of the tent with many entrées and desserts. He walked over to the table and picked up a small plate and filled it with different kinds of sweets. He had a sweet tooth.

Princess Serene entered with a beautiful lady wearing a gown that had spreading branches of oak leaves with acorns embroidered in gold, silver, and copper bullion thread on a white satin background. As Ron looked in admiration at the lovely lady, Princess Serene said, "Prince, I would like to present my favorite aunt, Queen Melusina from the Aquatic Warsaw Kingdom."

Ron put his plate on the table and walked over quickly to the queen and bowed and said, "Your Highness. This is an extreme honor to finally meet you. Your niece keeps on chewing my ears off with auntie this and auntie that. Your niece really loves you and thinks about you all the time."

"Thank you for the kind words, Prince Element. Please, let's be informal. You can call me Melusina. No bowing is necessary, and a handshake will be just fine."

The princess walked over to Ron and gave him a light slap on his shoulder, and with a big grin on her face, she said, "Squealer—I can't tell you anything."

"Sorry, Princess, I didn't mean to embarrass you. But it's true, and the queen—oh, I mean Melusina—had to know that she is blessed with a niece who loves her dearly, just as I am honored to finally have a sister who I know is not only a sister but a lifelong friend. There, I said it! Indict me!"

"Kiss my fanny, Prince. And come over here and give me one of your famous bear hugs. I need one now before you make me cry."

Ron rushed over to the princess and gave her a big hug. Then the princess grunted, "Prince, I need you to leave a little air in me before you crush me."

"Sorry, sis. Sometimes I forget my own strength."

As Ron stepped away, he pulled one of the chairs out from around the table and offered a seat to the queen. She thanked him as she sat down. Ron did the same for the princess. They sat and talked about Ron's abilities, and he was able to learn from the queen and the princess how to use his telepathy and extrasensory perception to a higher degree.

He learned how to use the Internet without a computer in his head, and he could see various television programs around the world without having to use a television. He also learned that the flaming sword also had transmutation abilities. Upon command, the sword would morph into whatever Ron required at the time. Examples include a shield, a parachute, a rope, a necklace, a bracelet, or a ring.

They told him he didn't need to have a secret base because he had the ability to serve a variety of functions in himself. He was his own command center, control room, crime lab, or laboratory. Because of the Internet, he had his own research library, information center, or communications center.

Why would he need a safe house when he could become invisible at the first sign of trouble? Why would he need additional weapons when he had the five elements and the flaming sword?

"So I guess I am a full-service hero with all the accessories and frills," Ron said jokingly while the others smiled and laughed.

Later that afternoon, Prince Steven joined the round table.

As the evening went by, Ron sensed that maybe Prince Steven had a crush on the princess, but he kept his mouth shut in case he would be accused of being a squealer again. Ron could hear the people enjoying their feast around the campfires and the joy of the music. Their songs and the hymns of praise for him started to put a solemn look on his face.

The queen saw this and asked, "Prince Element, what's wrong?"

Ron turned toward the queen and replied with his head slightly bent down, small tears dripping from his eyes, "I do not deserve these peoples' admiration. What I do is because I have been given these abilities, nothing more, and nothing less. I didn't deserve them. All these people believe in me, and I do not want to fail them. Do you understand what I'm trying to say?"

The queen got up along with the princess, each holding one of his hands; and with loving eyes toward Ron, the queen said, "You truly are a noble knight, a man of honor and virtue. Your humbleness shows the nobility in your character. There is no shame in feeling this way. Prince Element, I am a warrior of the ancient order, and I would be honored to fight by your side—anyplace, anywhere. So dry up those tears and let us rejoice. Come on now, let's celebrate!"

48

War Room and the Battle Begins

It rainstormed all that night. Ron stepped out of his tent, and he saw the wind had driven the rain everywhere in the campground. There was standing water and mud all over. Now it was early dawn, and the rain stopped, and Ron saw the natural wet spring jungle with clouds over the tops of the large trees and the green mountaintop hills and the sound of his tent roof. It was wet and dripping.

The sun came out once that early morning and shone on the decorative avocado woods beyond the ridge and waterfall before it went down. Ron watched the smoke puffs from the campfires into the sky above the tents of the royal guards near the king's tent, soft puffs with a blackish-gray flash in the center.

The celebration yesterday and the sight of the area now in the early morning took on a different aspect since all the guests left before nightfall, and no signs of the banners and flags that flew so proudly yesterday promenaded today. Ron thought, *All things must come to an end.*

Only the royal guards and a handful of troops were present at the campsite. Before Ron reached the large tent of the king farther down from the waterfall, the sun came back up. As Ron approached the tent, the four guards who protected the entrance saluted him with their right fist striking smartly the area of their chest.

As he entered the tent, he paid his respects to the king. "Your Majesty," he said as he bowed down. "What do you have for me today?"

"My prince," the king said, looking over a large map of Guyana on the wall of the tent, "come over here please, and take a look at this map."

In the tent, there were four generals of the king's army, who were over a large table in the center of the tent with another map outlining more details than the map on the tent's wall. Ron always wondered why his dad used to teach him military tactics and strategy when he was just a teenager. He never knew why he would ever need it. *Dad, I guess you knew what you were doing*, Ron thought.

He could see that this tent was a TOC; that is, a tactical operation center or a command center—in other words, a war room. Ron knew that this was a place where order was maintained, especially if the world around it was falling apart, which was likely to take place real soon.

His eyes started to scope the areas in the tent, and he could see twelve people sitting around a large table in the left side of the tent, monitoring large laptop computers and passing information to the generals. They were monitoring the environment in Guyana and reacting to events from the relatively harmless to whatever major crisis that came about. Their discipline caused them to use strict predefined military procedures in providing information to the generals.

Ron could see that it was the king who provided the leadership and guidance, ensuring the proper service and that military orders were maintained.

Ron remembered his dad's lesson when he talked about the different wars in history and the campaign that led up to these wars. His dad made it a point to emphasize that command centers should never be viewed as a mere information center or help and service desk. It was not a place where switchboard operators helped an organization's members maintain routine communications with one another.

While Ron walked toward the map area, he heard the king say in a strong but calm voice, "Give me a progress report on the second area."

It came from one of the generals. "No one has shown up there yet, and we have the place surrounded. It's a fortress."

The king nodded and said, "Good, that is excellent news." The king turned around to look at Ron and then smiled and said, "Son, did you have breakfast this morning?"

Ron told him no and that it was okay, but the king instructed one of his lady soldiers to bring coffee and a nice-size breakfast portion for the prince. And then he said, "Prince, we believe the evil spirits are heading in this direction near the Temple for Ages, which is located in this area."

He then pointed to an area near the northeast coast of Guyana. The king was pointing to New Amsterdam, located in the East Berbice-Corentyne region, about sixty-two miles from the capital of Georgetown, and it is one of the largest towns in Guyana. Looking at the scales of the map, Ron saw that it was located four miles upriver from the Atlantic Ocean, mouth of the Berbice River, and on its eastern bank, immediately south of the Canje River.

Ron could see that the jungle was intense in that area and very hard to penetrate outside this town. No wonder this area was picked for the temple, Ron thought.

Then a new report came in, and the generals' faces were solemn: "We have a report that there is a raven coming from the area of New Amsterdam and flying toward Georgetown—wait, the raven landed on a brown ship heading toward New Amsterdam. It looks like Dier is aboard."

"Who is Dier?" Ron asked as he faced the king. "And what does a flying raven have to do with this operation?"

As Ron was speaking, the lady soldier entered the tent along with four servants holding a pitcher of hot coffee and three trays of breakfast foods with plates, utensils, and cups. They set the breakfast items on a large table near the left side of the entrance, which had four chairs around it. The servants left, and the king motioned to Ron to sit down and start having some breakfast before he spoke.

Ron moved to the chair farthest away from the entrance as he faced the area of the maps. He wanted to say something, but the king smiled and put his right index finger on his mouth and moved his head left to right.

I guess that mean no, Ron thought.

Ron then poured a cup of coffee and extended his arm out with the cup to see if the king would have any. The king smiled and nodded and walked over to Ron and sat down.

After Ron gulped down his coffee and ravished five pancakes and eggs, he looked at the king with his eyes wide open; and with his head leaning toward the right, he smiled and let out an inquisitive look.

The king let out a robust laugh that shook his small belly. "Son"—he said in between his laugh—"you are very funny, and I'm so glad you are here. Okay, I will tell you."

The king explained to Ron about the three evil spirits that now possessed human bodies. One of them was named Dier. "We knew for sometime that he has attained the body of a congressman in Georgetown. The raven means that they have already killed the guard who was protecting the temple. So now we know that their next step will be to attack the second tribal area."

"Why should we wait until they attack the next area when we can start an offensive action now to avoid more bloodshed?" Ron said as he stood up from the chair and walked toward the map, focusing on the temple and seaport area. Ron looked at the king and said, "We could flank them—yes, we could flank them. All we need is two forces, one over here and the other over there, and I'll come over this area to draw them in." He pointed the location for the offensive action on the map.

The king and the four generals walked over to the map and looked at one another with surprise and nodded in agreement.

The king said, "This could work. Son, you are a tactical genius. To make this work fast enough for us, we would need the new spirit guards from Diyu. They could be there within the hour."

Ron looked at them and said, "We have time. The way you describe them to me, they would first celebrate their victory and rest the night in the area. The best time to get them is at an early morning raid."

Ron finished talking and went back for another serving of breakfast while the generals scrambled to the monitors to advise the underworld of their plan.

The king looked at his new son and was proud of what he saw. While Ron was sipping his coffee, both their eyes met. With a little nod from the king, attached with a grin, they both knew this new father-and-son relationship was off to a great start.

After he finished breakfast, Ron inquired of the king if there was anything else that was needed since he needed to call his wife and see how his father-in-law was doing.

The king thanked him and told him that he did a fine job, and if anything else came along to change the attack plans, he would send one of his guards to call on him.

As Ron stepped out of the tent, the sun was beating down hard, and he could see some of the puddles drying up. As he walked toward the rippling water and the roar of the waterfall, he smelled a heavily perfumed scent.

The scent resembled the smell of clove spice.

Ron looked down at the plants, which were growing on one side in a rosette pattern and color. The different leaf colors ranged from maroon through shades of green and to gold. On the other side, they were spotted with purple, red, and some cream, while the others had different colors on the tops and bottoms of the leaves.

A golden frog was leaping around the plant. Ron thought, *Mr. Frog must live here, so I guess these plants are bromeliads.*

Then Ron bent down, and with his right hand, he tried to pet the golden frog, saying, "Nice Mr. Golden Frog, come and say hello to your new friend. Tomorrow my hands will probably be stained, so let me pet you, my little friend, before the blood of the battle begins."

49

The Long and Winding Jungle Road

The rain was slacking, and the light infantry armies were moving along on a makeshift dirt road. The jungle area was thick with vines, brushes, and thorny hedges. The scout raised his right hand in a fist-like motion, signaling the column to halt.

After the general got his bearings, they started to move again; but seeing the rate of progress in the daylight, the general knew they were going to have to get off this makeshift dirt road someway and go across the jungle if they ever hoped to reach the site where they could flank the evil ones.

In the night, many more troops from Diyu had joined the column from the other dirt roads of the jungle; and in their columns, there were carts loaded with three cages, spears, hooks, and nets—all tied to the carts, being hauled by two black stallions on each cart. On some carts, the young student soldiers sat huddled from the rain, and others walked beside the carts, keeping as close to them as they could.

There were wild dogs who roamed the jungles, barking at the columns, keeping themselves dry under the wagon as they moved along. The road was muddy. The ditches at the side were high with water, and beyond the trees that lined the dirt roads, the open swamp field looked too wet and too soggy to try to cross.

The general, after looking at his map, told the driver to stop and give the two black horses a rest while he got down from the cart and walked up the road a way, looking for a place where he could see ahead to find a side road they could take across the jungle.

The map indicated that there were many side roads, but he did not want one that would lead to the camp of the evil ones.

The general then decided to ask the scout, but the scout was no real help because he could not remember this area since he always passed it quickly while riding his horse, and they all looked much alike as he rode in the breeze of passing trees.

The scout knew he must find one if they hoped to get through. No one knew exactly where the evil ones were or how things were going, but the general was certain that if the rains should stop, then their sound could carry, and the evil ones could probably hear them.

The rain was not falling so heavily now, and the general thought it might clear. The scout went ahead along the edge of the dirt road. And when there was a small dirt road that led off to the north between two swamp fields, with a hedge of jungle trees on both sides, he thought that they had better take it, and he rushed back to his cart. He told the scout to turn off and went back to tell the others troops.

"If this road leads nowhere, we can turn around and cut back in," the general said.

One of the drivers who were stuck in a muddy ditch worked his way out of the ditch ahead and moved along the narrow dirt road between hedges. It led to an old house on stilts. The house was low and long with a burial wreath over the front door.

There was a water well in the yard, and one of the student soldiers was getting water to fill up everyone's canteens. The old house standing on its stilts was deserted.

The general turned his head and looked back down the road. He saw that the old house was on a slight elevation above the plain, and he could see over the swampy plains the dirt road, the hedges, the sugarcane fields, and the line of jungle trees along the main dirt road where the troops were passing.

Two soldiers were looking through the house. One of the soldiers came out with a gold candlestick in his hand.

"Put it back," the general said.

The soldier looked at him, went in the house, and came back out without the candlestick.

"Where's your partner?" the general said, looking distrustful.

329

"He's gone to the latrine around the back."

The general ordered everyone back to their position and move out.

Just before dawn, they were stuck in a muddy road, and as nearly as the general could figure out, they were about a quarter mile to the ambush site. The rain had stopped, and the general ordered the gear and provisions to be unloaded from the carts and start to organize the area with troops on either side of the main dirt road and formulate the positions for flank movements.

Amabo watched the stars as they came out one by one and the moon as it rose, round and pastel, and moved like an empress across the sky. The night took its time to wear away, and the stars grew soft, and the moon dropped to repose in the wasteland of waters.

And at daydawn, Amabo looked toward the west; and midway between sky and sea, he thought he saw a figure of a man wielding a flaming sword, gliding above the land mists. And then the object seemed to float upon the edge of the sea, moving nearer and nearer.

Amabo looked at Isolep and Dier, who were also looking at the object. With a sense of fear moving up and down his newly possessed body, he said, "Oh shit—he's here!"

The evil ones grabbed their gear and started to run toward the muddy dirt road that led to the interior jungle. Amabo told the others to spread out, and they would meet later in New Amsterdam at the Little Rock Hotel. All agreed. Dier's little skinny body huffed and puffed his way through the jungle, praying that the person wielding the flaming sword would go after the others and not him.

They kept running down the muddy dirt road while the jungle vines and hedges on either side heard the splashes of their worn-out shoes in the puddles that aligned themselves with the road.

"I order you to halt," the general said.

Isolep stuck her tongue out to the general. She then grinned and showed him her fanny, and they just ignored the general and ran a little faster into the jungle.

The general opened up his holster, took the pearl-handle pistol, aimed at the one who seemed to be praying while running, and fired. He missed, and they all started to run in zigzag motions. He shot three more times and dropped one.

He blew his whistle, and the net fell on the two who looked like they were getting away. The one he dropped got up and went limping through the hedges and was out of sight. He continued to fire at him through the hedges as the injured person limped across the field. The pistol clicked empty, and the general put in another clip. He saw it was too far to shoot at the limping person. He was too far across the field, limping away, his head held low and his long black hair fluttering in the wind.

The general commenced to reload the empty clip and put his pistol back in his holster and said, "That's a lucky long-haired son of a bitch!"

PART XII

New Amsterdam and a Silent Run

50

New Amsterdam and the Dump
in the Pants

The hot Guyanese sun liquefied the earlier damped afternoon and what was left of the wet and soggy night while the clean brick pavements after the nights washing had Ron wondering what occurred the day before and in the early morning briefing and interrogation.

This small town he was in, consisting of three main roads and about a dozen cross streets, and had at least seven hotels rising up in the town's landscape, but the newest one built was called the Little Rock Suites on Main Street, not to be confused with the Little Rock Hotel in Vryman's Erven, which was now under their surveillance. The other hotel, the one on Main Street that had a similar name, brought about an additional conflict they needed to avoid.

Dier told Ron that the evil ones were supposed to meet up at the Little Rock Hotel; but to be on the safe side, they watched the Little Rock Suite, just in case Dier—after being under interrogation—made a mistake, which he did, in his pants.

Ron thought about the interrogation procedure, which should have been called a scare-shit-in-the-pants procedure. That went on this morning as he threatened Dier by shape-shifting into a large bear, whose teeth was beginning to penetrate the skinny man's throat.

Dier was so scared that he not only gave up Amabo's hideout, he also gave up the spirit who set their release in the underworld. He also told them that Amabo didn't help the Buddhist priest achieve his goal, but instead, "he threw him under the bus," as Dier explained it.

Dier was so scared he would have given up his father, mother, and any other brothers and sisters in the underworld he had left.

Before coming to New Amsterdam, Ron did a little information gathering on this town. He read on the Internet that it had a mayor and, as he could see while walking down the street, a thriving market.

He needed to know the escape routes out of this town. One could get to Crabwood Creek, which was about forty-five miles away via the Corentyne or to the East Canje area of Berbice. There was also a road that leads up the Berbice riverbank to the town of Mara, and that was about twenty-five miles south.

The logistics of knowing any escape plan in advance was another lesson his dad taught him. *Thanks, Dad, again*, Ron thought while a smile lingered on his face.

Since Amabo was wounded, he wouldn't go to a hospital where he could be found; but in case he did, the hospital was also under their surveillance.

New Amsterdam has a government-run hospital and has one of the nicest seaports too, Ron thought.

As Ron walked through the town, he saw many old colonial buildings, some dating back to the time of Dutch colonization. He saw a mission chapel that had been designated a national heritage site. This he found out by using the Internet.

Earlier, he went into a restaurant and used the bathroom, and he had to give a thumbs-up for being one of the best bathrooms he had used since he has been in this country. *They say New Amsterdam is known for having the best bathrooms in all of Guyana. I bet Dier would have loved to use it before we got a hold of him.* The thought of Dier's last expression brought a sweet smile to Ron's face.

As Ron walked around town, he passed the main schools in New Amsterdam, which was Berbice High School, and he saw the Berbice Educational Institute. He walk past Vryman's Erven Secondary while scooping out the hotel where Amabo was supposed to be in.

The last two schools he saw were the Tutorial Academy and New Amsterdam Multilateral High School, which the Internet said opened since 1975.

Ron then decided to sit down on the manicured lawn in an area called the Esplanade. That was the name of an open public ground west of Esplanade Road and immediately opposite an area called the Gardens.

To the senior citizens in this area, it would have evoked many pleasant memories of the time when it was immensely popular as a picnic resort and meeting place for the people of Berbice. Ron, looking at the stage platform in these public grounds, imagine that the bandstand there saw many splendid and well-attended performances of the British Guiana Militia Band.

Ron's mind wandered to yesterday after leaving the king's war-room tent, when he called his concerned wife. He was happy to hear that his father-in-law was recovering well from the operation, but it bothered him to hear that his wife had cried when she saw her dad in the recovery room looking lifeless on the bed, with the breathing apparatus attached to his face.

She had never seen her dad so helpless before, and the sight of him lying there with the oxygen mask over his face haunted her into heavy tears. She and her mother spent the day at the hospital until her dad told them to go home and relax and get some sleep. She was happy to see that the operation went well and that the results showed that there was no sign of recurring cancer in the area that was removed.

All her dad needed to do was rest, and full recovery would take its own time.

Just then, a squelching noise came over the earpiece Ron was wearing, and he heard the surveillance team at the hotel say that the subject was limping into the front hotel lobby with a large bag from the pharmacy in town. They wanted to know what they should do. Ron used his walkie-talkie and told them to stand down.

He then proceeded to walk toward the hotel. They had a makeshift command center in a building across the street overlooking the hotel. Ron had the other surveillance team abandon their previous observation areas and surround the Little Rock Hotel and have at least a five-block radius reconnaissance.

"Prince, how do you want to handle this?" said the general while looking with his large black binoculars through the window of the new command center.

"Have you seen any evidence of him carrying the *Book of the Dead* and any papyrus?" Ron asked as he went over the transcript of the information Dier gave them earlier during the interrogation.

"None was spotted on him. He may have hidden it, or it could be in his room," the general replied. He was receiving a call from one of his surveillance team members, and then he said, "He is in room number 6, my prince, and it is overlooking an alleyway in the back that he could try to escape through if cornered."

"Just cover the alleyway, and I have an idea on how to find the artifacts. Just tell the surveillance team that the prisoner Dier would be assisting us in capturing Amabo, and do not try to stop him while this prisoner enters the hotel. Please confirm all stations that you have understood this command."

"But, Prince, the prisoner is at the other headquarters, and how—"

Ron cut off the general and told him to just do as he instructed.

The general had a little inquisitive glance toward Ron but did as he was told to do.

All surveillance teams acknowledged back that they all understood the message. Then Ron looked at the general and told him to walk with him to the next empty room that overlooked a back stairs, and he closed the door.

In front of the general, Ron smiled and then slowly shape-shifted into the prisoner Dier.

The general took a step back. Eyes and mouth wide open, he said, "Mary, Joseph, and baby Jesus—what just happened here? My prince, are you still here... how ..."

Ron, in his new transformed body and still in his regular voice, told the general, "I'm still here, General. Don't be alarmed. It's a gift I possess, and very useful in tactical situations. As you can see, Amabo would think when he sees me that Dier has escaped, and then hopefully, he would provide me the information about the missing artifacts."

"Do I still call you *my prince*? And what do I tell the other soldiers in the next room when they ask where you are?"

"You tell them that I have stepped out to handle something else and that you were given this prisoner to accomplish the mission. Now you must make like I am the prisoner Dier and treat me like I was him. At no time will you reveal what has happened here. I will now change my voice to match his pattern of speaking and transform my clothes to look like the clothes we captured him in, minus the *poop* in his pants." Ron looked at the general, flicking his eyes up and down; and with a silly grin, he finally said, "Do you understand?"

The general nodded in acceptance and, at the same time, scratched his head. Then with his right hand, he tried to compress and comb back the receding hairs on his head. He then grabbed Ron by the arm and led him into the command center and spoke to the soldiers manning the communication and surveillance lines, "This is prisoner Dier, and I want him to be treated with respect while he is here. He is a major asset for the completion of this mission, and I would court-martial anyone who does differently. Am I read loud and clear?"

Everyone stood at attention and, in unison, said out loud, "yes, sir!"

51

The Little Hotel That Rocks

"The news said, 'Gunmen rob owner, staff of Little Rock Hotel, and TV station.' Okay," said Ron as he approached the Little Rock Hotel, "let's see what else the Internet provides on this hotel."

> Gunmen launched an attack on the Little Rock Hotel in New Amsterdam on Friday night, escaping with cash, jewelry, and other items valued in excess of $2 million.

That's got to be Guyanese dollars, Ron thought.

> According to the reports, the attack started just before midnight when a man walked into the hotel's bar and started checking out the people who were there. He then walked outside and joined three other men, who were masked and armed with handguns. They ran in…

All right, this hotel seems to be prone to arm robberies. Let's see what other information is available.

A big fire damages the Little Rock Hotel: Vryman's erven, New Amsterdam—The speedy action of the Guyana Fire Service prevented what could have been a tragedy when fire began at the Little Rock Hotel and Television Station in Vryman's Erven yesterday.

"I thought something was a little off when I saw the large antennas on the building. I can see before walking in that the TV station is located on the first floor. Let me see what else is on the article," Ron thought out loud.

The fire may have started in the area of one of the rooms on the first floor of the building that houses Channel Ten...

The fire service is still probing the cause. There was a media personality staying there, and she said that she was sleeping in her bedroom when she heard the loud screams earlier that morning, and then she observed the smoke. Another lady with her husband, who was returning from a celebration, saw the fire service getting to the hotel on time and preventing any additional damage, even though the loss seems to be very substantial.

When the other news reporter arrived on the scene, the fire was quenched, but the first-floor area of the building was seriously blackened on the external areas.

Bedroom furnishings and other items were being carried to another building across the street by the staff and those who resided in the hotel. Channel Ten was off the air for several hours, but no one has claimed that the television station suffered any damages.

Ron continued reading other information regarding the hotel. He saw that the hotel began operating around the 1980s, and then it expanded in 2005 with the Little Rock Suite on Main Street.

He was happy to see that the entrepreneurial spirit was still alive in Guyana. All entrepreneurs, when they try to be successful in their business, seem to come under the "Ron's prone theory." They are either *prone* for more government regulations and taxes, or they become *prone* for arm robberies. Either way, they are susceptible to persons or entities that are envious and greedy—the government bureaucrats who want to take from what they *can't* build and the criminals who take from what they're too *lazy* to build.

Ron thought that the owners of this company must be strong leaders, strong enough to deal with the robbers and gunmen who seemed to plague society—a problem now spreading all over the globe.

The people should have a voice in government, especially the poor. But the poor are being led by people who claim they have their interest at heart. They are led to believe that putting money into a problem would help alleviate the situation. For decades, the government of the United States has been doing just that. Money, money, and more money—and the poverty rate hardly moves. Why?

The politicians who are using that method of solution know that they can continue their excuses since the people who they are supposedly trying to help—the poor—are now just focusing on who is dancing with the stars or who is on the tonight shows. The "what's in it for me" attitude is destroying all the nations in the world.

It is the entrepreneurs who provide jobs so that the poor can have an opportunity to lift themselves out of poverty. But government tries to destroy this type of thinking by running down any ideas that take away government dependence and entitlements. So the rich must pay their "fair share" so that the government can keep controlling the poor.

Every time Ron heard the words *fair share*, he knew what followed was a government scam or a politician who wanted to be elected. Ron knew the judicial courts also had a problem. When judges are appointed and not elected, they are also *prone* to legislate from the bench. They ignore the people's will and put their own two cents into legislative areas where they don't belong. They fulfill their own personal agendas. So what about the poor? Is there anything they can do?

Then there is education. It is controlled by most societies from the government. And if not by the government directly, then by major unions that pay the government's politicians to rule or legislate what is in the union's best interest. The union then claims to the public that they are for the children. But the children are then being used by the government at an early age, with a curriculum that teaches them to conform to the government's ways of thinking. This procedure and the government's indoctrination then gradually remove, little by little, the parents' rights over their own children. A sad state for any nation.

"Okay enough," Ron whispered to himself. He knew that this criminal on the loose needed his undivided attention—*now*!

Ron knocked on room number 6, and a voice on the other side said, "Who is it?"

And Ron said, "It's me, Amabo... Dier. Hurry up and open the door. I don't want to be seen standing out here all day."

Ron heard the movement of a heavy object behind the door scraping its way toward the side of the door, and then the sound of the latch moving. There was a slow peekaboo opening of the door, an arm reaching out to him, grabbing him and pulling him into the room, shutting the door, putting the latch in place, and moving the dresser to barricade the room's door.

"What's wrong with you, Amabo? Are you becoming paranoid?" Ron said to him as he walked over to the bed and plunged himself down on it.

"How did you get out? I saw you and Isolep get captured. Where is she?" Amabo said, his eyes wide open and his hand gripping his sword very hard.

"You know Isolep with her emotional behavior and her defiance of authority. She kept sticking her tongue out to everyone and finally pulled her pants down to show her fanny, which was great, because she distracted the soldiers and gave me a chance to slip away without being noticed." Ron smiled and opened his eyes wide to show how clever that move was.

Amabo thought for a second and nodded. He laughed and said, "That Isolep, she is great, always full of tricks. We are going to have to get her back."

Then Amabo's face became very stern as he looked at Ron and said, "How did you know what room I was in? I never told you the room number, and you couldn't have gotten it from the front desk because I registered under another name—so how?"

"Relax and take a chill pill, boss. I was watching the hotel, and I saw you come in with a bag. Then I followed to see what room you were in. Then I waited awhile to make sure you were not followed or compromised," Ron said as he walked to the bathroom to make like he was going to take a piss.

347

"Okay, that makes sense," Amabo said, limping back and forth around the room, trying to think.

"How are you feeling, boss? Were you able to fix the wound in your leg?" Ron said as he washed his hand in the sink then exited from the bathroom and sat down on one of two chairs next to a table in the corner, whose window above overlooked the back alley.

"The leg is okay. It's just a flesh wound. Hurts like a son of a bitch, but I cleaned the area with peroxide and bandaged it up," Amabo said as he limped over to the refrigerator and poured himself a glass of orange juice. He then looked at Ron and said while sticking out the orange juice container, "Want some?"

"No, thanks, boss," Ron said, eyeing the room.

This hotel offered basic hostel-style rooms, no air-conditioning, but it came equipped with a refrigerator, television, and phone. The bed seemed clean, and the walls were plain, and the rug had a fresh smell.

Ron said, "Boss, why the cheap accommodation and next to a TV station? Couldn't you at least get a room with air-conditioning?"

Amabo, with his head low and in a deep concentrating mood, looked up nonchalantly and said, "I needed a place off the main road and, at the same time, be in a high-volume profile place to fool whoever may be tracking me. Now shut up! I have to think." He got up and looked out the window.

Even though the room was a little larger than a prison cell, Ron thought that Amabo had a step up for now and

that the future room life was grooming him for—*hello*—
would be a step down cell. The thought put a smile to
his face.

"What are you smiling about? There is nothing funny
about this situation," Amabo said as he stared at Ron.

"Boss, I was only smiling about Isolep and her wagging
her funny tongue. Come on, boss, lighten up. By the way,
where are the artifacts? Are they in a safe place?"

"Yeah, yeah, they are safe. Don't worry," Amabo replied
as he continued to look out of the window.

"Safe…where are they?" Ron said insistently.

"They are buried near the Berbice River adjacent to
Waterside Street, close to the Buried Field. Don't worry,
we'll get them, but first I need to figure out how we can get
Isolep out. Let me think!" Amabo limped over to the bed
and plunged down on it.

Ron gave Amabo a few minutes to think as he looked at
the room. *At least there are no roaches camped out here*, Ron
thought. He then said, "Boss, if we had the *Book of Going
Forth by Day*, we would have maybe the power to get Isolep
out and accomplish our mission. What do you think? Could
that be the answer we need? Hmnn?"

"You're a genius, Dier, a real genius."

Amabo got up and gave Ron a big wet kiss on his head.

Ron thought this was the second time someone called
him a genius this week, and he smiled like a little boy so
that Amabo could see Dier's skinny face reflect a smile,
which made his little head look awkwardly silly.

Amabo limped over to the bathroom and poured cold water on his face, patted it dry with towel, and said to Ron, "Let's get the artifacts and move toward the second site." He pushed the dresser away from the door and grabbed his gear. "We're out of here."

As Amabo limped down Vryman's Erven, his face gleamed while his long black hair limped along with him. He believed that there was a light in the tunnel, and it was shining on them right now. Their goals were going to be achieved.

They just passed the Buried Field, and they waited for the cars to pass and then started to cross over Waterside Street. The Berbice River, with its blue-colored water, jumped out to greet them, saying, *Hello. What a nice day for a swim.* The hot Guyanese sun patted their sweat-filled clothes down as a policeman patted down a criminal before taking them to jail.

A small empty shack by the river was the landmark for the buried treasure. Six steps limping toward the north and six steps limping toward the west marked the location for the buried treasure.

As Amabo took out a small collapsible shovel to dig out the items, he told Ron to be on the lookout for strangers or cops. Pulling out a large bag from the sandy shore, Amabo raised his limping body up and started to move toward the empty shack to look inside the bag to make sure everything was there.

"Dier, we got everything, and now we can get to the second site and have the power to release Isolep. Isn't that great? We will see her real soon."

Amabo's back was turned away from Ron. While Amabo kept talking, Ron changed back to Tex Element with the catlike face and said to Amabo with a smile on his face, "You are right about seeing Isolep. I'll make sure you will have a bird's-eye view in the cell next to her."

"What are you saying, Dier?"

Amabo turned around, his eyes wide open with a look of astonishment on his face. He then said, "Oh shit—it's you again."

Ron continued his smile and said, "Shit happens."

52

The Silent Run to Nowhere

A careful silence surrounded Diana Diamond. Her dad being operated on, a psycho stalking her, and a husband out saving the world wasn't what she thought she had signed up for. Life's many turns created different paths, and three of them seemed to be encountering dark clouds and much indecision.

Her husband called to let her know everything was going as planned and that he would be home soon. He asked about her dad and wondered how the business was going without him and if they missed him. She told him he was missed, and as soon as he got back, they should spend a little alone time together. He loved the idea, and then he said before he hung up that he loved her, and then his voice lingered as a faraway echo of a previous life.

She ran through the cut grass on her property and went down and around the back roads across County Road 23, a favorite place for her to run. There was no sign of any other person in the area on this April day, a much-needed day off.

She ran down toward Crystal Lake Road and made a left, a familiar path in the crest of the forested hills lined with trailers and log cabin homes and beside the rippling ten-mile river waters. The cool air was warmed by the early sun on the hilltops, and in the deep shading area, it was suddenly cool. Sometimes the air was warm on her face and cool on her legs at the same time.

The world these days was not quite still beneath Diana as she walked. It seemed steadier when she ran.

As Diana ran through the sunny day, bright sparkles of light danced through the leaves. The path had flashes of light and, in other places, lined with the shadows of thick tree trunks. Ahead of her were five deer on the go, four were babies, and one of them was a pointed buck clearing the path for the little ones.

They all raised their backside, showing off their little white streamers while they bounced themselves away through the deep green forest road. Delighted seeing them all bounce, Diana smiled and hopped herself.

Motionless as a deer with headlights focused on it, Glen sat among the rotten, fallen tree logs on the hillside above the river. He could see two hundred yards of the running path, the lenses of his field glasses flashed against the reflection of a home-produced metal sheet covering a hidden well down by the road's path.

He was the one who first saw the deer jump, and as they passed him up the hill—and for the first time in several days watching the area—finally he saw Diana Hemingway in the flesh, jogging with a purpose that radiated in her face.

Below the binoculars, his face did not change expression, but his nostrils flared with a deep intake of breath as though he could catch her scent at this distance. He would breathe in and hold it for a moment. Then, little by little, he would release the air through his mouth while a hiss passed through his lips.

The breath brought him the smell of the forest leaves with a hint of mint in them, the beading grass beneath, and the gently decaying forest mast, a trace of rabbit bits from yards away, the deep stench of a shredded skunk skin beneath the rotten tree trunks, but not the scent of Diana, which he could have identified anywhere, since their presence was parked outside his house.

He saw the deer go ahead of her, and he saw them leaping long after they had left her sight. She was in his view for less than a minute, running easily, not fighting the pavement of the road. An insignificant day pack on her shoulder, with a bottle of water cupped at its side, made her seem like she belonged to the forest roads and the trails to nowhere.

Tracking her with his binoculars, he picked up a sunburst off a shiny object by a trailer home below, which left him seeing spots for at least one minute. She disappeared as the path tilted down and away. The back of her head was the last thing he saw, the tied ponytail bouncing like the streamer of a white-tailed deer.

Glen remained still, and he made no attempt to follow her. He had her image running clearly in his head, and he could run that image in his mind for as long as he chose to do so. He then lay back in the brush and fallen branches with his hands behind his head, watching the heavy foliage of a pine tree above him shivering against the sky. So dark was the sky it seemed as if it was almost green.

Glen closed his eyes to see again the deer romping ahead of Diana. He imagined she was the deer dancing down the path, shadowing the golden sun behind her, but this image was the wrong deer being her. This little deer should have an arrow in it, pulling against the rope around her neck as he led it to the axe. And then this little deer would stop tormenting him with her presence.

Yes, yes, yes.

The thought was so delicious in his mind that he could not be still anymore, and he got up, his hands and mouth stained with a killing desire. That taste wandered while his mouth turned down in a shape of a sobering child. He looked again for Diana down the path while he took a deep breath through his nose again, but this time, he took in the cleansing scent of the forest.

He stared at the spot where Diana disappeared. Her path seemed lighter than the surrounding woods, as though she had left a bright place behind her; but for her future, he knew a dark place was being crafted in front of her.

He climbed quickly to the ridge and headed downhill on the other side toward the parking area near the mechanic shop where he had left his truck. He wanted to be out of this area before Diana returned to her home, which was about a tenth of a mile away from the mechanic shop and down County Road 23.

Glen then parked beside an old abandoned Chevy parked in a driveway in a white vacant Cape Cod home. He left his motor running. He crossed the roadway and saw that her car was locked and looked hunkered down over the driveway pavement as though it were asleep. Her gray car amused him.

He looked around both sides. Not seeing anyone, he unfolded his flat steel slim jim and slid it down into the door above the lock.

Alarm? Yes? No? Click. No.

Glen got into her car, into air that floated Diana Hemingway's scent around intensely. The steering-wheel cover was very cute, he thought. It was a black red-dress-waving-kitty-design wheel Cover. It was black in color featuring a waving Hello Kitty in a red dress and a bow. He then stared at a designer sticker on her dashboard.

He looked at the design with his head tilted like that of a parrot, and his lips formed the words *Hello Kitty*. He smiled and took another deep breath.

356

He then sat back on the front seat covers, which were pink and black with pink hearts, coupled with foam back feel, featuring three hearts in the middle.

He moved his body, grinding down slowly in the seat covered with a high-polyester and machine-washable cover. He closed his eyes, breathing deeply again, his eyebrows raised. He moved his head back and forth, as though he was listening to a classic Steppenwolf music. Then the pointed pink tip of his tongue appeared, as though it had a small rattlesnake mind of its own—hissing, finding its way out of his face without modifying his facial expression.

Glen's thoughts were mindfully floating in the air, unaware of his movement, as he leaned his body forward, inaugurating the steering wheel cover by scent and licking with his tongue the areas where Diana's palms would rest while driving.

He tasted with his mouth the sweet scent of her sweating hands on the designer Hello Kitty wheel cover.

Then he leaned back in the seat, his tongue slowly moving back in the cradle where it belonged. While closing his mouth, he moved his tongue in the hidden crevices of his mouth as though he were savoring fine wine.

Before exiting and locking Diana's Nissan Altima, Glen took a deep breath and held it and did not exhale until his truck was out of the area. He wanted to hold her scent in his mouth and lungs until it became the right time for him to exhale her life forever.

53

Rooms and a Burger

While the prisoner was being transferred to a holding cell, Ron thought he might take a break and enjoy a little relaxation in New Amsterdam. A little sleep wouldn't be bad for a start. He started to check out the advertisements on the Internet.

> Guyana is nestled in the Amazon jungle that is teeming with wildlife and barely touched by mankind. Nearly 80 percent of this country is tropical rain forest, and it is the perfect vacation destination for outdoor adventurers. Outdoor enthusiasts will enjoy pristine rivers, cascading waterfalls, and breathtaking vistas, and may even spot some rare wildlife. After wrapping up your day of adventure, check into one of the area hotels.

Okay, that seems like a good idea, Ron thought until he saw a blog about a hotel.

Wilhelm Vision Hotel: WORST hotel in Guyana!!

Had to stay in New Amsterdam for 2 nights recently since I live thirty miles away and was traveling with college friends. We made a choice based on web available information and Man-oh-Man we finally arrived at the bottom-less pit!

So we are writing this blog to prevent others from having this horrible experience, don't get me wrong, there are other places nicer and a lot cheaper within a block's range!

Guyana's Hotel are great but this one has gone the way of 'pigs playing in their pens.'

All right, maybe I'm better off going back to Grandpa's home or back to the campgrounds at the King Edward VIII Falls. As he started to go to the makeshift command center, a growling in his stomach indicated he needed to eat. He then again checked the Internet, and he saw the following:

BB Burgers (City Mall)

Okay, to begin with the City Mall's food court is always packed and hectic. It is hard to find a seat which is always problematic there. But that was not the biggest problem. The cashier at the BB Burgers' stall has to go!

I mean, when people are frustrated or angry I tend to tell myself they had a bad day so I should be less of a bother. I approached the scary-looking cashier to order, "A chicken burger, with cheese and fries, and a drink" – the classic.

I thought she was just the cranky type but at this point it appeared she was the unprofessional type. Right after I stated my order she ignored me, turned around to talk to the cooks behind her then had the audacity to ask, "Wha you seh you want?"

I never answered, just walked away – she was lucky I wasn't that hungry because some good Guyanese answers would have come out.

I wouldn't recommend eating in the mall with your family; you can if you're alone or with a couple of friends but geez! That lady! If you want a BB Burger which to me is one of the best, I recommend you go to their Waterside Street location, beautiful atmosphere, scenic and some really great staff. (John Ramos)

Okay, then I'll go to the Waterside Street location, Ron thought. As he arrived, he saw a three-story building that housed the BB Burgers fast-food service on its ground floor and the Heavenly Cocktail Bar on the top floor. He saw that it was a fairly new building. As he approached the counter, there were two customers in line before him.

Looking around, Ron saw one of the corner white tables with green edges. There was a man who sat there eating. He was short, fat, almost bald, who had a "Born to be Wild" short-sleeve shirt. His belly spilled over his tucked-in shirt and tight belt. His face looked like the triple chin of an overweight man with a high-blood-pressure trouble ready to explode. To make matters funnier, he wore a tattoo on his right arm that said, "Born to eat."

Every time he breathed, his chest would expand, and the sounds from his lips were like that of a heavy snorer. He had short hands and stubby fingers, and one of his hands was grappling with the burger while the other was busy picking his nose and pulling at hairs in his nostrils.

Ron turned around and walked out of the establishment, thinking, *I guess today I'm born to go hungry.*

As he walked down Main Street and passed the marketplace, a squelching noise came over the earpiece he was still wearing, and he heard command center calling him in. The thought of going back to the center was enticing for Ron since they had coffee, coffee cakes, and other pastries he could munch on. He smiled to himself and thought, *I guess now* hunger *is not part of my vocabulary.*

He picked up his pace with a little bounce and a smiling face. He whistled the Spanish tune "O' Solo Mia," which meant "only mine," thinking about the pastries he'd be gulping down today.

PART XIII

Good-byes and the Battle

54

Time to Say Good-bye

The day was forecast to be sunny and clear. Ron rose early, even before the sun, to check his equipment and pack his little waterproof traveling bag and reflect on how everything went.

The king and all the royal dignitaries' bade Ron Godspeed with a festive roast the night before. Medals were bestowed to Ron from the king, the ruler of Diyu, and the other royal families. All the toasts had been made and farewell said—all but one.

In the doorway of his tent, Princess Serene handed him a waterproof pouch. In it was a change of clothes, bread to eat, and fruits to munch on. "The trip may be boring," she said. "I should get you some books to read."

Ron stopped her. "Princess, remember I use the Internet."

"Then I should pack some more food for you."

"Food is not a problem."

Ron thrust out his chest, along with a silly grin on his face. "People will be eager to feed a prince."

She stopped and smiled at his uniform. "You don't look like much of a prince now. You look more like a hero type."

Ron stood before her, ready to leave, smiling tenderly toward her.

"There's one more thing," the princess said with a start. "Please wait."

She hurried to the table inside her tent. She came back a moment later with a gold chain and a shield-shape locket with the king's and her picture in it. The locket belonged to her mother. Ron knew she valued it more than anything in her life.

"Take this with you, my prince."

"Thanks," Ron tried to joke, "but where I'm headed and what I'll be doing, a locket isn't something I usually wear."

"Where you're headed, my prince, you will need it all the more because we will always be with you. This locket also has special powers that, in the future, you might need."

Ron thanked her and put the locket and the pouch she gave him inside his traveling bag.

"I never thought I would ever say good-bye to you," she whispered, doing her best not to cry. "I thought we would have more time, like brother and sister, together here."

Ron drew the Princess close and tenderly kissed her on her forehead. He felt her body tremble in his arms. He knew she was trying to be valiant. There was nothing more to say.

"So…" Ron took a deep breath and smiled. They looked at each other for a long while, and then he remembered his own gift. He went into the traveling bag and took out a framed picture drawn by Raj. He told Raj to draw a picture of Princess Serene and him together like brother and sister since he knew he had seen her before.

Raj was able to capture her essence in the drawing, and the likeness of Ron was also remarkable. He had it delivered on a same-day messenger service to New Amsterdam, and then he had it framed and waterproofed.

She took it. Her bright brown eyes were moist with tears. He threw his pouch over his shoulder and tried to drink in the last sight of her beautiful, glistening brown eyes. "I love you, sister."

"I love you too, my brother. I can't wait for my next drawings." She jumped up and down like a little child.

Ron started toward the dirt road by the river and turned around and took a long last look at the campgrounds, the tents with its royal banners, and the roaring waterfall.

He was happy here. He gave a last wave to the princess. She stood there, hugging the picture close to her body. Then Ron did a sliding dance-walk, like a salsa move, to break the mood. He continued to walk; then he swung around a final time to catch her laughing.

Her long dark hair down to her waist and over her dress of white satin and silver tissue and crusty silver lace, with that courageous smile accompanied by a tinkling little-girl laugh, was the image he wanted to carry with him back to the realm of Narrowsburg.

55

The Battle of the Giants Took Its Course

She came to, to the sound of rushing waters and the gentle tweet of birds singing the early morning praises of the warm sun above.

She opened her eyes slowly. It was still morning. She had fallen into a deep ravine, far below the level of County Road 23. Her back was twisted against a tree, and she could barely move. A wound ached horribly on the side of her head.

Why am I here? Am I dreaming? What happened? Diana kept repeating those questions in her mind.

Then she remembered leaving home early this morning to go to the post office and to get a quick bite to eat in town. She remembered starting her car and pulling out of the driveway. She remembered that she was doing around fifty-five miles per hour before reaching the curve that went downhill. She applied the brakes to slow the vehicle down to the appropriate speed, and then a popping sound.

Her brake pedal hissed its way to the vehicle floor and just died there.

Instead of slowing down, her vehicle accelerated down the steep hill, and she tried to control the steering wheel while frantically pulling up the emergency brakes to slow down the vehicle speed. All she heard was metal rubbing against metal, but the speed still continued.

She then shifted the gears to low drive, and the sound of the transmission screamed to be set free.

She saw what was up ahead, another small curve and the crossing bridge over the brook before Luxton Lake Road turned off.

The vehicle did slow down a little, but she knew she could not control the steering wheel at this speed. The speedometer read eighty-five miles per hour. She released her seat belt, opened the door, and jumped out screaming, "Geronimo!"

And that was the last thing she remembered.

Her back that was twisted against a tree was starting to grow numb, and she tried to move, but she ached. The wound that ached horribly on the side of her head was now dripping blood. She tried to be positive in this situation, so she smiled and said to herself, "I'm alive…so what else could go wrong?"

As soon as she thought about it, a disturbing roaring sound seemed to be headed her way.

Maybe it's a small tractor purring its way up to me, she thought. *And maybe who is on it could help release me from the clutches of this gripping tree.*

She again tried to smile, but the ache seemed to travel from the side of her head to the area where her lips were located.

Again, she heard the deep rumbling from the woods.

"Who's there?" she shouted out. "Who is it? help!"

There was no reply. She tried to focus on the spot in the woods where the sound was coming from, trying to make out any silhouette.

Who would be out here so early in the morning? she thought, hoping it might be some roaming deer. *They are so pretty.*

Then, as she focused through the brushwood and trees, there was a set of eyes. Eyes not human at all but large as large brown eggs—buttery, narrow, and fuming. Her blood froze.

Then it moved! She heard the shrubs and dry leaves crunch under its feet. The thing took a step out of the forest and became very clear.

Dark brown, white tips, and hairy.

Holy shit! It's a grizzly bear! It was not thirty paces away.

Its buttery eyes were trained on her, and she wondered if he was protecting his supply of food or inspecting her as if she were its next meal. She heard a growl. Then it was deathly still.

371

This five-hundred-pound entity, she knew, was about to charge! She was certain of it. She tried to clear the cobwebs in her head. She could not possibly fight such a monster. With what? It stretched almost six and one-half foot high, and it could slash her to pieces with its razor-like claws.

Grizzly bears, she knew, are especially dangerous because of their strength and their bite. She was once told that a bite from a grizzly could crush a bowling ball. The thought of her head and that of a bowling ball didn't inspire happy thoughts.

Her heart was pounding rapidly, and at this moment, it was the only sound she heard other than the beast's low-slung growl. It took another step toward her. The bear's homicidal eyes never left her own. It was deliberate, and it was tracking her little movement.

God, help me. What can I do?

She couldn't flee. It would run her down at the first moment she tried. She looked quickly around. There was no one to hear her shout for help.

Her eyes searched for any strong tree to climb, but she didn't want the grizzly to figure out her intent. She could sense its fierce, hot breaths. She remembered the Sub Commander mini boot knife—two and a half inch, with a satin double-edged blade—that Ron bought her so that she could practice the combat moves he taught her. Even though it was five inches overall, the blade was only two and a half inches.

She slowly grabbed the knife from her right boot. She didn't know if it would hold up against the grizzly's hide, but then again, it was a weapon—sort of.

The bear grunted twice and flashed its teeth at her. A pronounced hump appeared on his shoulders; rich saliva drippings came from its jaws. He was big, bad, and determined.

"I do not want to die. Not like this. Please, God, do not make me fight this thing," she kept repeating to herself.

She felt so much *alone.*

Then, with a last deep roar, the grizzly seemed to understand that—and it charged.

All she could do was pull herself behind the tree that her back was twisted against. She barely escaped the first wave of violent gnash of the grizzly's terrifying teeth.

She stabbed and thrust wildly at the bear with her knife. She was able to tear at its face and neck and, at the same time, doing everything she could to repel its growling jaws. The bear's appetite for her made him lunged savagely. He kept coming again and again, and she kept piercing him with her knife—again and again. All the while, she kept backing around the tree until the bear's jaws ripped into her left boot, and she cried out until the air deflated from her lungs.

"Oh my God, oh my God!" she cried out in pain.

There was no time to inspect the wound on her left leg. The monster kept slamming into the tree and into her again, but this time, goring her left hip area. She screamed out in pain and shouted out, "Lord, please help me!"

She tried a karate-kick at it and continued to slash and thrust her blade. The beast backed away for a second and then lunged forward. Its teeth fastened on her left leg again and started to shake its head back and forth, as if it was trying to tear her leg out of its socket.

With her right foot, she kicked herself away from the bear. She tried to get up and run, but her legs had no power. She could see her blood being spattered everywhere.

Somehow she was able to limp across a bush area with more trees cuddling together, providing better cover for her defense, but her strength was nearly worn out. Her left hip area was in pain and felt like it was on fire.

This is it, she thought.

She fell to her right side and pressed her body up so that her back was against another tree, waiting for the end to come.

Beside the tree, she saw a one-inch round branch that was five feet long with leaves attached to it. It must have broken off from the tree from her fall. She reached for it, even though it didn't seem much like a weapon, and quickly cleared the front leaves off it with her knife and made a pointed end on it.

When she was done with it, she stared back at the angry, growling bear and said, "Come now, you piece of shit. I can't wait to tear you a new asshole. What are you waiting for? Come on, chicken shit. Finish what you started!"

Her mind flashed to her training, which seemed like yesterday. She held the tree branch like a spear.

"Come to Mama, Papa Bear," she shouted at the bear again. "Come and fuck with me. I am ready. Let's see who wears the cojones here. Take your best shot."

As if to please her, the beast made another charge.

Diana controlled her breathing; it was still. She offered no defense except to raise the new spear at the form soaring toward her. Harnessing all her remaining power, she thrust the spear-like tree branch with all her might at its eyes as she shouted out loud, "Take that, you son of a bitch. Who is your daddy now?"

The beast stood on its hind legs and raised his head up to the sky while letting out a blood-chilling cry. He was wounded, and she knew she had actually hurt it. The spear stuck in his right eye while the bear was taken aback. It shook its head wildly up and down and sideways, trying to rid itself of the spear in his eye.

She then lunged at the bear, grabbing her knife in her right hand, and with whatever strength she had, stabbed at its throat and face, at anything she could strike, while shouting, "Take this, you motherfucker—and eat this, you piece of shit!"

Again and again, she thrust and slashed the beast with her knife.

The blood oozed out of its dark-brown fur, each knife thrust striking home, while its roars and painful cries started to diminish.

The grizzly bear stumbled while still trying to swing its head free of the spear. With a newfound strength, Diana jumped on the bear like one who was possessed and, at the same time, continued to slash, thrust, and tear every dark-fur part of this creature.

The beast's blood now mixed with her own, like a baptism of blood. It became airborne, and the timberland had a new dusting to go along with the active stream. Finally the grizzly's hind legs crumpled, and his body crashed and fell to the earth. Diana took the spear out of the grizzly's eyes and forced it deep into the bear's skull. A dying snarl came out of its dreadful sharp-toothed mouth.

Diana just knelt next to the fallen body, washed out of all her strength. She was stunned and lay there quietly as if time just stood still. Then she let out an exhausted shout, "Thank you, Lord, for the victory. Thank you…"

Her head and body plunged down on the earth's bloody ground.

Diana was badly wounded, and her blood ran freely from her left hip area and left leg. She had to make it out of the ravine, or she knew she would die there.

Ron's face appeared in her mind as she approached the crossing bridge. Ron knew. She smiled as she reached out to touch the invisible him. *Here is the way*, he whispered. *Come to me now.*

Her limp body gave out while her mind swam in oblivion, and the battle of the giants took its course.

"Is she dead?"

A voice crept through the haze. A woman's voice. Diana opened her eyes, but she couldn't make out a thing, only a fluctuating blur.

"I don't know, honey," another said.

"But her wounds are severe. She might not make it. Did you call 911?"

"Yes, they are on their way," remarked the first.

Diana blinked, her brain slowly starting to clear. It was as if there were flickering curtains reflecting her sight.

Am I dead? Where am I?

There was a nice young man's face leaning over her. Black hair, long and thick, dropped over his black leather jacket. He smiled. It warmed her like the sun.

"Ron?" she muttered. She reached out to touch his face.

"You are hurt," replied the man. His voice was soft and caring. "I'm afraid you are mistaking me for someone else."

Diana's body was so numb that she felt no pain. "Am I in heaven?" she asked.

The man looked around and saw the dead grizzly bear and the area where the battle took place. He was amazed. His head moved up and down at the thought of this young lady fighting a bear and was still alive and talking.

The man smiled again. "If heaven is a world where all wounded warriors resemble a bloody turnip, then, yes, this must be heaven."

She felt his hands cradle her head. She blinked again. It was not Ron, but someone caring, speaking with a Spanish accent.

"I am alive," she uttered with a sigh.

"For the moment, yes…but your wounds are serious. Are you from this area? Do you have family?"

A loud siren and flashing red lights appeared over the crossing bridge, voices and movement trying to make its way through the ravine.

She tried to focus on the man's questions. It all became too fuzzy and vague. She was tired, and she needed to rest just for a little while, so she just said, "Yes."

56

The Book of Thoth

It was a little chilly for a spring night in Anna Catherina, Guyana. A breeze blew over the backyard gardens of 207 North Street. Harry Kincade brought a light sweater from inside the house and placed it around his wife's shoulders.

"Thanks, Harry," Hanna said.

"You're welcome, my love."

Ron was walking ahead of the Kincade's and talking with Bali. They were going over the details of the past few days. Beefi was in the kitchen preparing some sweets and evening snacks. One could hear the pots and pans clanking and moving around, the stove burning hot water for evening tea, and Beefi sticking her little head out through the back window every now and then, seeing them walking back and forth in the garden. She started to talk to herself in a manner that only she could accomplish.

"If yuh eye nah see, yuh mouth nah must talk." This meant, *You must see for yourself before you talk*. Beefi again slid her head out of the window and murmured, "Nah tek yuh mattie eye fuh see." This meant, *See for yourself and form your own conclusions instead of relying on the reports of others.*

While Beefi was in her own little world, Ron explained to Bali that there was more to the artifacts in the second area. That area also had the five-thousand-year-old book of magic and wisdom. It was the book that was said to have inspired the Freemasons. It was the book that contained the wisdom behind the tarot cards as they are known today. Many of the 1960s revolutionists were seeking this knowledge. This ancient book is called the *Book of Thoth*, and it was located in the second area. If the three evil ones got a hold of it, then who knew what spells could take place and what condition this crazy world would be like.

Bali then called out to his wife to see if the evening snacks and refreshments were ready. Beefi stuck her head out of the window and shouted back, "Nah one time a fire mek peas boil."

Hanna, Harry, and Bali laughed so hard that tears came from Hanna's eyes.

Ron looked at them and didn't understand why they were laughing. He looked at Bali and said, "Why are you guys laughing at what Grandma Beefi said?"

Bali was laughing so hard he couldn't talk. Hanna, in between her laughter, said, "Ron, my mother told my dad that his request about the snacks and refreshments and if they were ready. She replied, 'Nah one time a fire mek peas boil.' This means, 'Some things take a long time to be completed.'"

Ron looked at them funny and said, "I don't get it."

Hanna, Harry, and Bali looked at one another, and they started to laugh again. Bali was in such pain that he doubled over on a big boulder in the yard and continued laughing.

Hanna then looked at Ron and walked over to her grandson. She gave him a big hug and kissed him on the forehead and said, "Ron, living in Guyana has certain benefits, especially knowing the creole language. When you have lived here for sometime, you get to understand the flavor and culture of our country. And there are things that are kind of funny—you know what I mean?"

Ron looked at his grandma with an inquiring look and said, "Grandma, I still don't get it."

Hanna looked at the others, who were still chuckling at Beefi's response, and then focused her eyes at Ron and said, smiling, "It's a Guyanese thing."

57

Good-byes Are Hard to Do

It was a cool morning as the sun broke through the light mist, low in the sky. Ron was having his morning run on the seawall next to the cemetery. He looked up at the blue sky and saw the passing white clouds making their way toward the seemingly endless sea—the Atlantic Ocean. He thought, *What a wonderful place to be brought up in.*

His adventures and the new friendship he had acquired here brought a little sorrow in his heart about leaving. Ron knew that his work was done here, and it was time to head back to Narrowsburg. He walked slowly back to the house to take a shower, have breakfast, and say the first good-byes.

Last night in the garden area, his grandparents agreed to stay behind in Guyana for a little while longer. When it was time to leave the next day, they hugged and promised to see one another in a couple of days. Ron needed Beefi to believe that a car was going to pick him up at North Street that morning. Hanna arranged for a car to pick her up to take her husband and herself to Georgetown to do a little shopping so that Beefi would think they all went to the airport.

Harry and Hanna were in the house ready to make the phone call to Ron's parents' home. For this plan to work, Ron had to walk to the seawall so that his great-grandparents would say their final good-byes there and Bali would accompany Beefi away from their home. Ron didn't like deceiving his great-grandmother, but they all knew his secret would be hard for her to keep.

Great-grandma Beefi and Bali came to the wall to say good-bye and give him his traveling bag.

Great-grandma Beefi leaned up and kissed Ron and said, "God bless you, grandson." Tears welled in her beautiful grayish-brown eyes.

"In this entire world, I hope to see you guys again," Ron said as he gave them their final hugs.

Ron hoisted his traveling bag on his shoulder and headed down the lane toward North Street, waving a final farewell at the end of the street. Pain tore at his heart. A great part of his new love now remained in this place. A tremor of panic that he might never see them again ripped through him.

And then, suddenly, another wave of panic hit him. But this was different. He sensed that his wife was in trouble. Something was wrong. He just knew it. He needed to be home now. He ran up the stairs, two at a time, and shouted out to Harry, "Grandpa! Something is wrong back home...I feel it... did you call my home or my parents' house?"

"No one answered at your place. Your wife might be shopping. Your dad and mom are home. Do you want me to make the call now?"

"Yes, Grandpa, and thanks for everything. See you back home soon, Grandma."

As soon as the other side's connection was ready, Ron looked at them with his head leaning to the right side and a silly grin planted on his face. His body and everything he was holding were disappearing slowly in front of their eyes.

With the same silly grin, he held his traveling bag over his left shoulder with his left hand and waved good-bye with his right hand. He opened his eyes wide as he disappeared and flickered them up and down and said, "Now you see me...and now you don't."

Poof.

PART XIV

The Chapel and the Need

58

Going to the Chapel

That night, Ray Diamond found Ron huddled by himself in the hospital's chapel. He was actually praying, praying about what to do and if there was indeed a God who would let his wife suffer through this painful ordeal. His wife was still in surgery, and the doctors told him she lost a lot of blood.

"God, why is this happening to us?" Ron kept murmuring to the lonely shiny gold-plated cross at the center of the chapel walls. He knew from the police report that her car was tampered with. His dad's agency was on full alert, and the investigative team was in constant connection with the law enforcements. Deep inside, he knew it was the plumber who tampered with her brakes.

"Why would God…" He looked at Mr. Diamond, with tears drowning out his inquiring look, and said, "How could God not know or let this monster, who loves to scheme, who is evil —I mean, *real evil*—tamper with my wife's car brakes? He didn't give a thought to whether my wife would live or die in this bullshit accident. Why, God? Why...I want to kill him, Mr. Diamond...he is scum...I am thinking of plunging a dagger in his heart.

I am sorry to say that, but I want to kill that son of a bitch and do it real slowly and painfully...I don't care if I lose my powers...that bastard has to die... even if I can't prove it... he is dead meat... a slab in the frozen meat locker!"

While Ron got up, Ray saw that his eyes were turning red, and his body was tense. Ray then grabbed Ron's wrist. "No more madness, Ron. I know you love my daughter. You have always been a loyal husband to her and a good son-in-law and friend to me. You have trusted me in the past, more than anyone could ask for, so I ask you to let me handle this. Believe me, he will pay, but you cannot bring this hatred inside you and let this emotional situation override your judgment. Trust me on this. This is between you and me. Promise me that no one will know what I am going to do. Remember that before she became your wife, she was and will always be, and still is, my little girl. And, Ron, nobody—I mean, nobody—fucks with my little girl. Promise me!"

Ron looked hard in his father-in-law's eyes, and Ron's tears stopped flowing. Ron staggered back in shock. This caught him off guard. Their eyes met, and it was as if some terrible knowledge had been passed between them.

Ron then gave his father-in-law a big bear hug and said to him, "I promise. You are the best, Mr. Diamond. I am sorry that I got carried away."

Then Ron turned around, facing the cross, and said, "I'm sorry, God, for my blasphemy. You have protected my wife and gave her the strength to fight off the grizzly bear. Forgive my sins toward you, and I pray that my wife will have a full recovery. I know I don't deserve it, but thanks for everything. And I pray that you bless my father-in-law too..."

Mr. Diamond smiled at Ron, and as they were leaving the chapel, he said, "Let's see how our little warrior is doing, okay?"

Ron nodded in agreement, and then his eyes opened up. "I forgot something..."

Ron then went back down toward the cross and knelt before it and prayed one more prayer. He got up and met Mr. Diamond by the chapel door.

Mr. Diamond looked at Ron and said, "What was that all about?"

"I needed to ask God for something else," Ron said nonchalantly.

"What was that?" Ray inquired.

"I told God that the bastard that hurt my wife, he's got to pay—big-time!"

Mr. Diamond looked at Ron and put his left arm around him. He nodded, smiled, and said, "Good prayer, I like it. Works for me."

59

The Need Is Gone

*N*o, no, no...it can't be. How could that bitch ever survive that accident? No, no, no. And then she fought a fucking grizzly bear? What's wrong with this world? That bitch should have been dead. No, no, no!

Glen paced back and forth in his bedroom, reading *The River Reporter*'s article about the accident. He shook his head right to left and back again and said in disgust, "What the fuck! They glorified that bitch. They should have felt sorry for the grizzly. Where are the animal-rights lovers? Why aren't they enraged! This bitch should have been jailed. What happened to cruelty to animals—shit, shit, shit! The bitch still lives on. Fuck, fuck, fuck!"

That night, Glen couldn't sleep a wink. He kept thinking what went wrong with his perfect plan. He cut the brakes just right so that after the first two or three steps on her brakes, it would have unleashed the hose from the brake cylinder, and the rest should have been history. This bitch led a charmed life, but he knew he was going to have to get up real close and personal and cut this bitch's life short. No more playing Mr. Nice Guy.

Days went by, and Glen acted as if nothing was wrong. He would follow up on plumbing calls and his regular routines and waited for the chance and moment to strike. His hunger was eating him inside.

He needed a kill. He couldn't afford to leave the area, but his *strong* appetite was scraping inside him to be set free. He needed a prey. He was eager for a new prey. The scraping need was making him want to kill. And he couldn't change it but only try to control it. Being cautious went beyond the actual killing, of course. Being cautious meant building a cautious life too.

He made his outward life pleasant for people to meet and acted out social pleasantries so that his life could have a longer expectancy. All of which he had done so very carefully. He was above suspicion, beyond criticism, and beneath the radar of the police. He chuckled as he thought of himself as the neat and polite monster. Everyone should know the nice boy next door.

Then the call came in from one of his buddies from the past. He had a desire to shoot a couple of deer, even though it wasn't hunting season. He knew about a vacant property near the state land, where plenty of these animals resided.

His friend had an extra rifle and cartridges that he could use to go after the game. Glen liked the idea and thanked his friend for thinking about him. His friend said that he was going to check the property out and that he would call back in a few days to set up the hunting arrangements.

Two days later, his old buddy called back, and they arraigned to meet tomorrow morning at the site. At midnight, Glen went to town and sat across the street from the post office and stared at the large melon-shaped moon, which was chuckling back at him.

The spring breeze was moving the gentle waves off the Delaware River.

He would again see the river with admiration, which brought joy to the moonlight bouncing off the water. The cold quiet thing within him laughed as the moon danced over the waves.

I'll have my kill, even if it is a small deer.

The need inside him cried out. The need, the strong appetite within, is very resilient now, waiting for it to be fulfilled, and yet it was very careful not to reveal itself. Oh, this wonderful crazy feeling inside him made Glen's loins stiffen to hardness once again. This *need* had been teasing and prickling him to find another one, find the next one, even if it was a fucking deer. He chuckled.

The bright moonlight would soon turn to sunlight, and the pressure of fighting the growing need within would be solved.

Tomorrow. Yes, tomorrow, I'll have my day.

He met his friend by the vacant property, and they decided to hide their vehicles around the corner where an old abandoned shack would hide their presence.

Going into the woods, they were able to find a herd of deer near a clearing by a small stream of water, and his friend lay down to steady his shot.

But Glen wanted to walk up close and get personal with the animals. Every step he made toward the herd, he would turn his head and look at his friend and grin and then slowly move closer.

When he was about thirty yards from the herd, he turned his head toward his friend, and he grinned for the last time.

A shot rang out, an open echo, birds flying toward the sky in different directions, the herd frightened. And a body, with its eyes wide open, looking up, fell slowly like a ragged doll, shivering, to the ground, watering the earth with blood from a hole newly created in the evil man's skull.

60

The Sniper

All the following days, Ray waited for dusk to fall. Time passed with agonizing slowness. Surveillance and covert photography had taken a toll on the older man. *A much older man*, he thought.

Time, shared only by yourself, makes your mind travel in places you once thought you had forgotten. Ray dwelled on many things: the friends in the Marines he left behind, the odd jobs he took, and the people he thought didn't exist anymore. Then there was Diana's safety. What would he do when he got Glen in his sight? He needed to be free from this burden. Its weight was too much.

His wife was staying over the Hemingways' farmhouse and spending her days and partial nights looking after their daughter. He told his wife that he desired to be alone for a few days, and he needed to recover on his own. She didn't like the recovery-on-his-own dialogue, but she knew once he had his mind made up, there was no talking him out of it. *Thank God*, he thought, *for a good wife*.

He rented a trailer and paid in cash for a month across the street from Glen's house, and he stocked it with TV dinners, eggs, ham, fries, milk, and all the essentials a growing old man needed. He chuckled inside.

Ray was in the midst of stabbing a piece of breakfast ham when the early morning light tumbled into the trailer's kitchen window. Sipping his morning coffee, he recalled when he was following Glen, he realized Glen was checking out a property next to a state land, which was used for game hunting. But this wasn't hunting season!

Why? Ray thought. He needed to check out this property.

He rented a black horse from a nearby farm house and brought along food rations for his trip into discovery land, as he called it.

Ray had traveled in the wooded forest for a day, riding during light, checking out the terrain and the game that roamed around until his back ached. Then once it was dark, he curled up in the brush high in the hills overlooking the terrain, and his mind raced as he drifted off to a troubled sleep. He needed to be free of this.

The following morning, after a light breakfast over a makeshift campfire, Ray pounded his left fist into the earth's dirt. He wanted this to be over, but he knew he had to breathe slowly and wait for the right time. Ray's eyes flitted desperately over the terrain from side to side as he estimated the probable outcome of any opposition.

The afternoon sun bathed the wooded terrain and empty field as he packed his gear and headed back to the trailer. The newly installed digital recorder he planted in Glen's house attached to his phone line produced the answers he needed for understanding why Glen was checking out that property.

He knew the time and place Glen would be tomorrow. Under his bed, Ray then pulled out a large metallic case. *Maybe freedom will come with this package*, he thought. *Let's see who will have the honor of passing through the asshole's skull.*

Ray took out two boxes of bolt-action cartridges as he continued to talk to himself, "Okay, let's see. The effective firing range of this 7.62 × 51mm is 875 yards, but the .338 Lapua Magnum's effective firing range is 1,640 yards. I guess you win, .338 Lapua Magnum. Let the evil man's skull have a new breathing apparatus attached to it."

He smiled at the thought.

In the large metallic case, he pulled out one of the Sniper Weapon System, an army rifle in the M24 series.

Let this burden finally be lifted, Ray thought as he wiped down the sniper weapon.

He knew he was still a shadow, a ghost in the terrain. He would be out there somewhere, waiting. Fighting a justice system—that, no man can win. But a single bullet in the brain *can*. One shot, one kill—and he thought, *I'm back!*

At early dawn the next morning, Ray dressed in a dark camouflage outfit, pulled his car out of the trailer's driveway, and headed toward the area of the ghost and his newly found *freedom*.

61

Joyful Reunion
and the Legend Continues

She sat up in bed, confused and upset. Where was her dad? Was he okay? Was her mom hiding something from her? She looked at her mom sitting near the windows doing her crossword puzzles. Every minute or two, she would look up and smile at Diana and say, "Is everything all right?"

Hearing no reply, Diana's mother's head went down, focusing on the next new puzzle to solve.

Diana was tired of sleeping, sitting up, and going to rehabilitation sessions. Hospital life and its food weren't Diana's cup of tea. She got up out of bed but managed to limp no farther than a couple of painful steps. Before her mother could say anything, there was a knock on the door. Diana's mom went to see who was there.

"I see our patient rises," Ron exclaimed, seemingly delighted. "How is our warrior today, Mrs. Diamond?"

Ron went over to give Diana a big kiss on her forehead. He lifted her up and put her back down on the hospital bed.

"Her ears are not injured. Nor is her tongue," Anna said, smiling and nudging at Diana until the latter started laughing.

"I don't like the TV in here. I'm not looking for entertainment. I just need to see how my dad is doing. Where is he?" Diana questioned, her eyes firmly on Ron. And then she looked at her mother.

There was silence in the room.

Diana rested for seven more days until most of her wounds had healed. Then Ron knocked on the door, entered, and seemed excited. He inquired as to her health, "Are you able to walk?"

"Yes, of course." Diana hopped out of bed to show Ron, though still a bit weak.

"That'll do." He seemed pleased. "Then come along with me."

Ron walked to the door, and Diana hurried, with a slight limp, to keep up with him. He led her through the hospital's halls, wide and high and adorned with beautiful wall hangings. He made a right and then down a steep flight of metallic stairs.

"Where are we going?" Diana asked, pushing to keep up. It felt good to be out of her hospital room.

"To view your new car, I hope," Ron said, smiling.

Out of the staircase windows, she saw her Nissan Altima painted brand-new, and the bodywork was pristine.

"Is this the same car? My favorite and first car I have ever owned."

Ron nodded and chuckled. "I knew you'd love it, and I was going to bring what you love back to you."

Diana tried to jump, but her limped leg was not ready to take on that new experience, so she dragged her feet into the loving arms of her husband and kissed him all over his face. And then she gave him a big bear hug and said, "I knew you were the one since the first day I laid eyes on you. You love me, and you show it to me every day... and I..."

The tears came down like water fountains as her body slumped over her husband's, and he held her up and said, "Hey, hey...this is supposed to be a happy moment. Come on, warrior. Show me my girl."

Hearing her husband's voice, she stood up straight—well, as straight as she could—with a little wobble in between and said, "Yes, sir." She stood at attention and gave her husband a salute and then said, "Is it okay for this Private Diana Hemingway to kiss her general?"

Ron took a step back and stared into her watery eyes and said, "Private, you are now commissioned as a warrior general, and if you don't give me a big kiss"—he pointed his right index finger to his lips—"now, I will have you spanked for being the biggest tease in this one-man army."

Ron then smiled, opening his arms for her landing.

She giggled and then leaped into his arms and said, "Do me…"

Ron then slowly and tenderly cupped Diana's face in his hand and gave her the biggest wet kiss ever recorded in human history.

Later that day and back in the room, Ray Diamond knocked and entered. Diana's eyes turned wide, and her mouth screamed out in joy, "Daddy! Oh, Daddy, I missed you…"

At the same time, she jumped up and down in her bed in the sitting position as her father came over to his daughter and gave her a big hug and said, "I missed you too, my munchkin."

Tears welled in her eyes as she looked at her dad sternly. "Where were you? You had me so worried. Not only me but Mom too." Diana looked at her mother, who quietly nodded in agreement. "You could have called. You turned off your cell phone. What was all the hush-hush about? Don't I count in your life? Don't you see I worry about you?"

She then hit her dad softly with both of her fists on his chest. She stopped and cried on his shoulders.

"I needed to do something, munchkin. You do count in my life, more then you will ever know. I'm here now. Can we be friends again?"

Ray Diamond grabbed his daughter by her shoulders, pulled her back slowly, and looked into her eyes, and said, "Can we?"

Diana smiled and nodded. She then gave her father a big bear hug while her happy tears flowed from her eyes. "Yes, we can, Daddy. Yes, we can."

That moment in the hospital was one of joy, laughter, and peace.

Lunchtime came, and they all said, "The hell with the hospital food." And they chuckled while Ray Diamond ordered delivery service from a Chinese restaurant in the area.

Later that day, both of Ron's grandparents and parents dropped by with flowers and balloons, all to wish Diana a speedy recovery and to just hang out.

New laughter, new jokes, and new hugs in the room with Diana made the festive afternoon go by quickly. Ray motioned for Ron to step out of the room for a moment.

Outside the room and with the door closed, Ray went into his right shirt pocket and gave Ron a clipping of a newspaper article and said, "Look at the bottom notice."

Cops Nail Hunting Violators

NARROWSBURG, NY—Police were busy locally during...

The Department of Environmental Conservation Police and state troopers at Narrowsburg made the following arrests for violations of the NYS Environmental Conservation Law during...

Alexander Faro, 51, of Ridgewood, NY, agreed to a civil compromise for illegally taking a deer with the aid of artificial light, illegally taking deer with the aid of bait, hunting without a license and...

In the Town of Bethel Court:

Mark Amsterdam, 25, of East Brunswick, NJ, was arraigned for illegal possession of a doe deer and for third-degree criminal possession of a weapon (a loaded .45 caliber pistol). Amsterdam was committed to the Sullivan County Jail without bail.

Glen Soros, 35, of Narrowsburg, NY, died of a gunshot wound to his head while illegally hunting deer out of season. Police are looking for another person of interest involved with this illegal hunting.

Ron looked at the article and then looked up at Ray. And then his eyes went back to the article and said, "Is this for real?"

Ray nodded with a slight grin on his face. "Son, you have your whole life to live. Live it well, and know that I will always be there for you and Diana."

Ron looked hard at his father-in-law's eyes and remembered the knowledge that had been passed between them in the chapel.

Ray put his hand out to shake Ron's hand.

Ron shook his hand real hard, and then they embraced each other.

Sounds of laughter between family and loved ones echoed through the narrow passages of the hospital's halls.

The story that we end today has had many narrators, and I'm afraid some will not want to hear their messages. But those who are *brave* and have a mind of their *own* will know the difference between fantasy and truth.

As the Wise One said, "The folklore will be yours to tell," and a novel adventure will soon be screaming out through new pages. But until then, my friends, we must wait.

This is the story legends are made of.

To be continued...

PHOTOGRAPHS

Roy Danza and Lee Ann Hemmingway

Roy Danza Hemingway

John "the Crusher" and Angelina Hemingway

Ray and Anne Diamond

The Family Colors

Harry and Hanna Kincade

Chief Master Sang Lee

Raj Ram

Felisha and Shadow the Cat

Diana Diamond (Hemingway)
Princess Serene and Kingdom of Caribbean

Princess Serene in the Lost World

Ronald "Tex" Hemingway, a.k.a. Tex Element

Age 12 Age 17

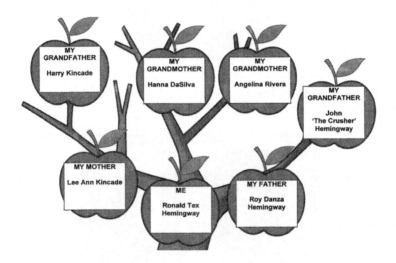

Ronald "Tex" Hemingway Family Tree

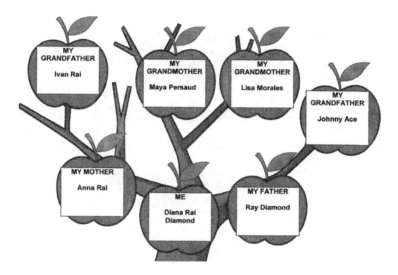

Diana Rai Diamond Family Tree

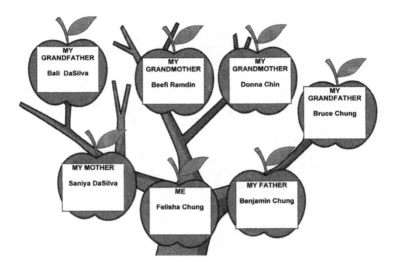

Felisha Chung Family Tree

Shadow the Cat

CPSIA information can be obtained at www.ICGtesting.com
Printed in the USA
BVOW06*1953060916

461309BV00003B/5/P